SECRET CODERS
Monsters & Modules

GENE LUEN YANG
& MIKE HOLMES

:01
First Second
New York

"It was this wonderful time between magic and so-called rationality."
—Wally Feurzeig, co-creator of the Logo programming language, on the early days of Logo

First Second

New York

Copyright © 2018 by Humble Comics LLC

Published by First Second
First Second is an imprint of Roaring Brook Press,
a division of Holtzbrinck Publishing Holdings Limited Partnership
175 Fifth Avenue, New York, New York 10010

Library of Congress Control Number: 2017957417

Paperback ISBN: 978-1-62672-610-9
Hardcover ISBN: 978-1-62672-609-3

Our books may be purchased in bulk for promotional, educational,
or business use. Please contact your local bookseller or the Macmillan Corporate
and Premium Sales Department at (800) 221-7945 ext. 5442 or by e-mail at
MacmillanSpecialMarkets@macmillan.com.

First edition, 2018

Book design by Rob Steen

Printed in China by Toppan Leefung Printing Ltd., Dongguan City, Guangdong Province

Paperback: 10 9 8 7 6 5 4 3 2 1
Hardcover: 10 9 8 7 6 5 4 3 2 1

Chapter

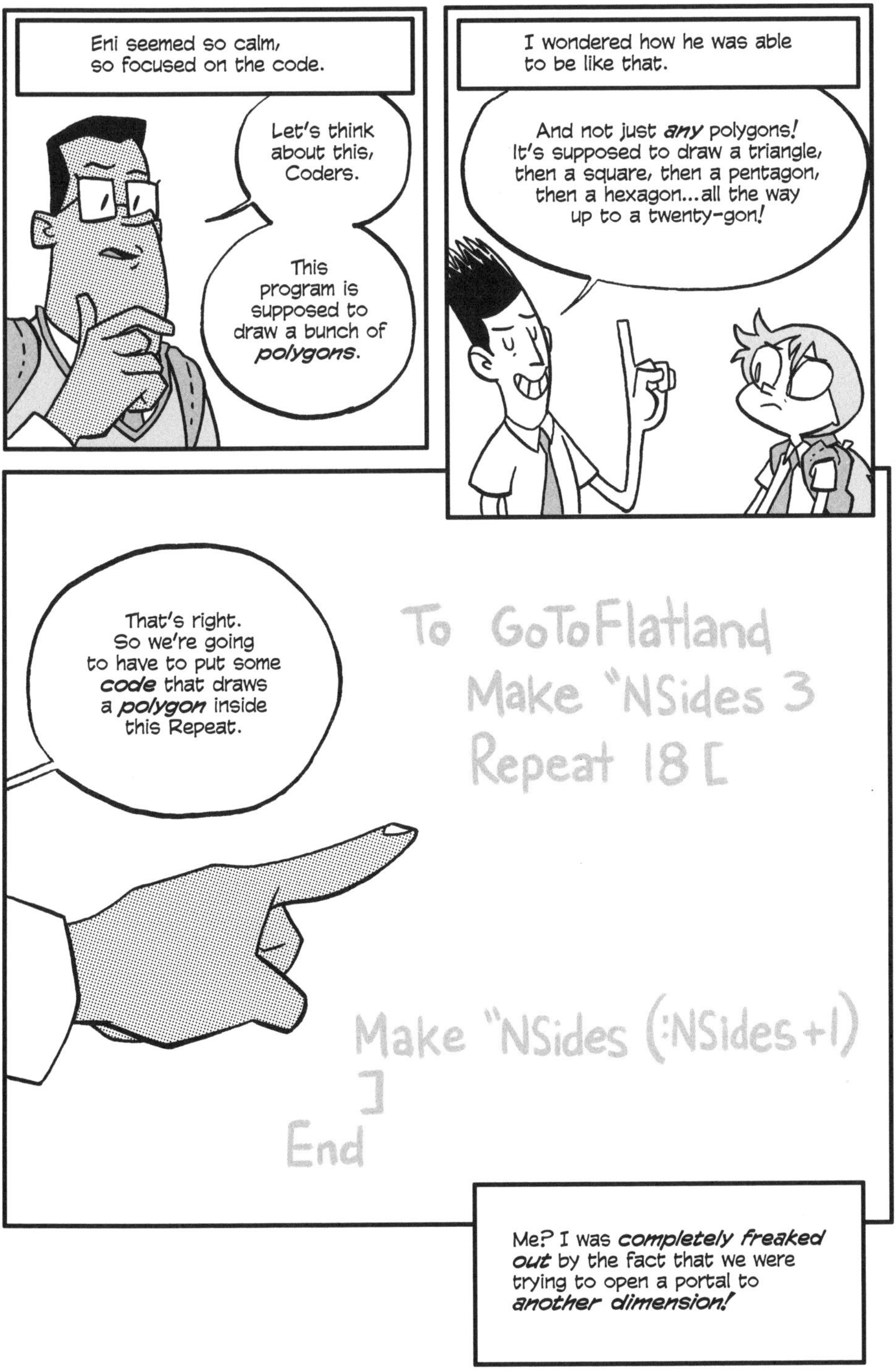
Eni seemed so calm, so focused on the code.
Let's think about this, Coders.
This program is supposed to draw a bunch of *polygons*.
I wondered how he was able to be like that.
And not just *any* polygons! It's supposed to draw a triangle, then a square, then a pentagon, then a hexagon...all the way up to a twenty-gon!
That's right. So we're going to have to put some *code* that draws a *polygon* inside this Repeat.
To GoToFlatland
Make "NSides 3
Repeat 18 [
Make "NSides (:NSides+1)
]
End
Me? I was *completely freaked out* by the fact that we were trying to open a portal to *another dimension!*

Or, as Professor Bee put it, one dimension less--a place called *Flatland*.

So were you able to do it? Were you able to write a program that draws all those polygons to open a portal to Flatland?

Wait. Code that draws a polygon... didn't we already do that?

```
To GoToFlatland
    Make "NSides 3
    Repeat 18 [

Make "NSides (NS
]
```

```
To DrawPolygon :NSides
    Repeat :NSides [
        Forward 10
        Right 360/:NSides
    ]
End
```

This code can draw a polygon with any number of sides, right? Can't we just copy it from *DrawPolygon* into the blank space in *GoToFlatland?*

Yes, that would work, children, but there is an *easier way*.

Come take a look.

+k
+k

4

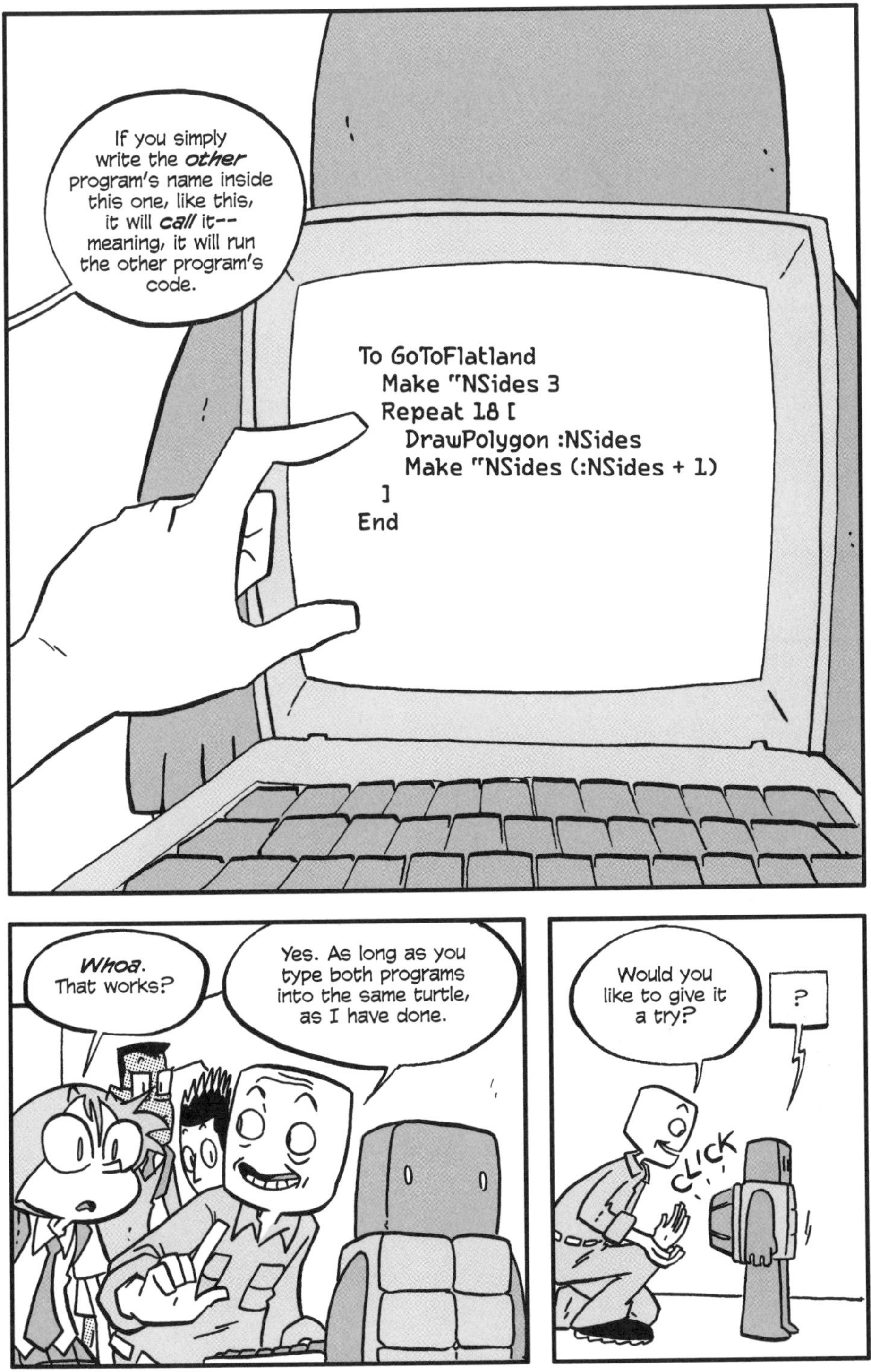
If you simply write the *other* program's name inside this one, like this, it will *call* it-- meaning, it will run the other program's code.
To GoToFlatland
Make "NSides 3
Repeat 18 [
DrawPolygon :NSides
Make "NSides (:NSides + 1)
]
End
Whoa. That works?
Yes. As long as you type both programs into the same turtle, as I have done.
Would you like to give it a try?
CLICK
?

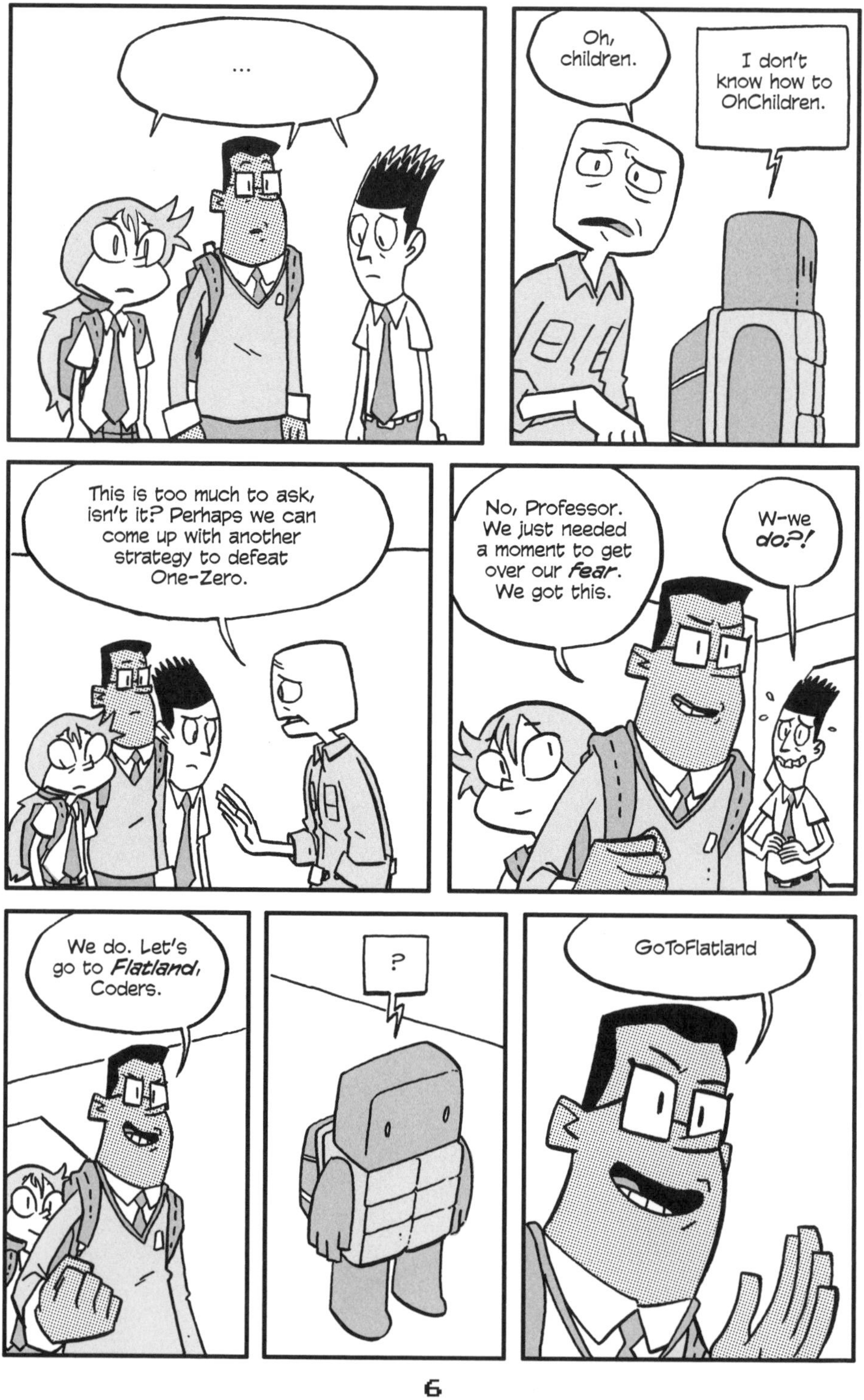
...
Oh, children.
I don't know how to OhChildren.
This is too much to ask, isn't it? Perhaps we can come up with another strategy to defeat One-Zero.
No, Professor. We just needed a moment to get over our *fear*. We got this.
W-we *do?!*
We do. Let's go to *Flatland*, Coders.
?
GoToFlatland

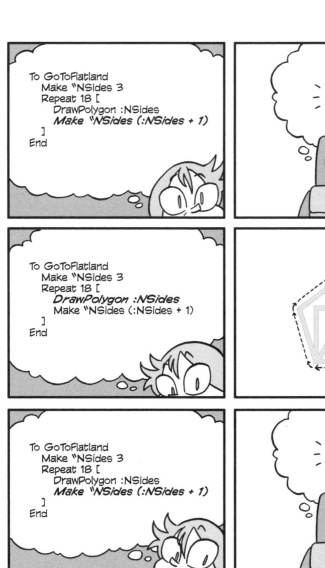

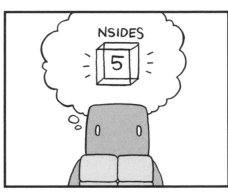

To GoToFlatland
Make "NSides 3
Repeat 18 [
DrawPolygon :NSides
Make "NSides (:NSides + 1)
]
End
NSIDES
5
To GoToFlatland
Make "NSides 3
Repeat 18 [
DrawPolygon :NSides
Make "NSides (:NSides + 1)
]
End
To GoToFlatland
Make "NSides 3
Repeat 18 [
DrawPolygon :NSides
Make "NSides (:NSides + 1)
]
End
NSIDES
6
To GoToFlatland
Make "NSides 3
Repeat 18 [
DrawPolygon :NSides
Make "NSides (:NSides + 1)
]
End

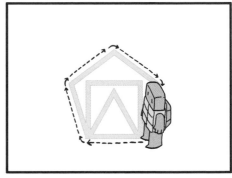

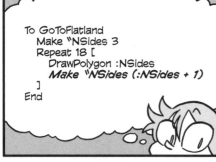

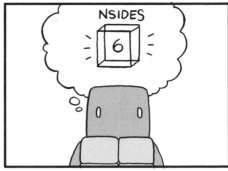

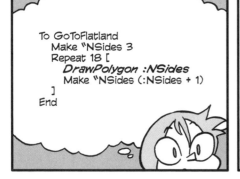

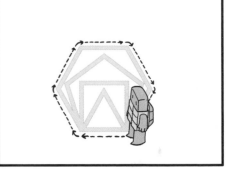

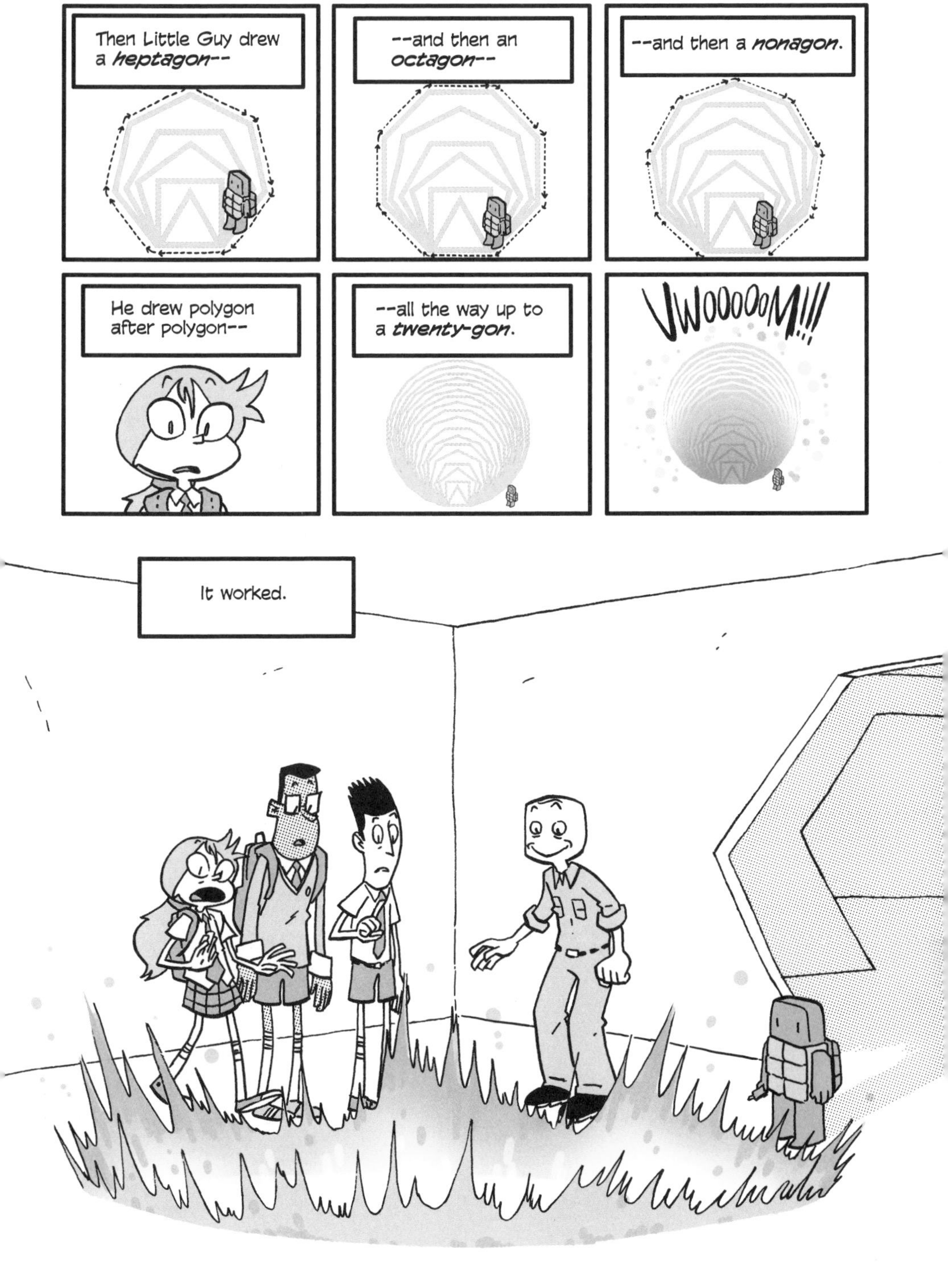
Then Little Guy drew a *heptagon*--
--and then an *octagon*--
--and then a *nonagon*.
He drew polygon after polygon--
--all the way up to a *twenty-gon*.
VWOOOOOM!!!
It worked.

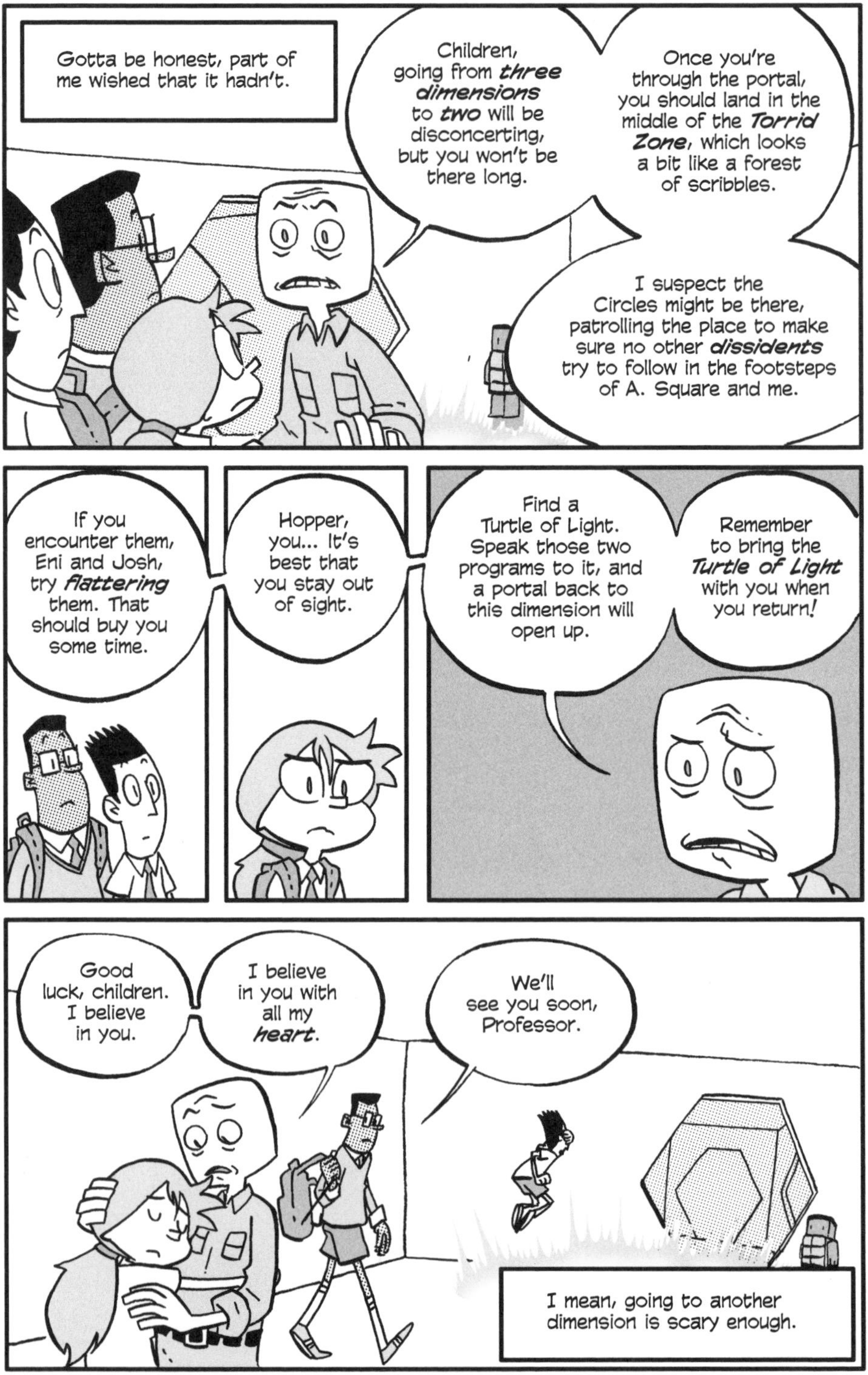
Gotta be honest, part of me wished that it hadn't.
Children, going from *three dimensions* to *two* will be disconcerting, but you won't be there long.
Once you're through the portal, you should land in the middle of the *Torrid Zone*, which looks a bit like a forest of scribbles.
I suspect the Circles might be there, patrolling the place to make sure no other *dissidents* try to follow in the footsteps of A. Square and me.
If you encounter them, Eni and Josh, try *flattering* them. That should buy you some time.
Hopper, you... It's best that you stay out of sight.
Find a Turtle of Light. Speak those two programs to it, and a portal back to this dimension will open up.
Remember to bring the *Turtle of Light* with you when you return!
Good luck, children. I believe in you.
I believe in you with all my *heart*.
We'll see you soon, Professor.
I mean, going to another dimension is scary enough.

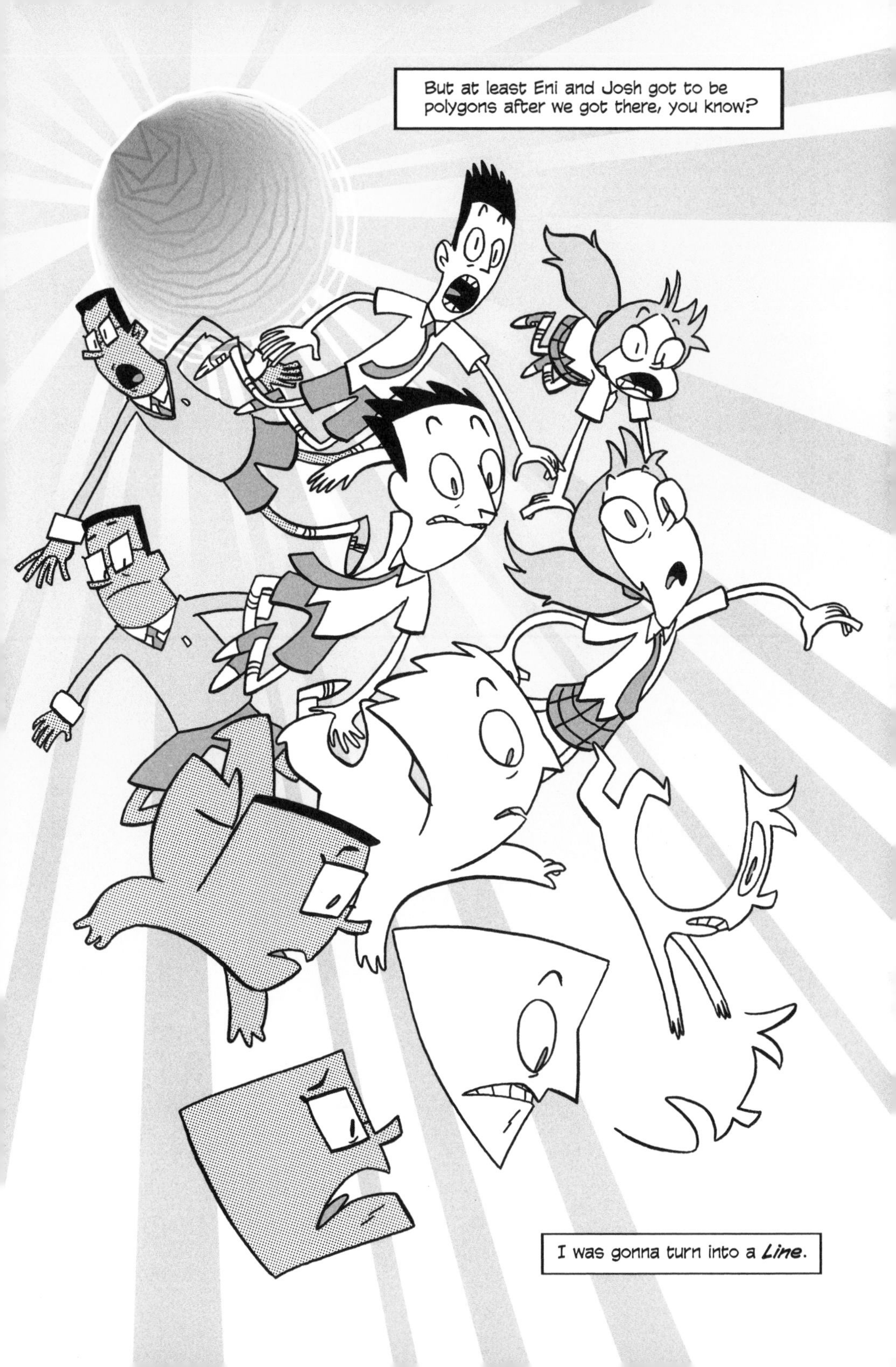
But at least Eni and Josh got to be polygons after we got there, you know?
I was gonna turn into a *Line*.

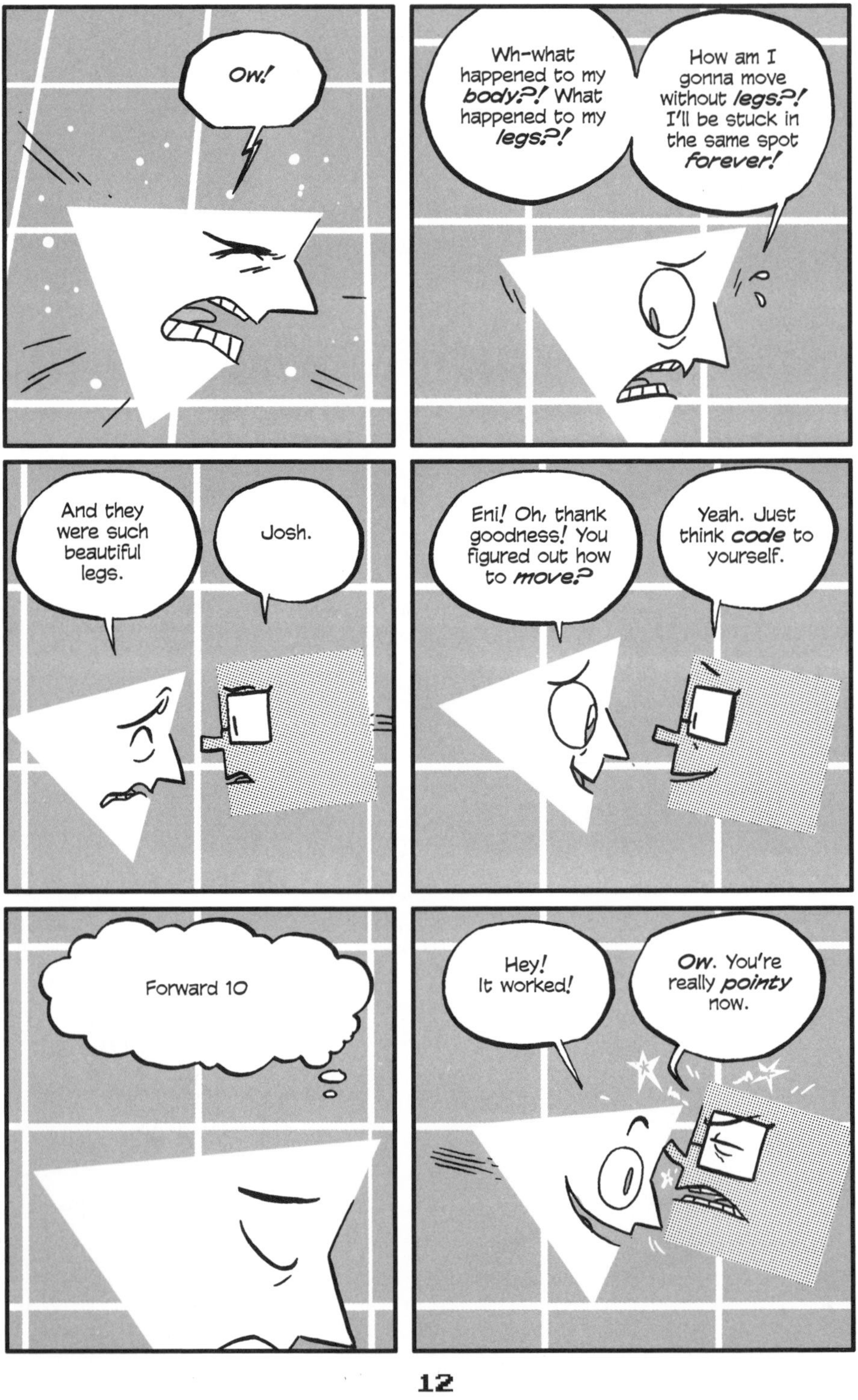
Ow!
Wh-what happened to my body?! What happened to my legs?!
How am I gonna move without legs?! I'll be stuck in the same spot forever!
And they were such beautiful legs.
Josh.
Eni! Oh, thank goodness! You figured out how to move?
Yeah. Just think code to yourself.
Forward 10
Hey! It worked!
Ow. You're really pointy now.

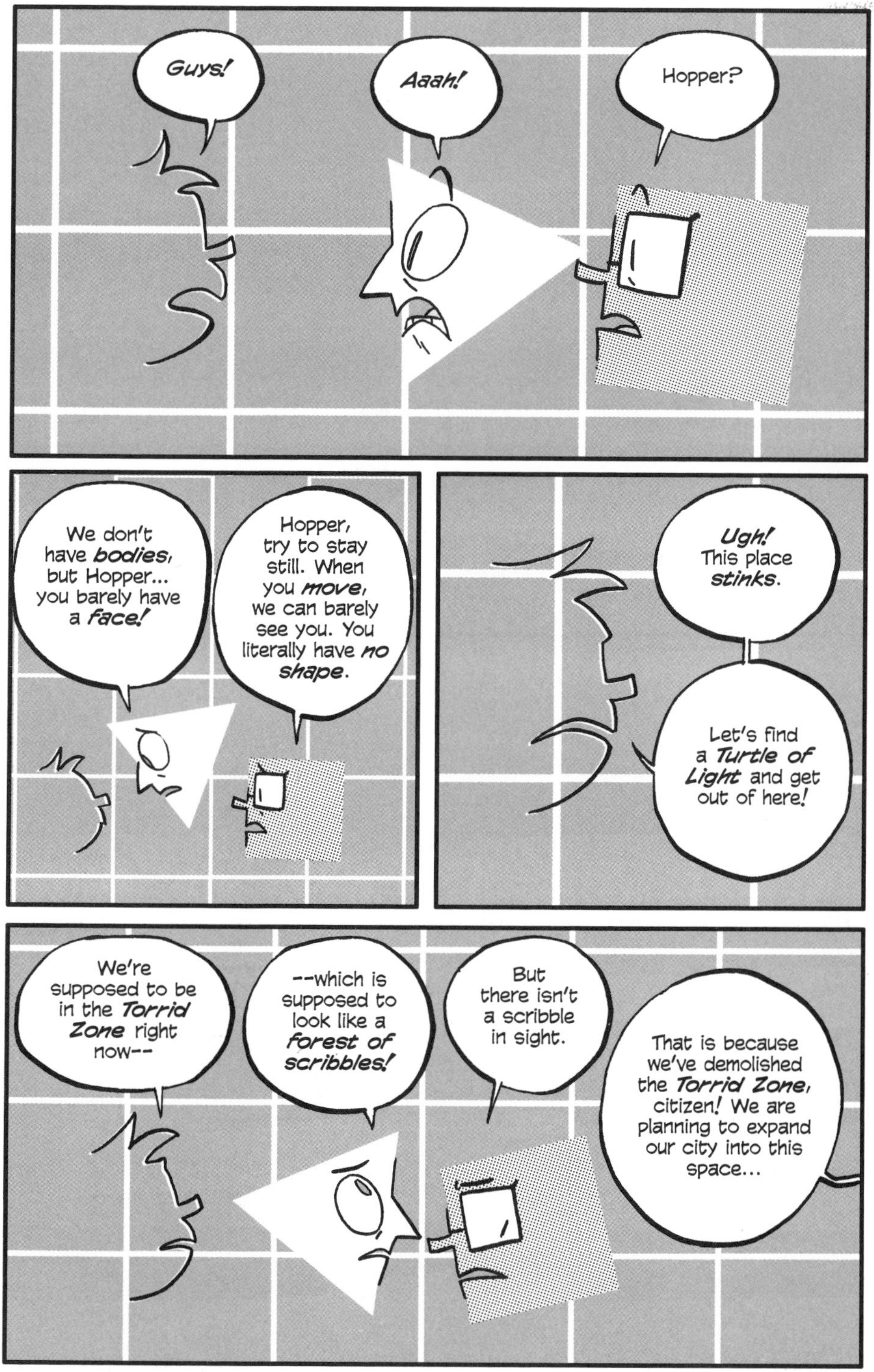

Guys!
Aaah!
Hopper?
We don't have bodies, but Hopper... you barely have a face!
Hopper, try to stay still. When you move, we can barely see you. You literally have no shape.
Ugh! This place stinks.
Let's find a Turtle of Light and get out of here!
We're supposed to be in the Torrid Zone right now--
--which is supposed to look like a forest of scribbles!
But there isn't a scribble in sight.
That is because we've demolished the Torrid Zone, citizen! We are planning to expand our city into this space...

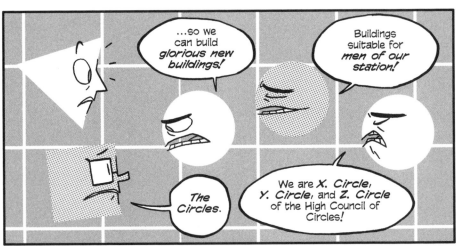

...so we can build *glorious new buildings!*

Buildings suitable for *men of our station!*

The Circles.

We are *X. Circle*, *Y. Circle*, and *Z. Circle* of the High Council of Circles!

Professor Bee said to *flatter* these guys!

I'll give it a shot.

Hello there, X. Circle, Y. Circle, and Z. Circle. You guys are so...uh... *circular*.

?!

Oh, geez! Step aside, Eni!

Oh benevolent Circles! How *wondrous* are your mighty deeds! I, a lowly Triangle, heard rumor of your *astounding achievements* in the Torrid Zone and wanted to see them for myself!

Ha ha. Very good, citizen!

Wow. Did you take a class on flattery or something?

I just say to them what I wish you and Hopper would say to me.

14

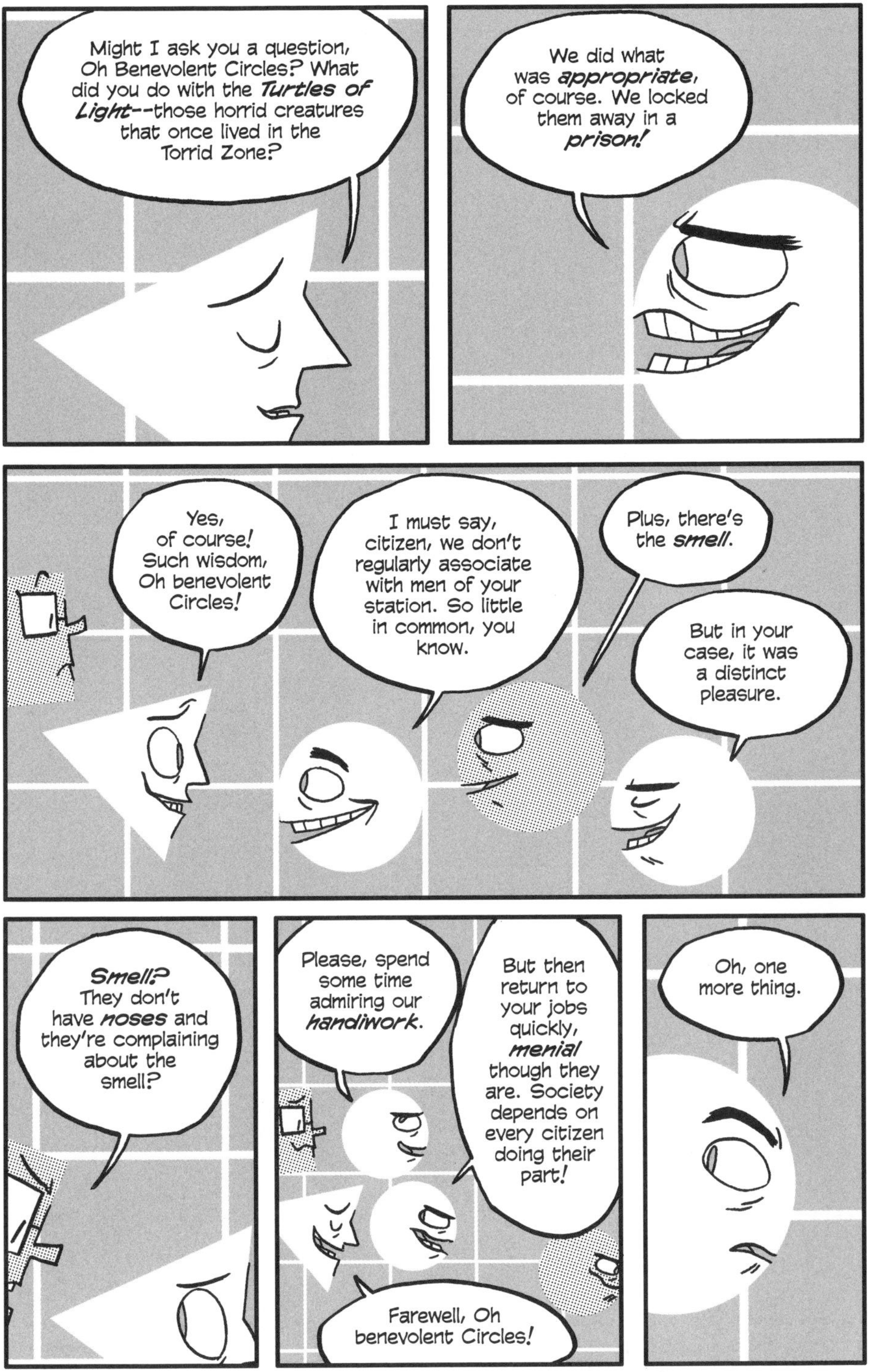
Might I ask you a question, Oh Benevolent Circles? What did you do with the *Turtles of Light*--those horrid creatures that once lived in the Torrid Zone?
We did what was *appropriate*, of course. We locked them away in a *prison!*
Yes, of course! Such wisdom, Oh benevolent Circles!
I must say, citizen, we don't regularly associate with men of your station. So little in common, you know.
Plus, there's the *smell*.
But in your case, it was a distinct pleasure.
Smell? They don't have *noses* and they're complaining about the smell?
Please, spend some time admiring our *handiwork*.
But then return to your jobs quickly, *menial* though they are. Society depends on every citizen doing their part!
Farewell, Oh benevolent Circles!
Oh, one more thing.

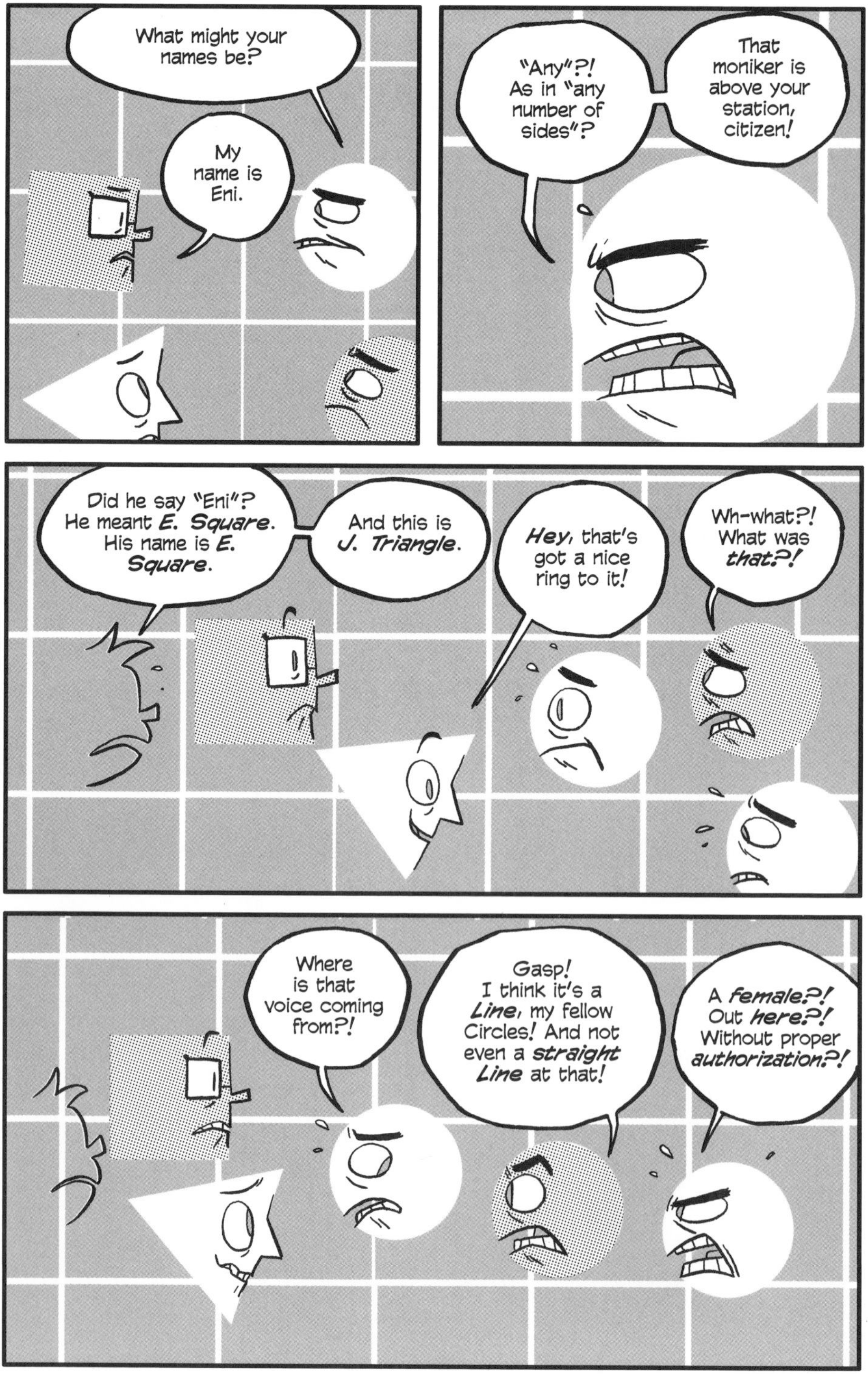
What might your names be?
My name is Eni.
"Any"?! As in "any number of sides"?
That moniker is above your station, citizen!
Did he say "Eni"? He meant E. Square. His name is E. Square.
And this is J. Triangle.
Hey, that's got a nice ring to it!
Wh-what?! What was that?!
Where is that voice coming from?!
Gasp! I think it's a Line, my fellow Circles! And not even a straight Line at that!
A female?! Out here?! Without proper authorization?!

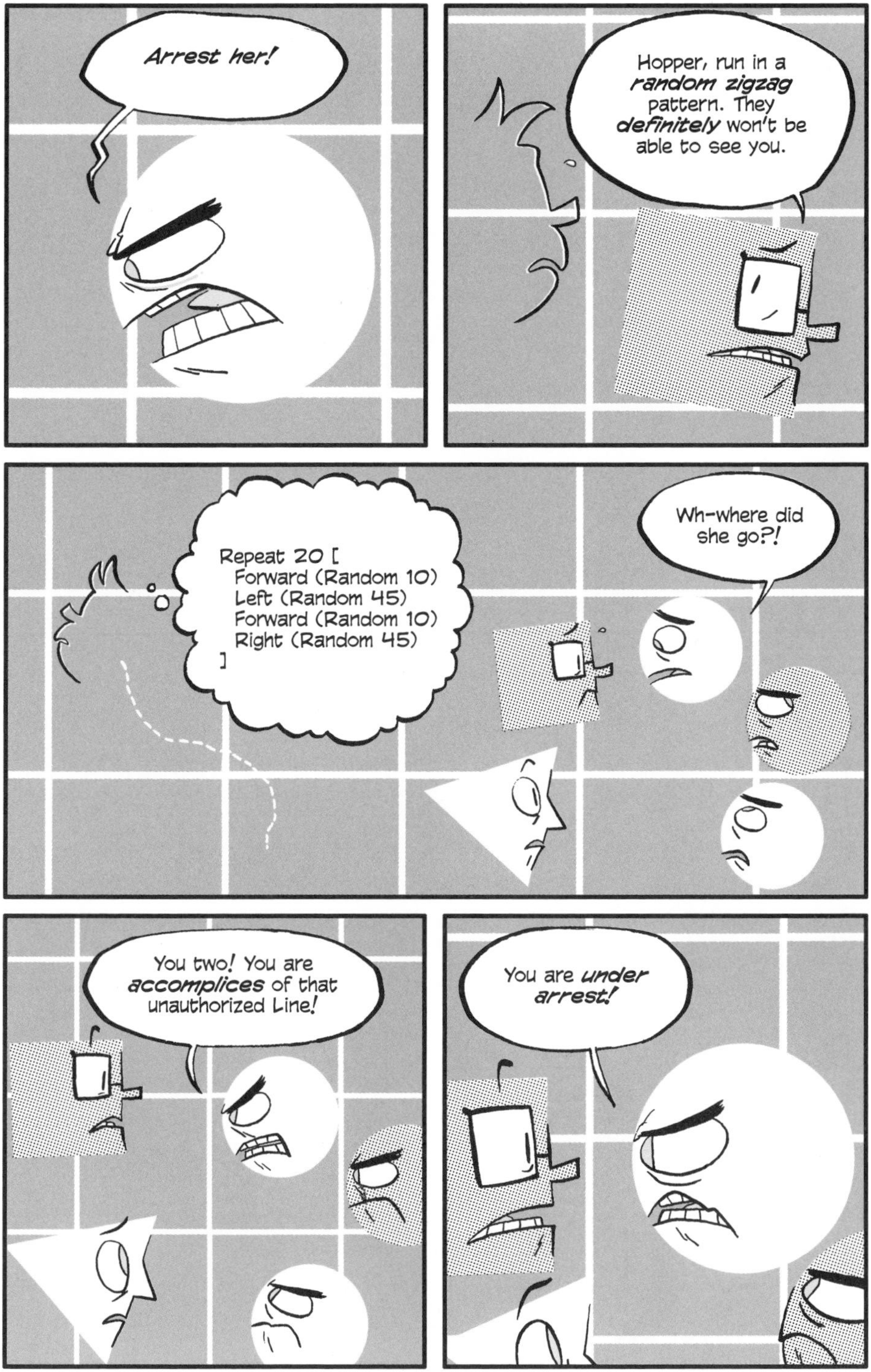
Arrest her!
Hopper, run in a random zigzag pattern. They definitely won't be able to see you.
Repeat 20 [
Forward (Random 10)
Left (Random 45)
Forward (Random 10)
Right (Random 45)
]
Wh-where did she go?!
You two! You are accomplices of that unauthorized Line!
You are under arrest!

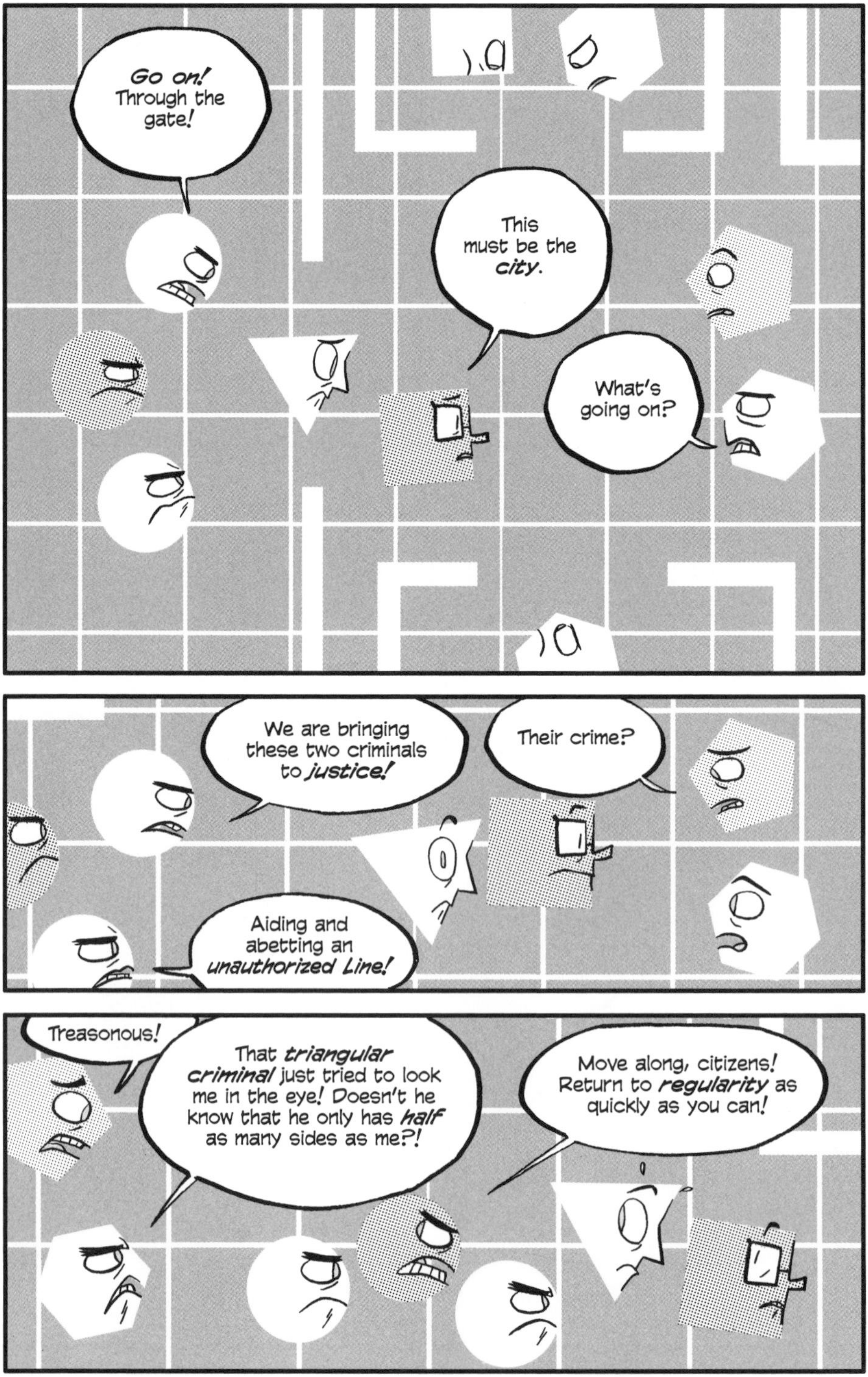
Go on! Through the gate!
This must be the *city*.
What's going on?
We are bringing these two criminals to *justice!*
Their crime?
Aiding and abetting an *unauthorized Line!*
Treasonous!
That *triangular criminal* just tried to look me in the eye! Doesn't he know that he only has *half* as many sides as me?!
Move along, citizens! Return to *regularity* as quickly as you can!

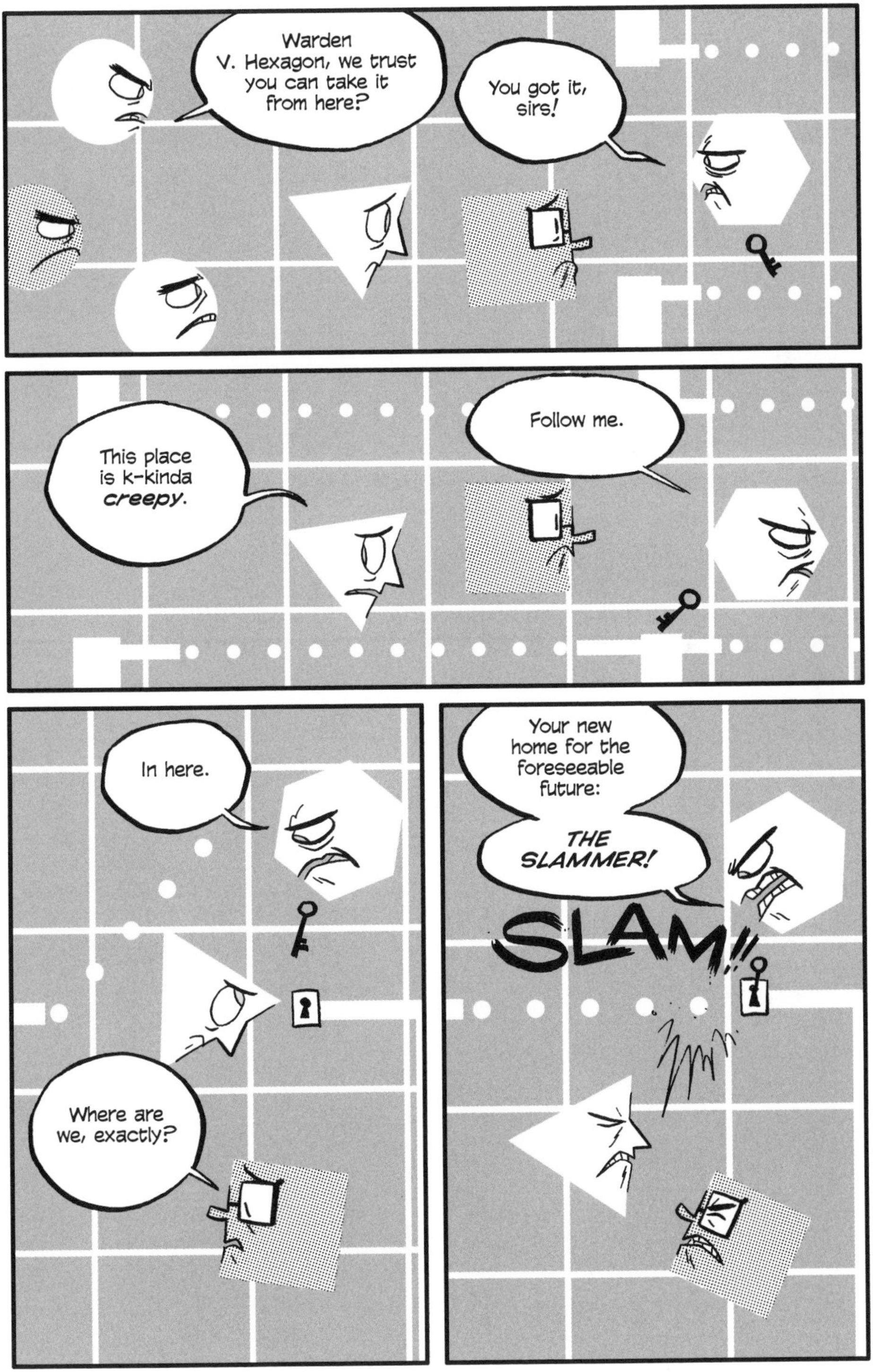
Warden V. Hexagon, we trust you can take it from here?
You got it, sirs!
This place is k-kinda *creepy*.
Follow me.
In here.
Where are we, exactly?
Your new home for the foreseeable future:
THE SLAMMER!
SLAM!!

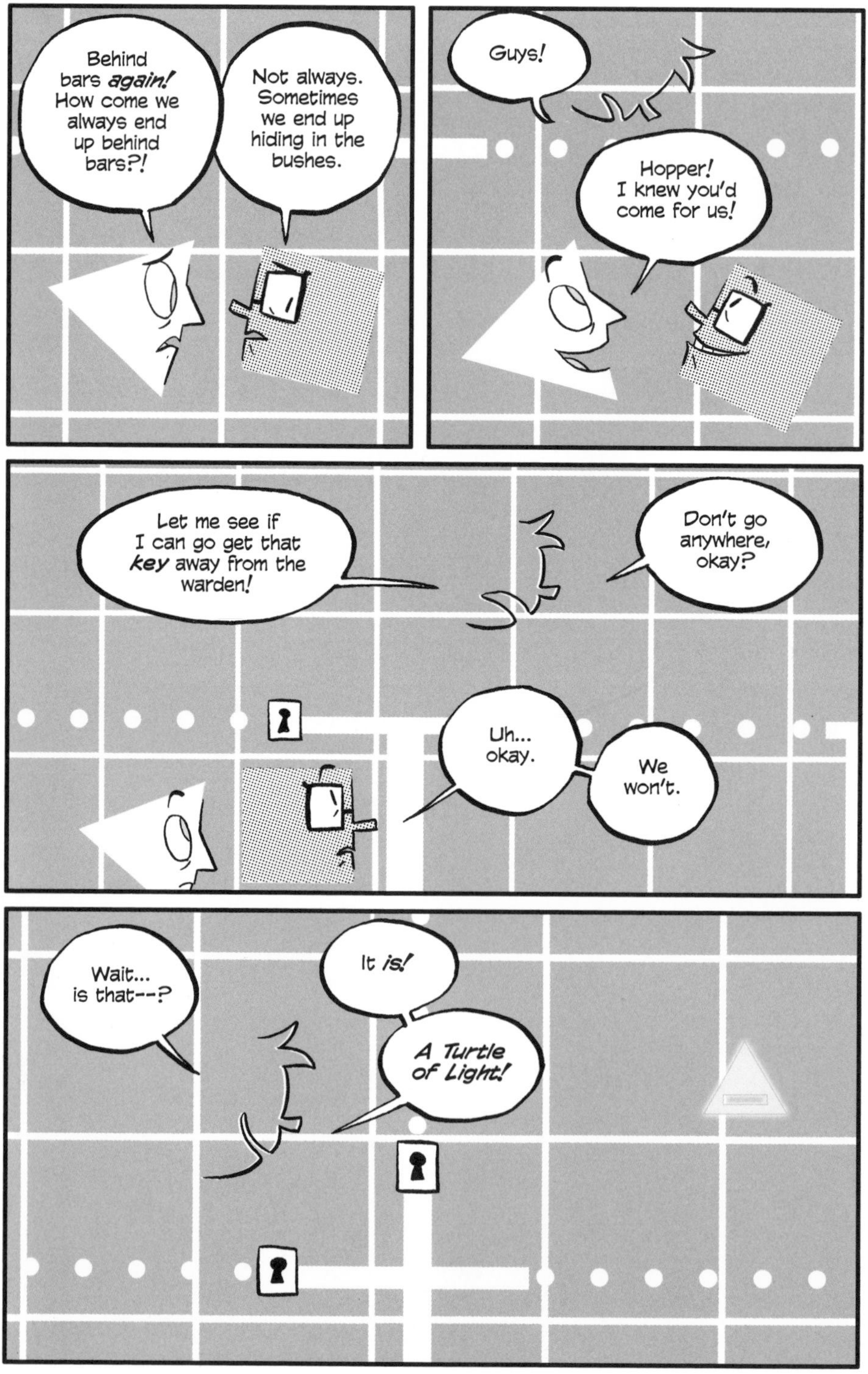
Behind bars again! How come we always end up behind bars?!
Not always. Sometimes we end up hiding in the bushes.
Guys!
Hopper! I knew you'd come for us!
Let me see if I can go get that key away from the warden!
Don't go anywhere, okay?
Uh... okay.
We won't.
Wait... is that--?
It is!
A Turtle of Light!

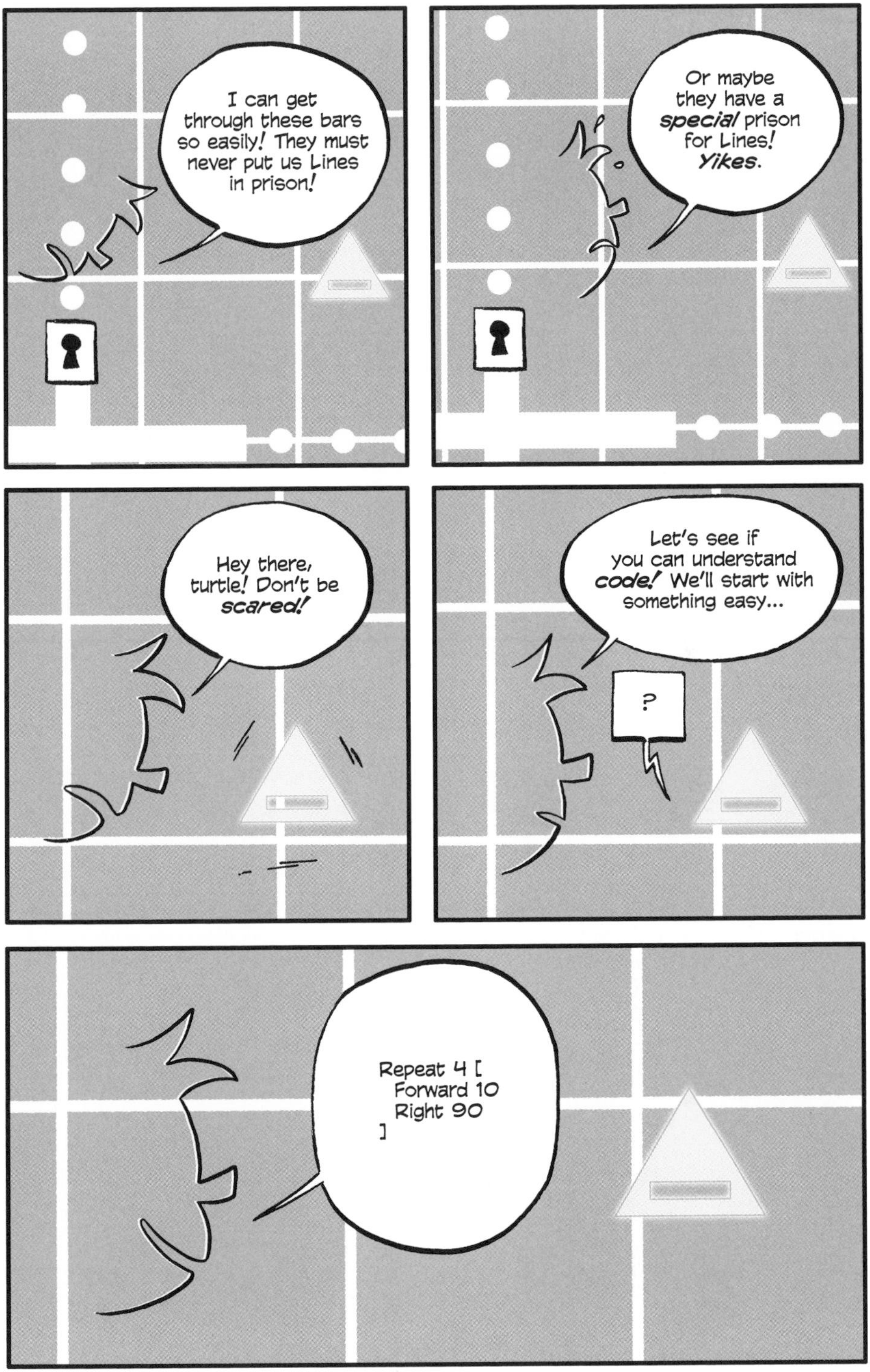

I can get through these bars so easily! They must never put us Lines in prison!
Or maybe they have a *special* prison for Lines! *Yikes*.
Hey there, turtle! Don't be *scared!*
Let's see if you can understand *code!* We'll start with something easy...
?
Repeat 4 [
Forward 10
Right 90
]

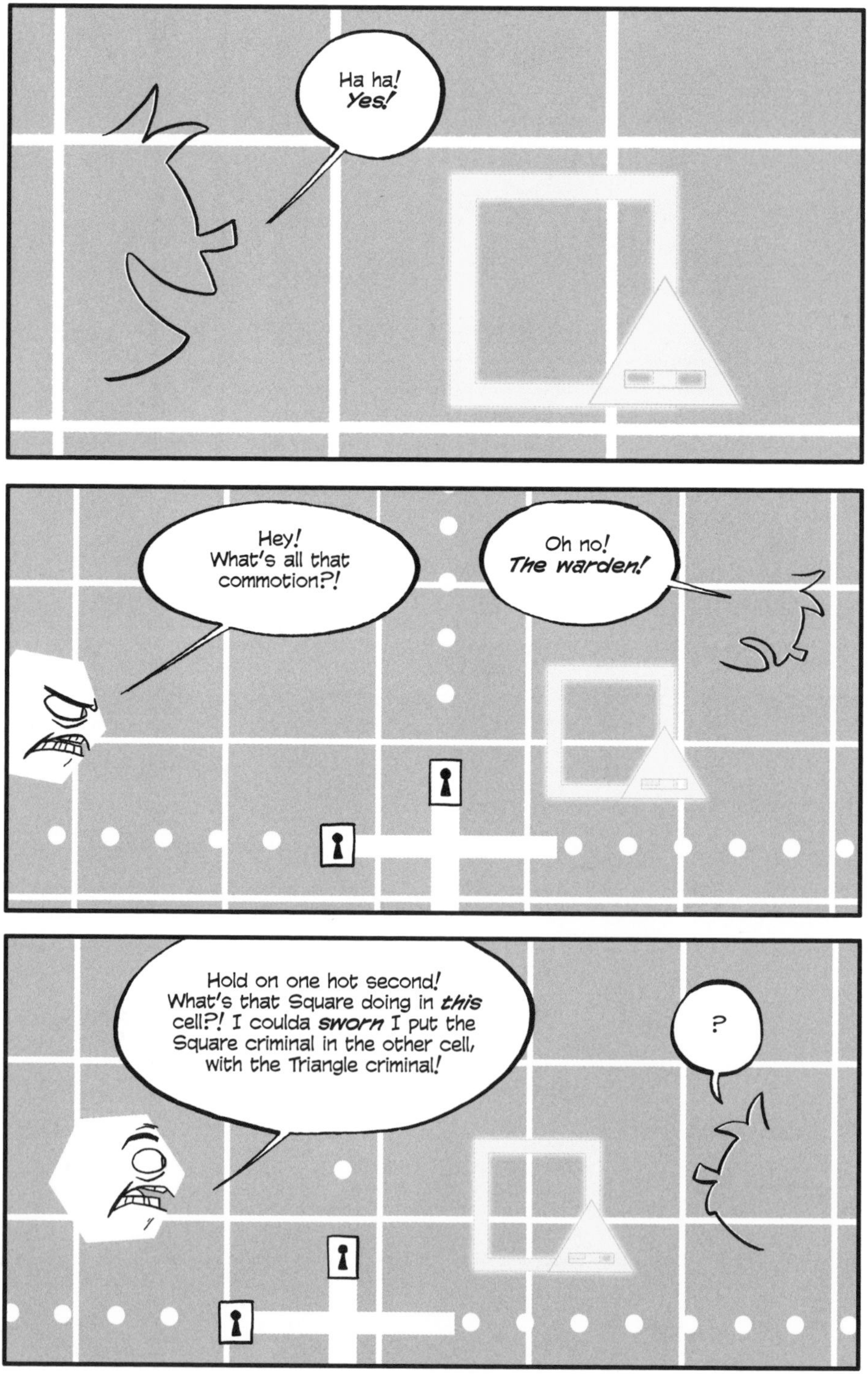
Ha ha! *Yes!*
Hey! What's all that commotion?!
Oh no! *The warden!*
Hold on one hot second! What's that Square doing in *this* cell?! I coulda *sworn* I put the Square criminal in the other cell, with the Triangle criminal!
?

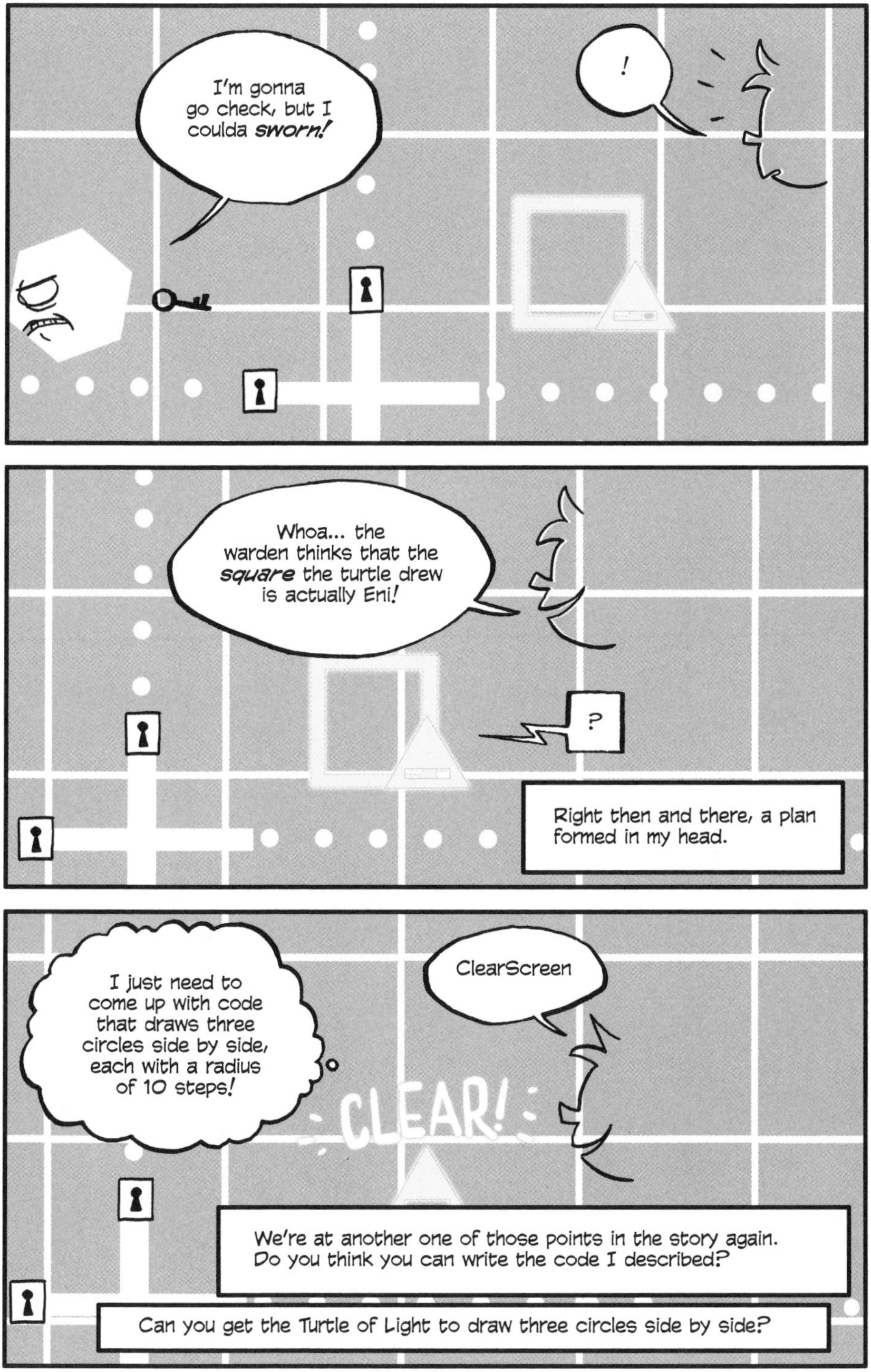
I'm gonna go check, but I coulda *sworn!*
!
Whoa... the warden thinks that the *square* the turtle drew is actually Eni!
?
Right then and there, a plan formed in my head.
I just need to come up with code that draws three circles side by side, each with a radius of 10 steps!
ClearScreen
CLEAR!
We're at another one of those points in the story again. Do you think you can write the code I described?
Can you get the Turtle of Light to draw three circles side by side?

Chapter

Did you do it? Were you able to come up with the code to make three circles?

To make one circle, I can use the *Arc command*, like this:

Arc 360 10

"The *360* tells the turtle to draw an *entire circle* because a circle has a total of *360 degrees*."

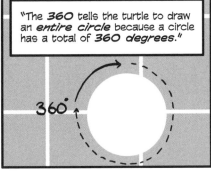

360°

"The *10* tells the turtle how big the circle's *radius* should be."

RADIUS!

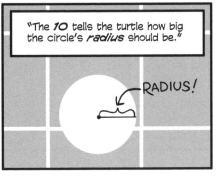

After drawing *one circle*, the turtle will have to get in position to draw the *next circle*, so I'll have it pen up, move forward 25 steps, and then pen down!

25

If I put all that in a *Repeat* that goes three times, I'll get *three circles!*

?

Repeat 3 [
  Arc 360 10
  PenUp
  Forward 25
  PenDown
]

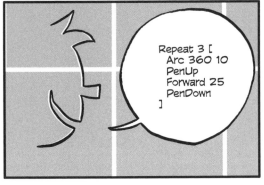

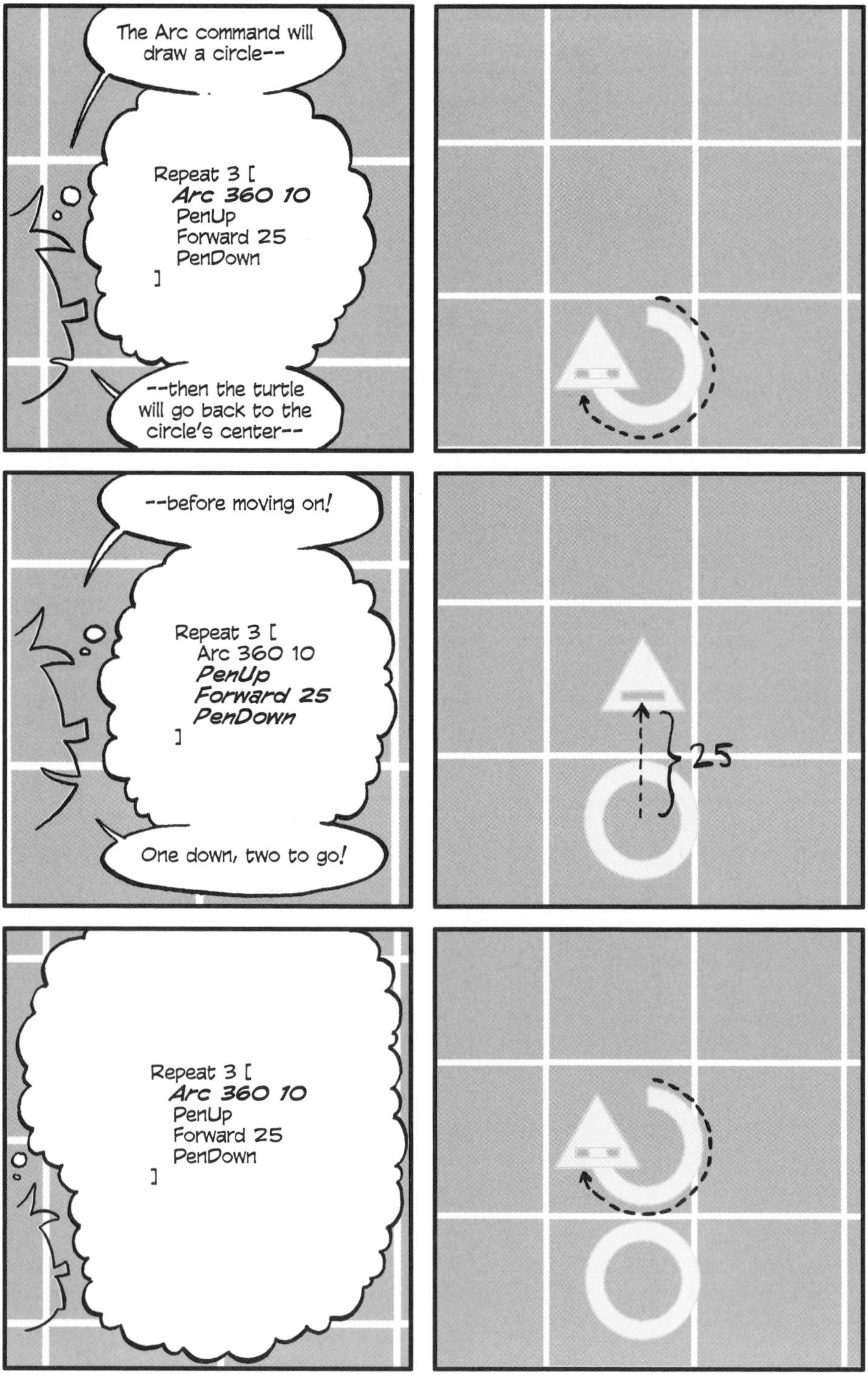

The Arc command will draw a circle--
Repeat 3 [Arc 360 10 PenUp Forward 25 PenDown]
--then the turtle will go back to the circle's center--
--before moving on!
Repeat 3 [Arc 360 10 PenUp Forward 25 PenDown]
One down, two to go!
25
Repeat 3 [Arc 360 10 PenUp Forward 25 PenDown]

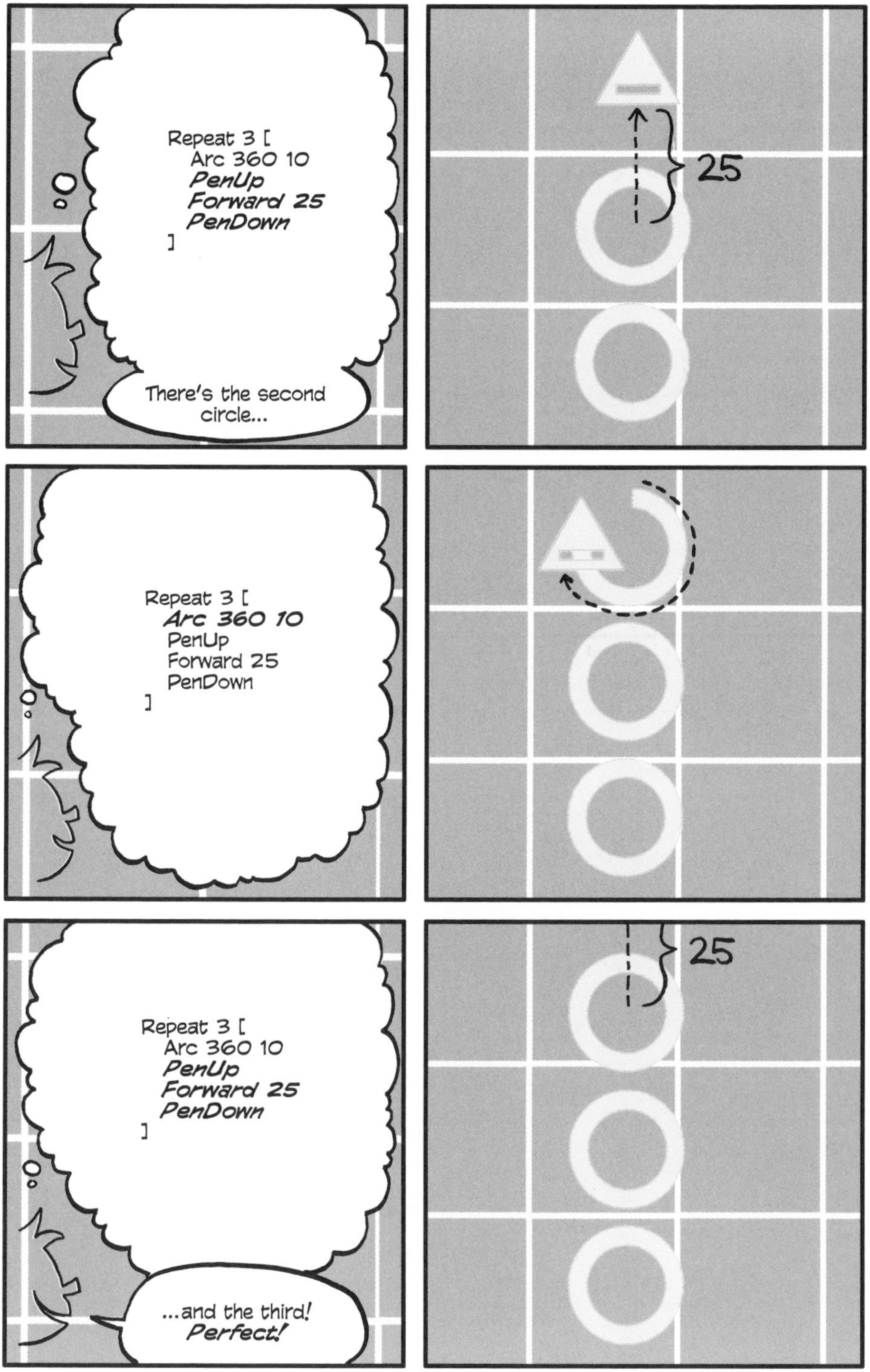
Repeat 3 [
Arc 360 10
PenUp
Forward 25
PenDown
]
There's the second circle...
25
Repeat 3 [
Arc 360 10
PenUp
Forward 25
PenDown
]
Repeat 3 [
Arc 360 10
PenUp
Forward 25
PenDown
]
...and the third! Perfect!
25

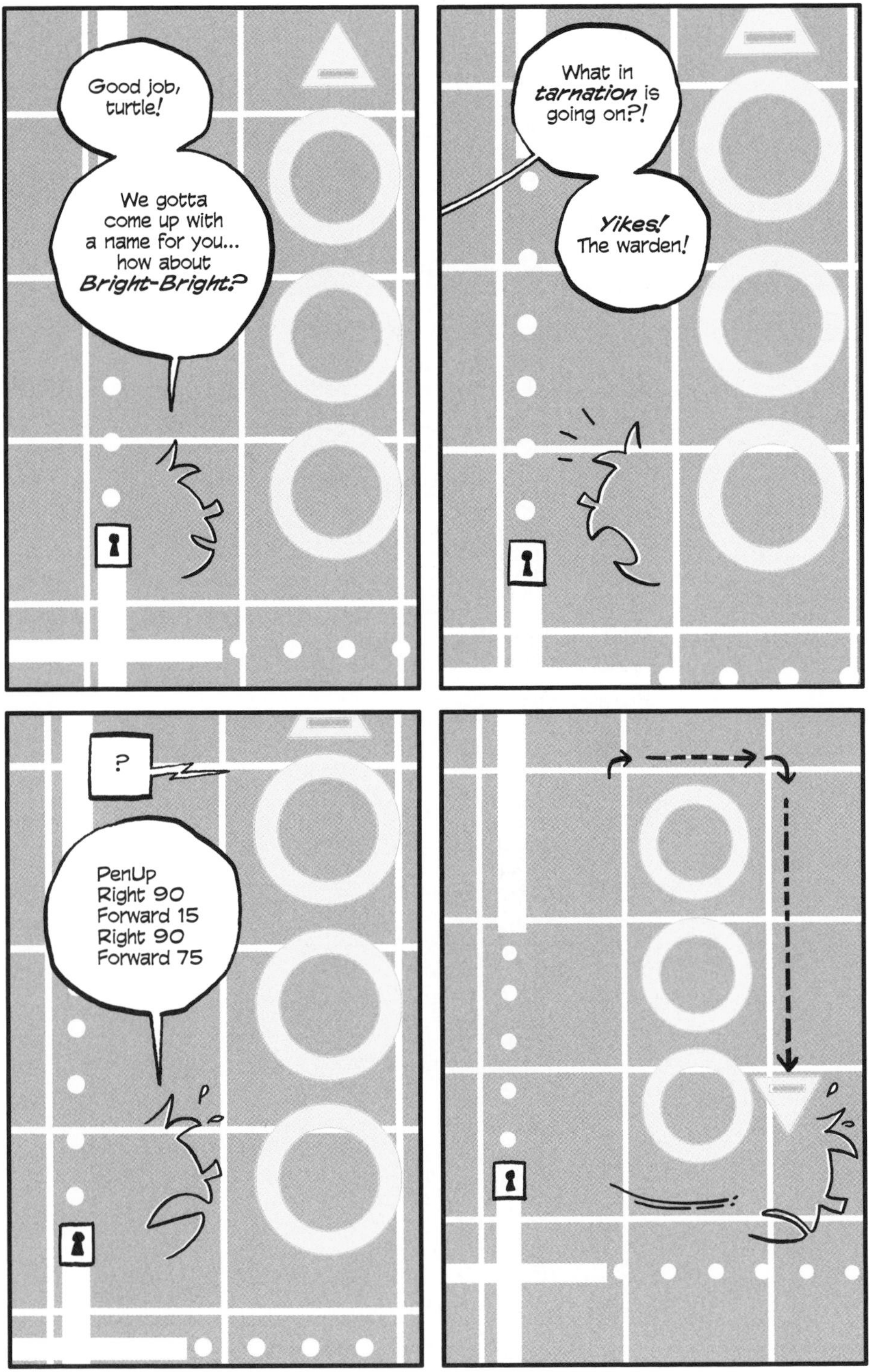
Good job, turtle!
We gotta come up with a name for you... how about *Bright-Bright?*
What in *tarnation* is going on?!
Yikes! The warden!
?
PenUp
Right 90
Forward 15
Right 90
Forward 75

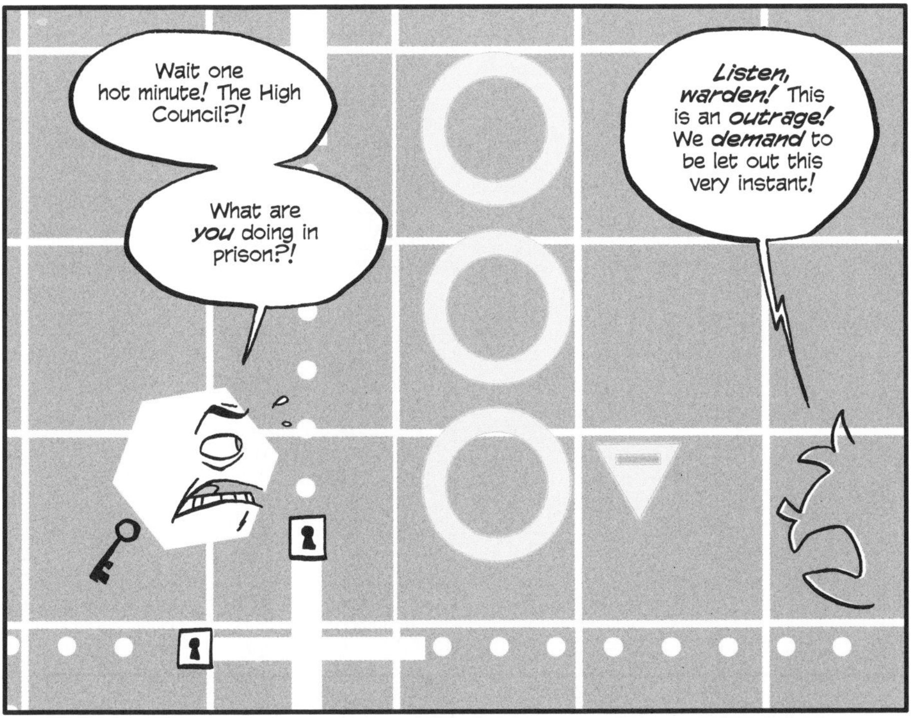
Wait one hot minute! The High Council?!
What are *you* doing in prison?!
Listen, warden! This is an ***outrage!*** We ***demand*** to be let out this very instant!

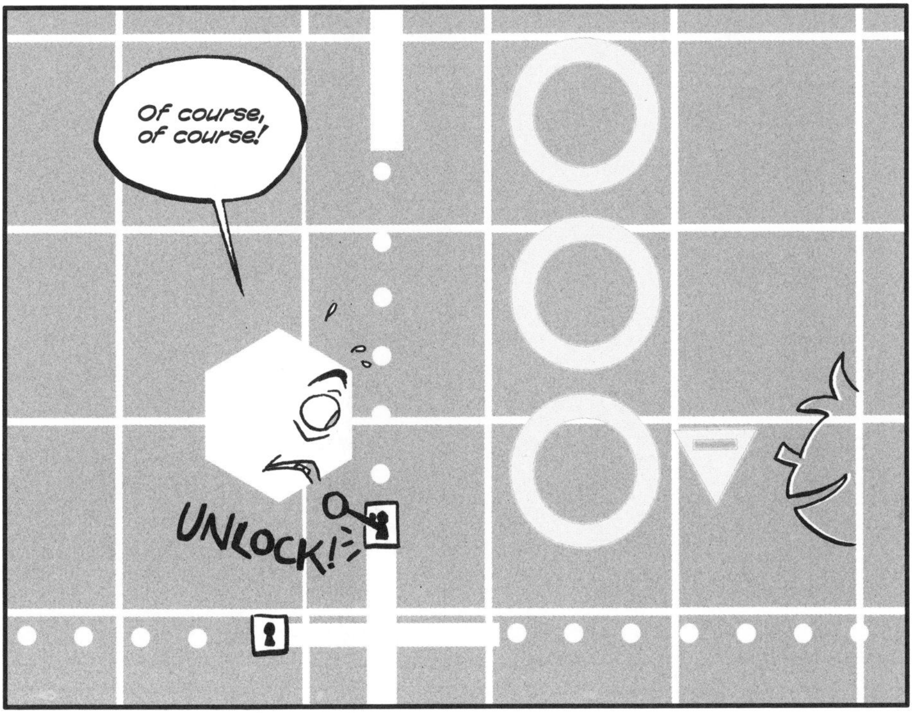
Of course, of course!
UNLOCK!

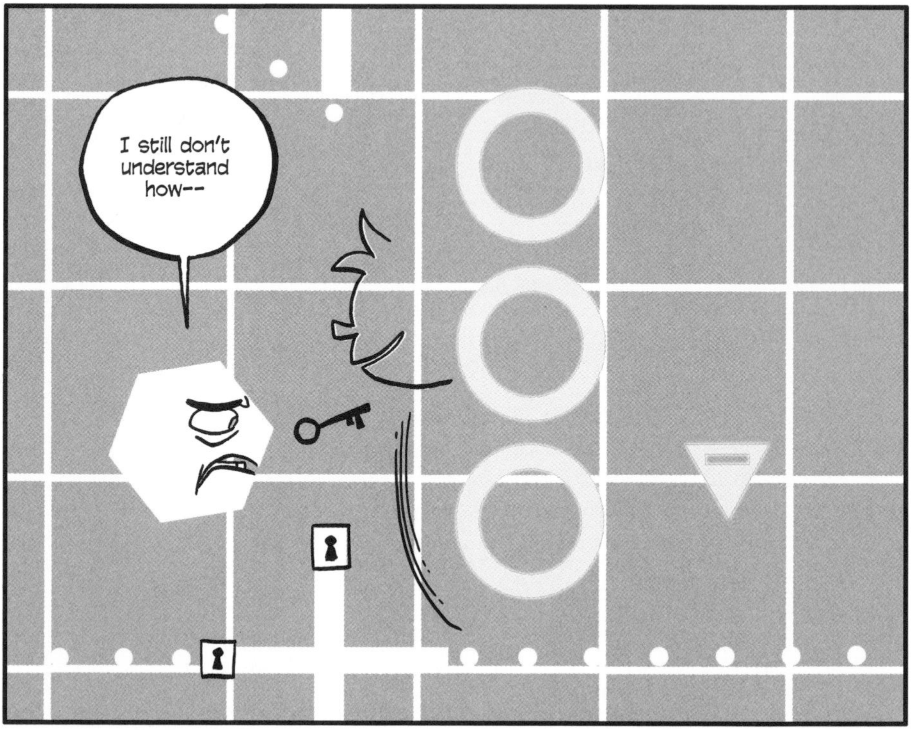
I still don't understand how--

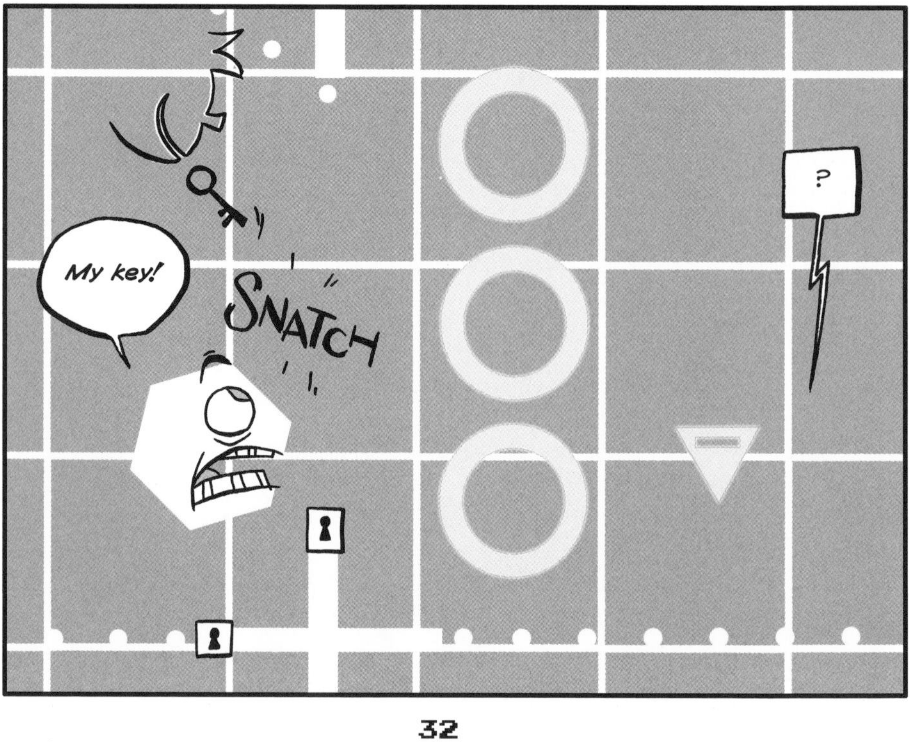
My key!
SNATCH
?

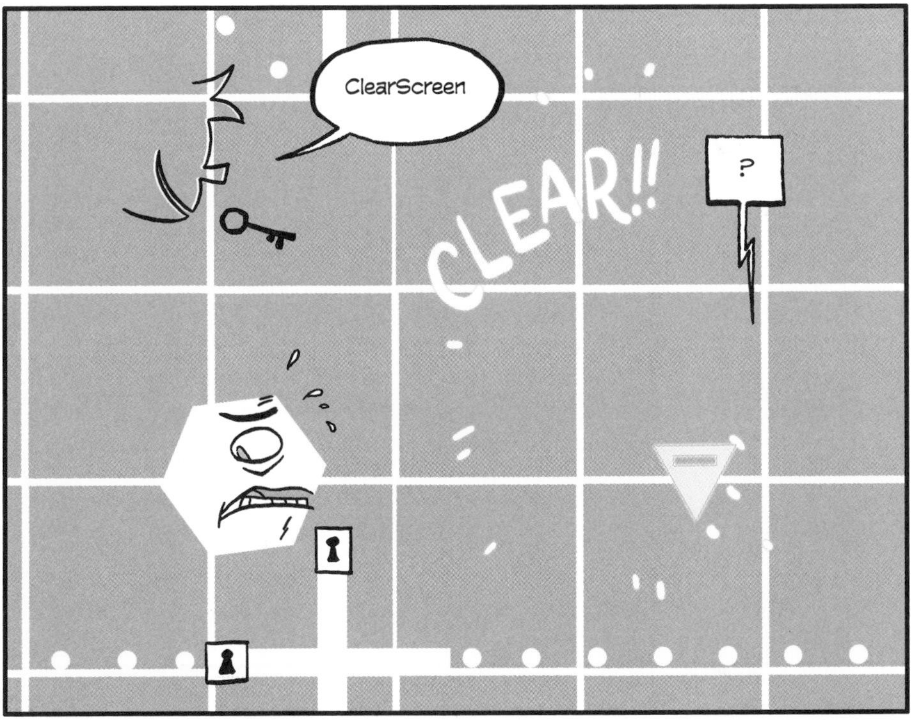
ClearScreen
CLEAR!!
?

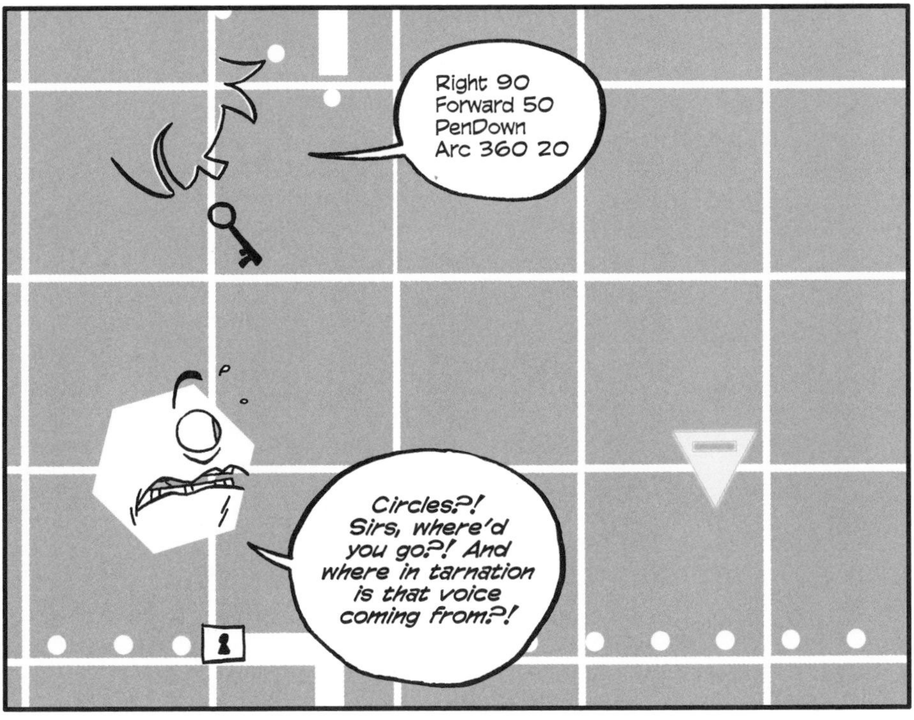
Right 90
Forward 50
PenDown
Arc 360 20
Circles?! Sirs, where'd you go?! And where in tarnation is that voice coming from?!

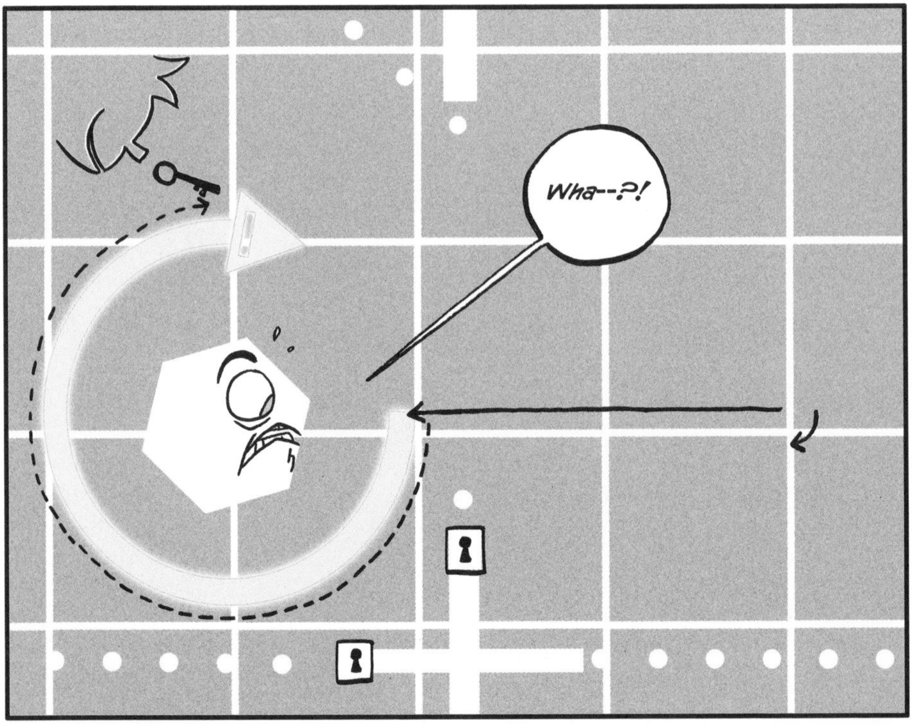
Wha--?!

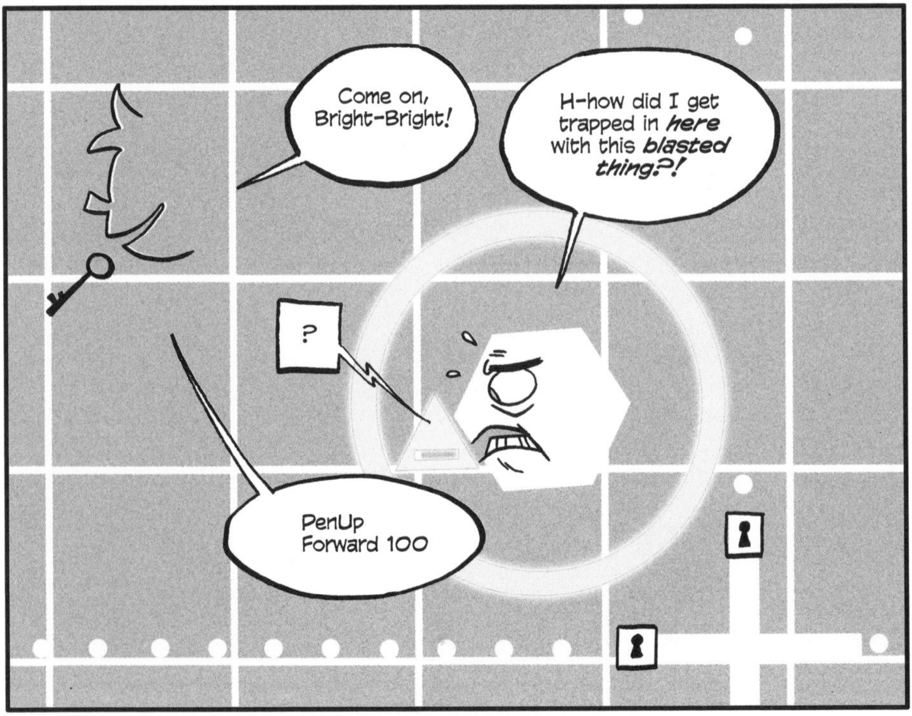
Come on, Bright-Bright!
H-how did I get trapped in *here* with this *blasted thing?!*
?
PenUp
Forward 100

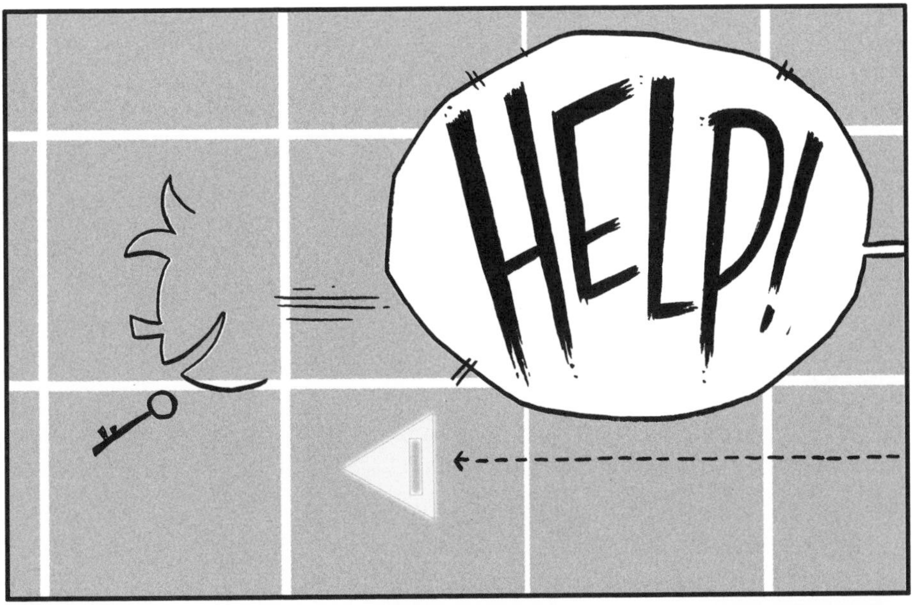
HELP!

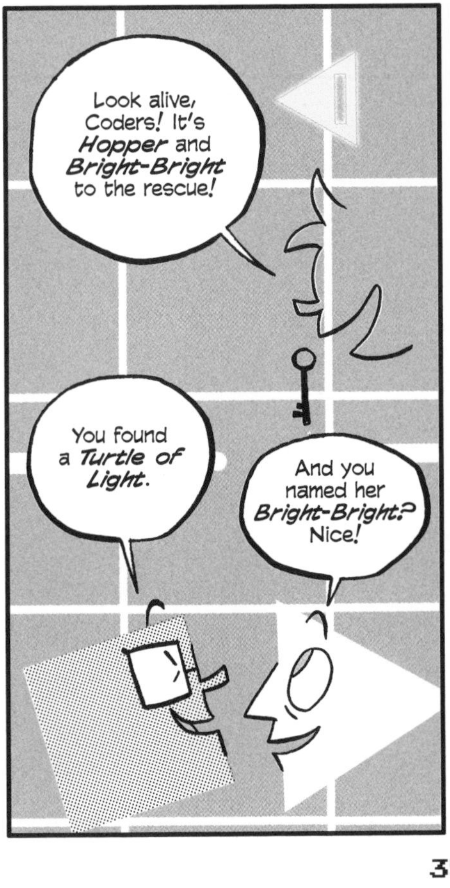
Look alive, Coders! It's *Hopper* and *Bright-Bright* to the rescue!
You found a *Turtle of Light*.
And you named her *Bright-Bright*? Nice!

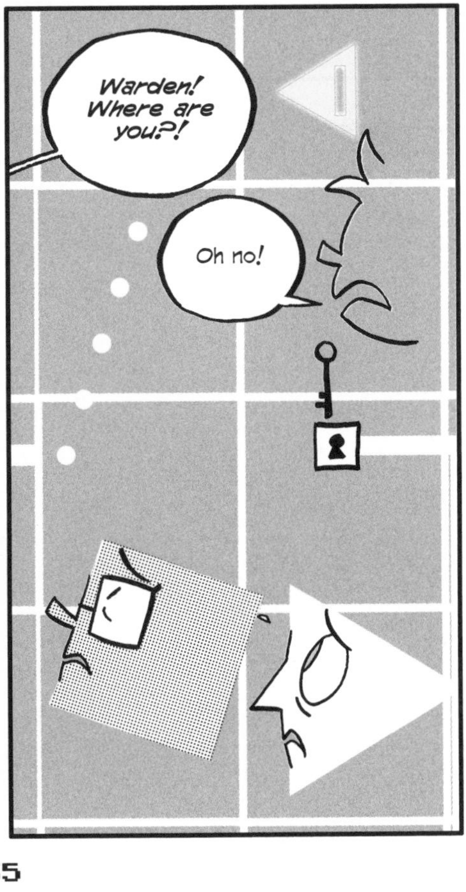
Warden! Where are you?!
Oh no!

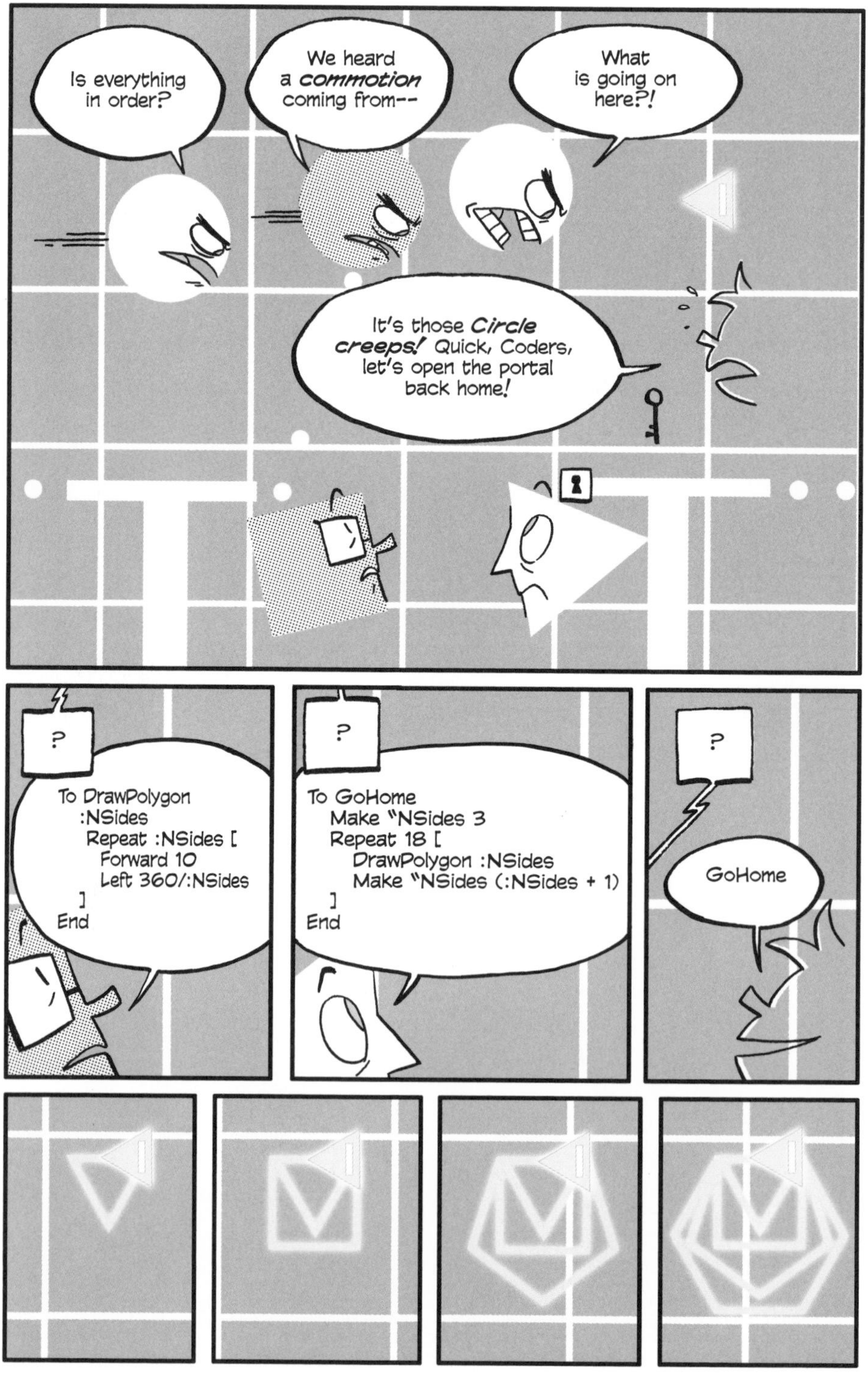

Is everything in order?
We heard a ***commotion*** coming from--
What is going on here?!
It's those ***Circle creeps!*** Quick, Coders, let's open the portal back home!
?
To DrawPolygon
:NSides
Repeat :NSides [
Forward 10
Left 360/:NSides
]
End
?
To GoHome
Make "NSides 3
Repeat 18 [
DrawPolygon :NSides
Make "NSides (:NSides + 1)
]
End
?
GoHome

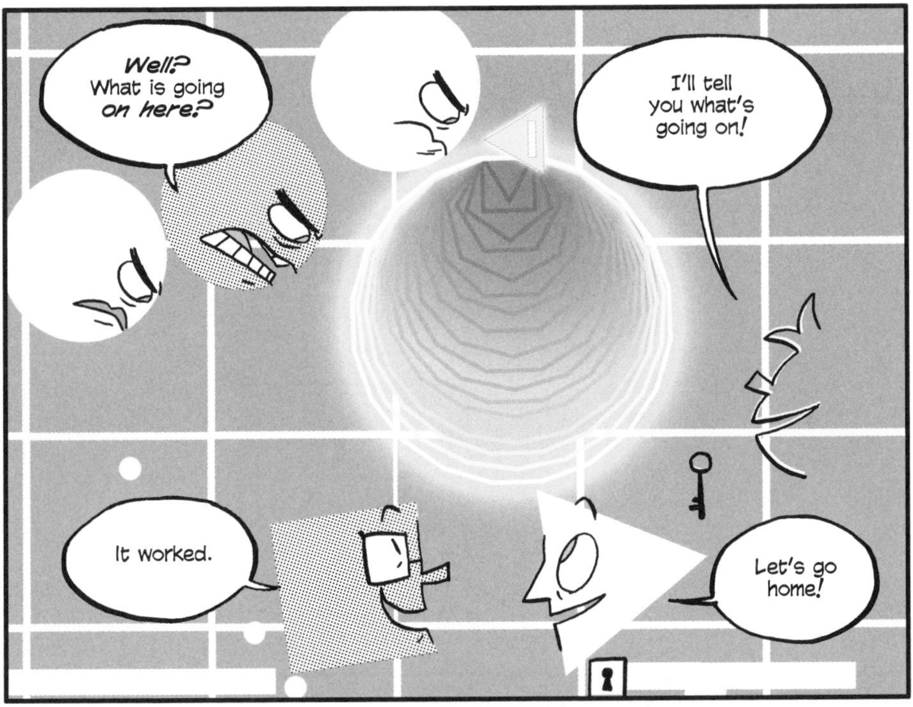
Well? What is going on here?
I'll tell you what's going on!
It worked.
Let's go home!

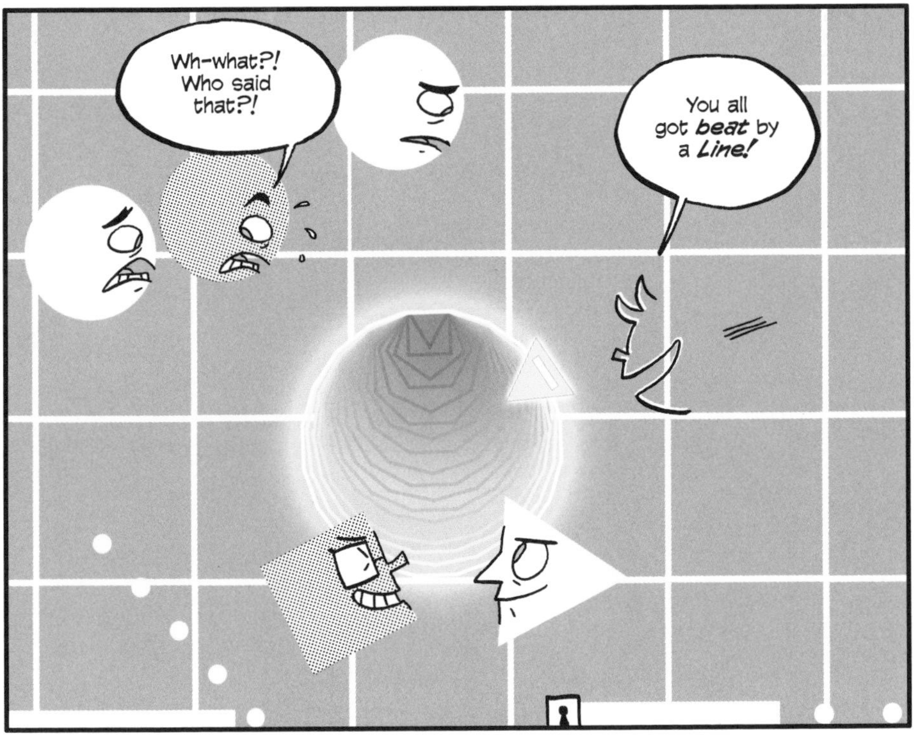
Wh-what?! Who said that?!
You all got beat by a Line!

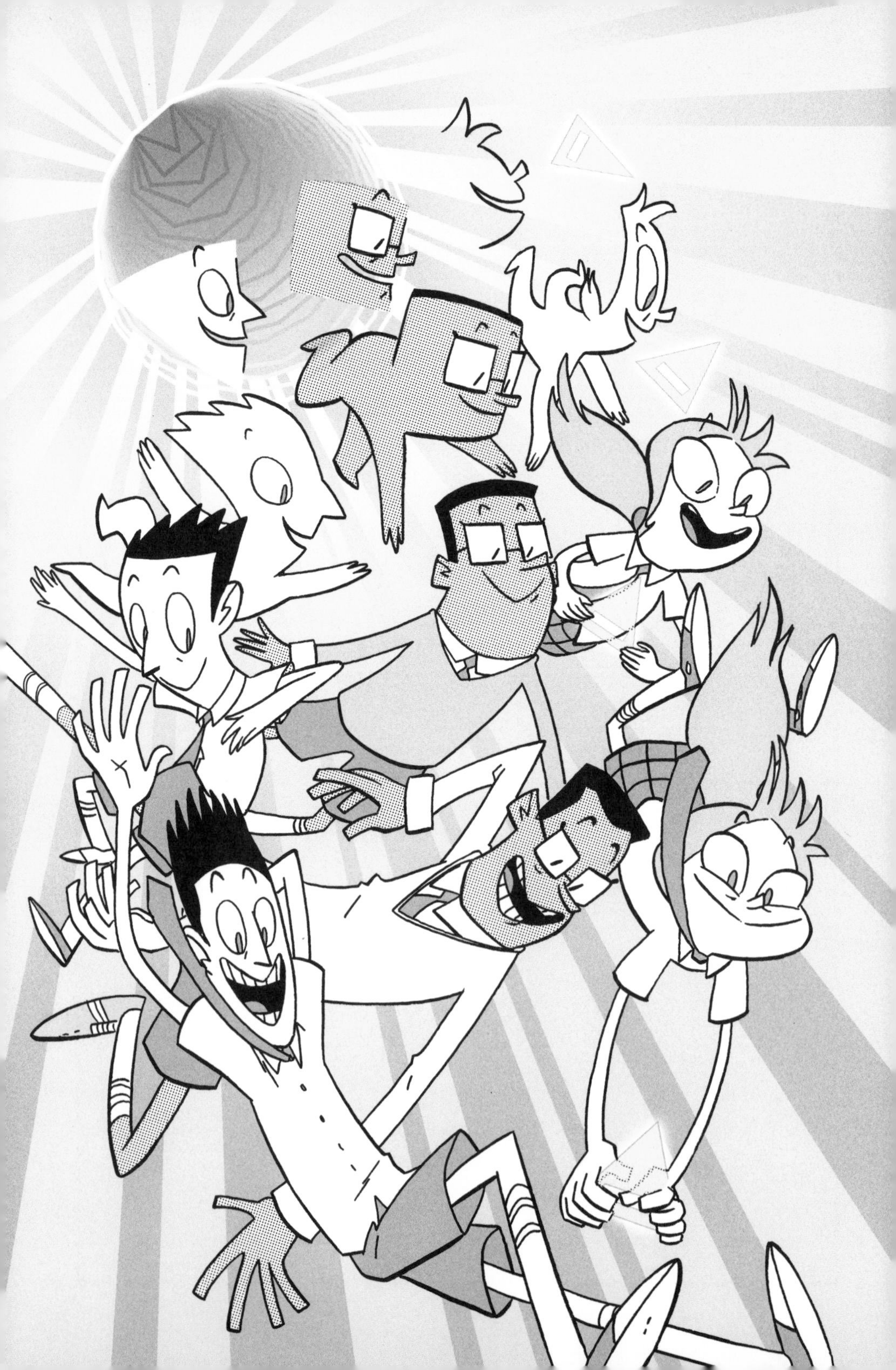

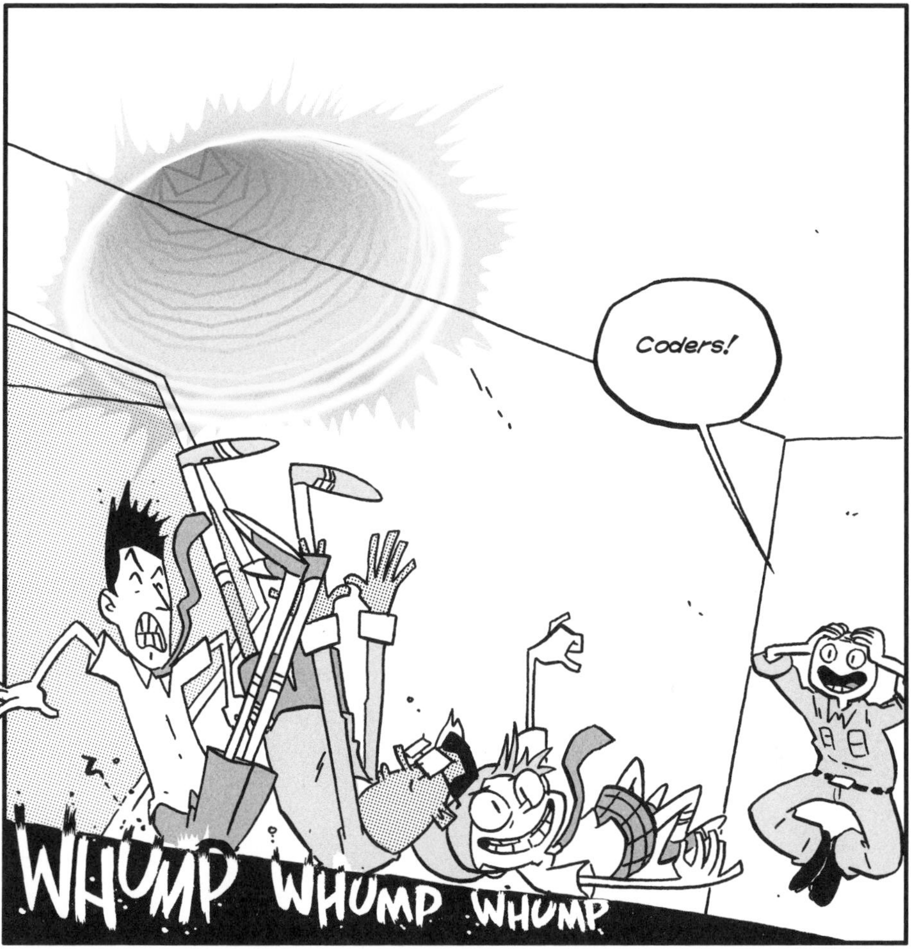
Coders!
WHUMP WHUMP WHUMP

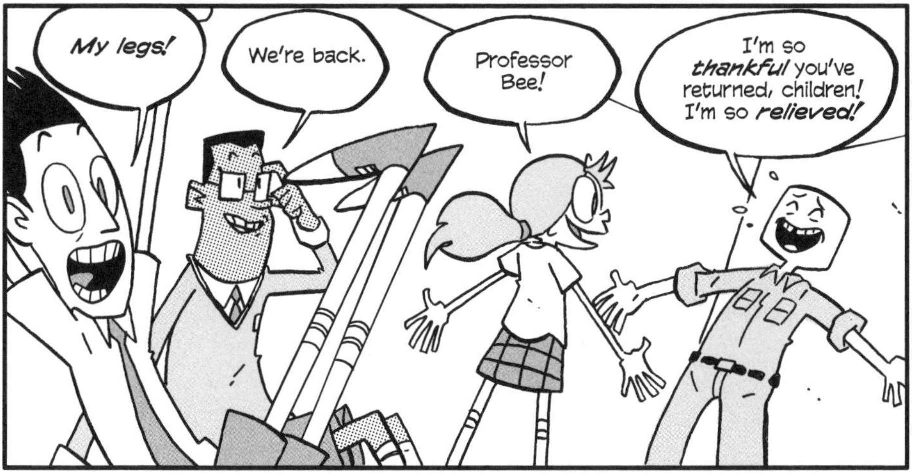
My legs!
We're back.
Professor Bee!
I'm so thankful you've returned, children! I'm so relieved!

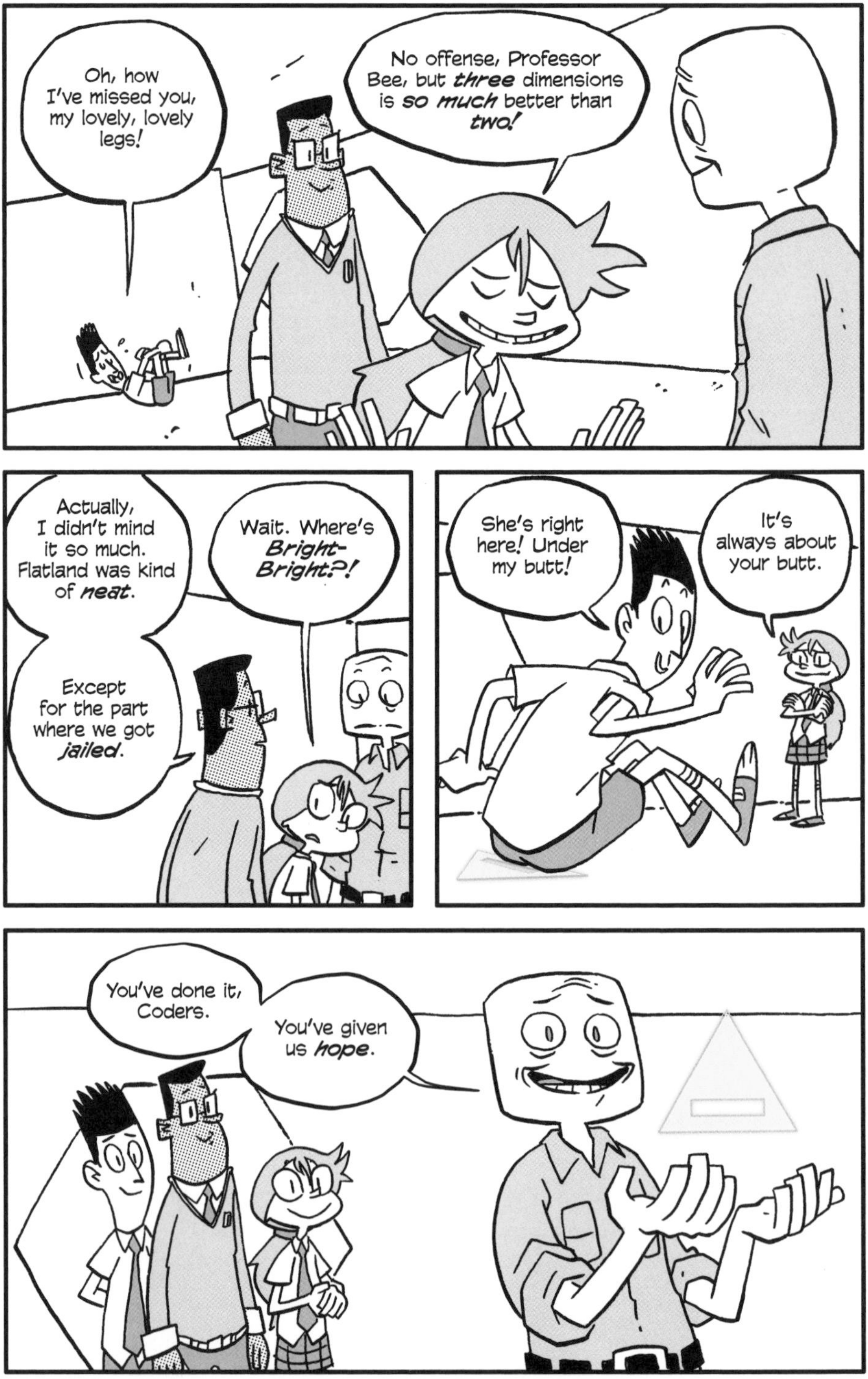
Oh, how I've missed you, my lovely, lovely legs!
No offense, Professor Bee, but *three* dimensions is *so much* better than *two!*
Actually, I didn't mind it so much. Flatland was kind of *neat*.
Except for the part where we got *jailed*.
Wait. Where's *Bright-Bright?!*
She's right here! Under my butt!
It's always about your butt.
You've done it, Coders.
You've given us *hope*.

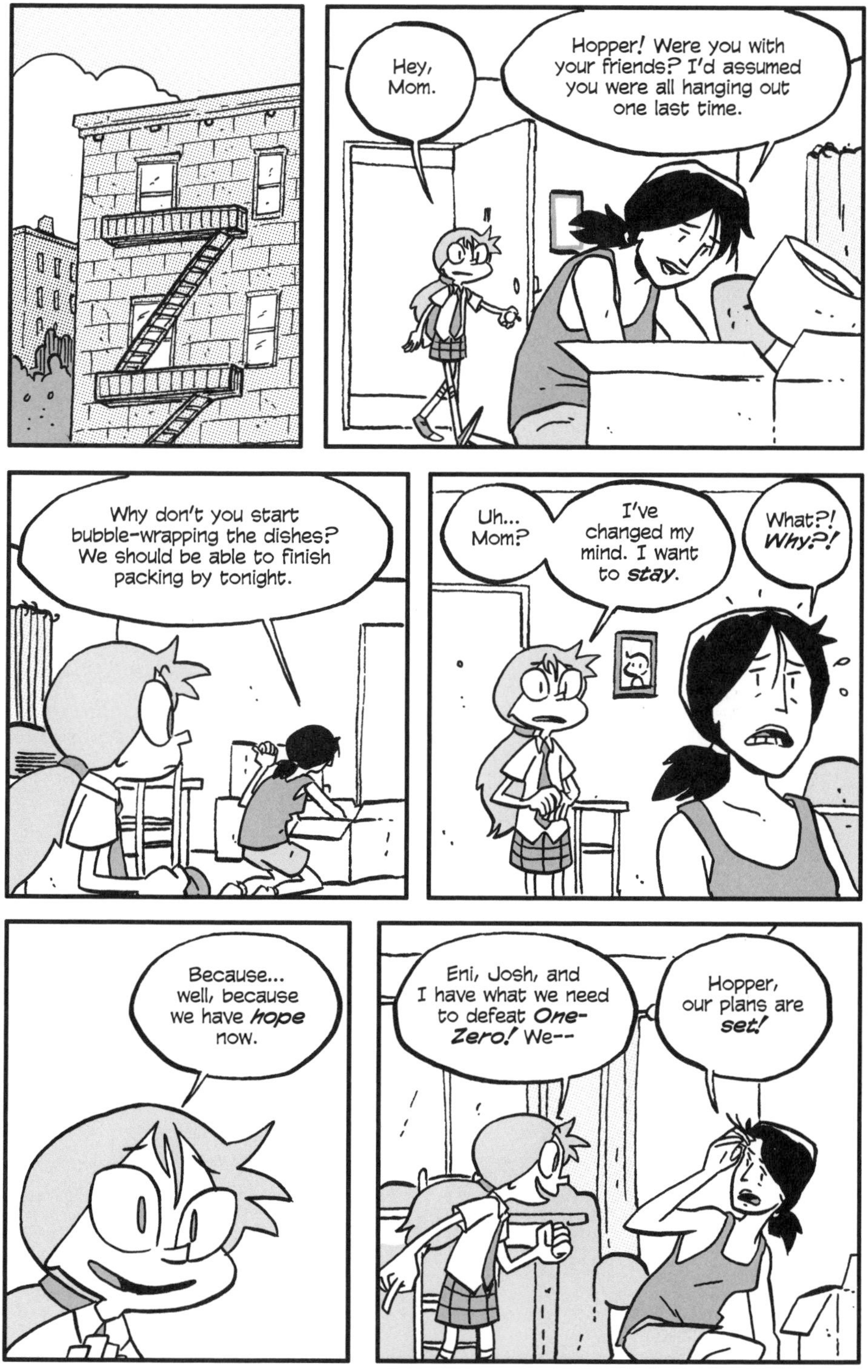
Hey,
Mom.
Hopper! Were you with your friends? I'd assumed you were all hanging out one last time.
Why don't you start bubble-wrapping the dishes? We should be able to finish packing by tonight.
Uh... Mom?
I've changed my mind. I want to *stay*.
What?! *Why?!*
Because... well, because we have *hope* now.
Eni, Josh, and I have what we need to defeat *One-Zero!* We--
Hopper, our plans are *set!*

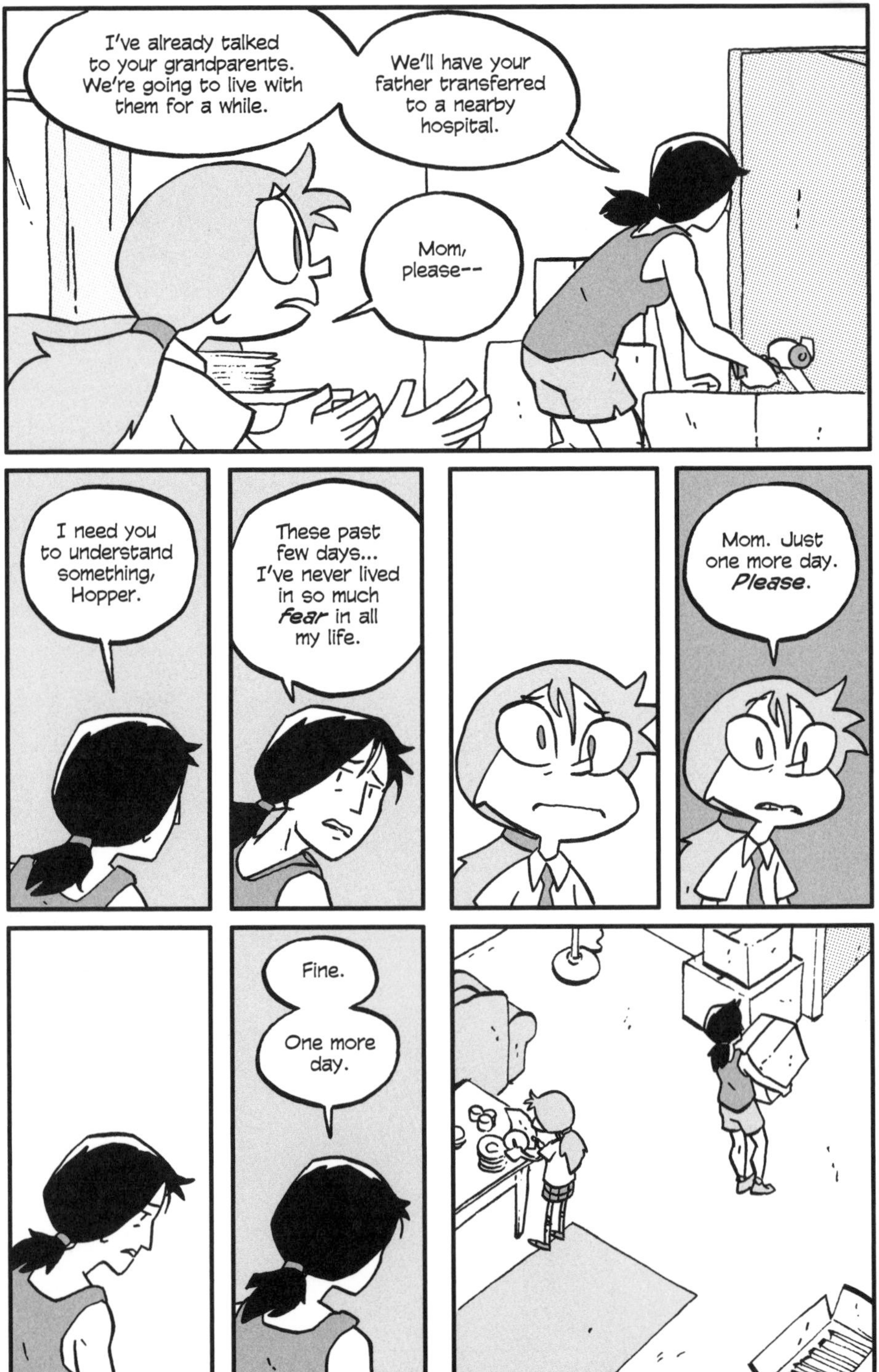
I've already talked to your grandparents. We're going to live with them for a while.
We'll have your father transferred to a nearby hospital.
Mom, please--
I need you to understand something, Hopper.
These past few days... I've never lived in so much *fear* in all my life.
Mom. Just one more day. ***Please***.
Fine.
One more day.

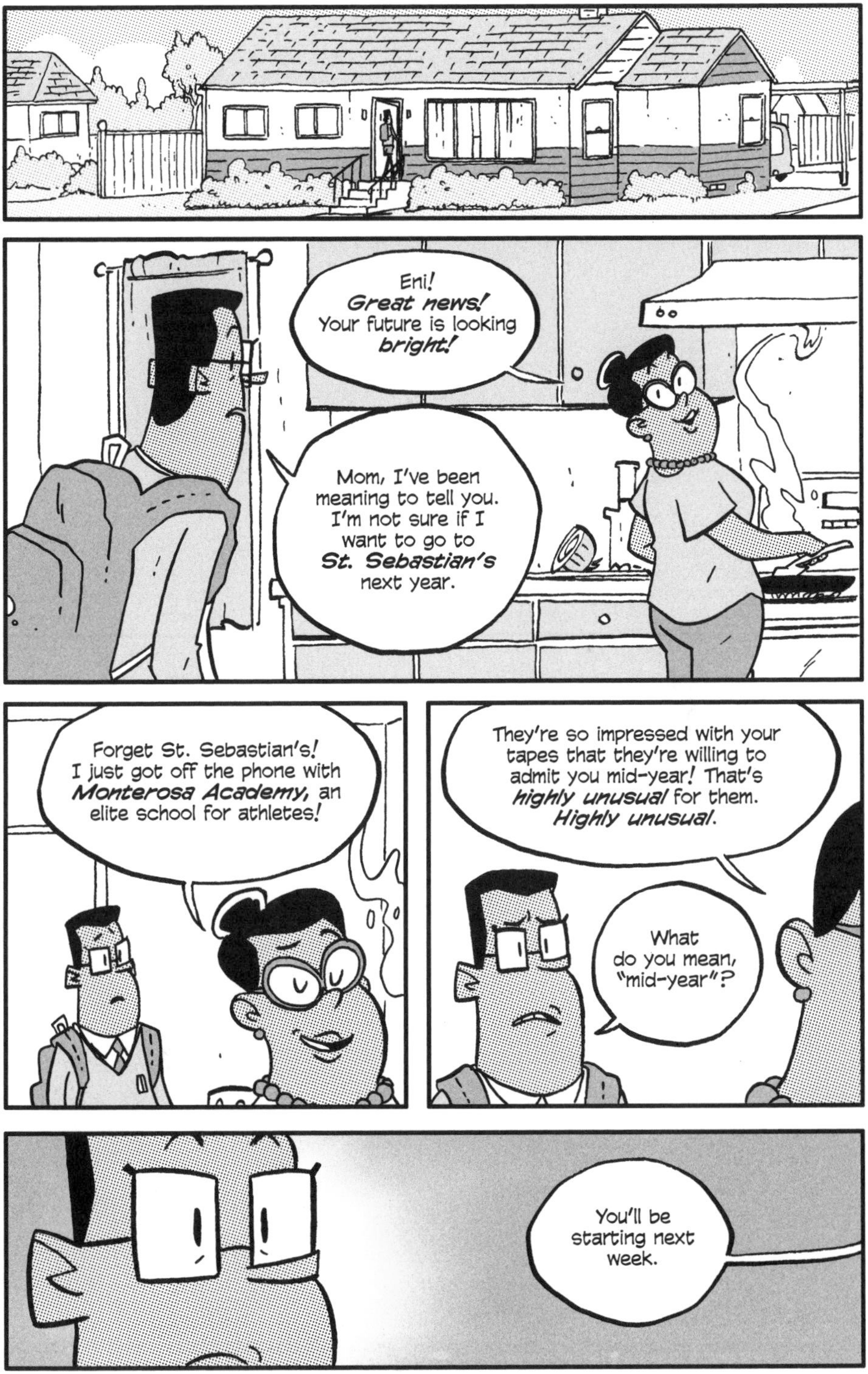
Eni! Great news! Your future is looking bright!
Mom, I've been meaning to tell you. I'm not sure if I want to go to St. Sebastian's next year.
Forget St. Sebastian's! I just got off the phone with Monterosa Academy, an elite school for athletes!
They're so impressed with your tapes that they're willing to admit you mid-year! That's highly unusual for them. Highly unusual.
What do you mean, "mid-year"?
You'll be starting next week.

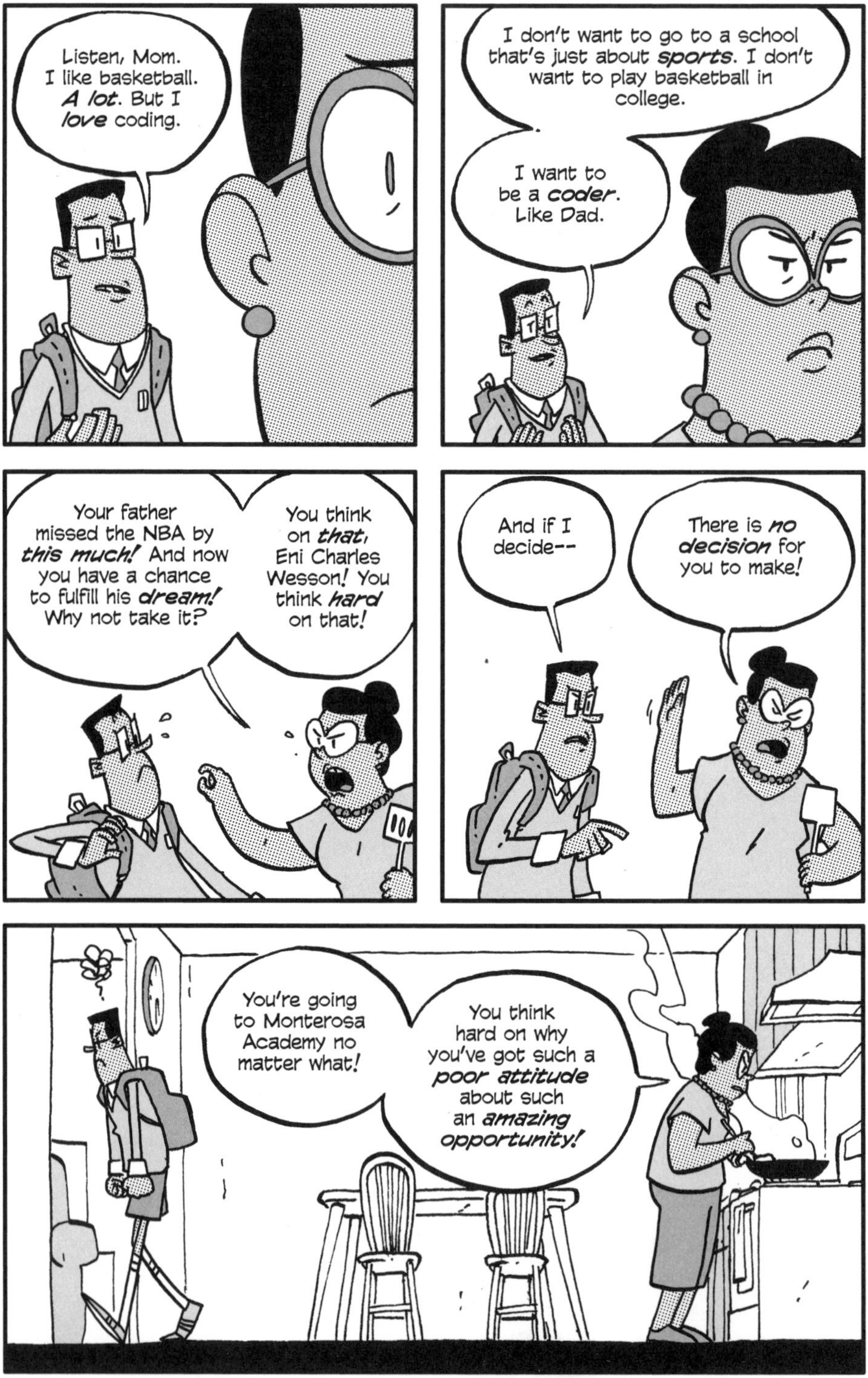
Listen, Mom. I like basketball. *A lot*. But I *love* coding.
I don't want to go to a school that's just about *sports*. I don't want to play basketball in college.
I want to be a *coder*. Like Dad.
Your father missed the NBA by *this much!* And now you have a chance to fulfill his *dream!* Why not take it?
You think on *that*, Eni Charles Wesson! You think *hard* on that!
And if I decide--
There is *no decision* for you to make!
You're going to Monterosa Academy no matter what!
You think hard on why you've got such a *poor attitude* about such an *amazing opportunity!*

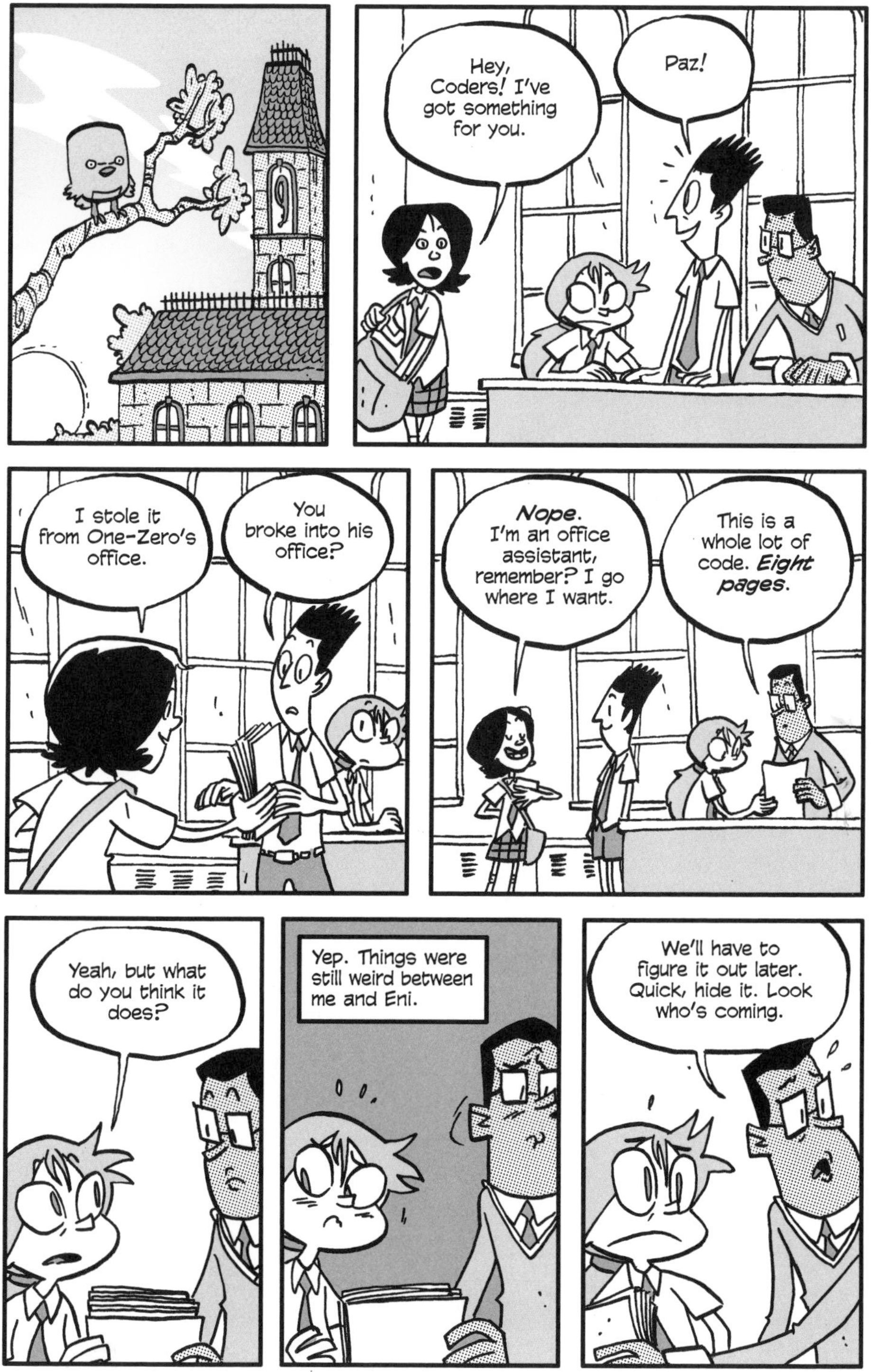
Hey, Coders! I've got something for you.
Paz!
I stole it from One-Zero's office.
You broke into his office?
Nope. I'm an office assistant, remember? I go where I want.
This is a whole lot of code. *Eight pages*.
Yeah, but what do you think it does?
Yep. Things were still weird between me and Eni.
We'll have to figure it out later. Quick, hide it. Look who's coming.

Good morning, class! Come, gather around! I'm going to teach you that *new lesson* I promised!

Wait, that looks like the same stuff we were making before!

Yes, but we're going to take it one step further.

This pellet turns *liquid* into *gas*.

We'll drop one in--

BLOOP

--then capture the results in an *elastic container*.

SSSSSS

SSSSSS

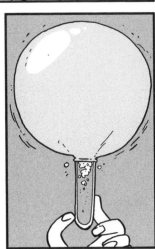

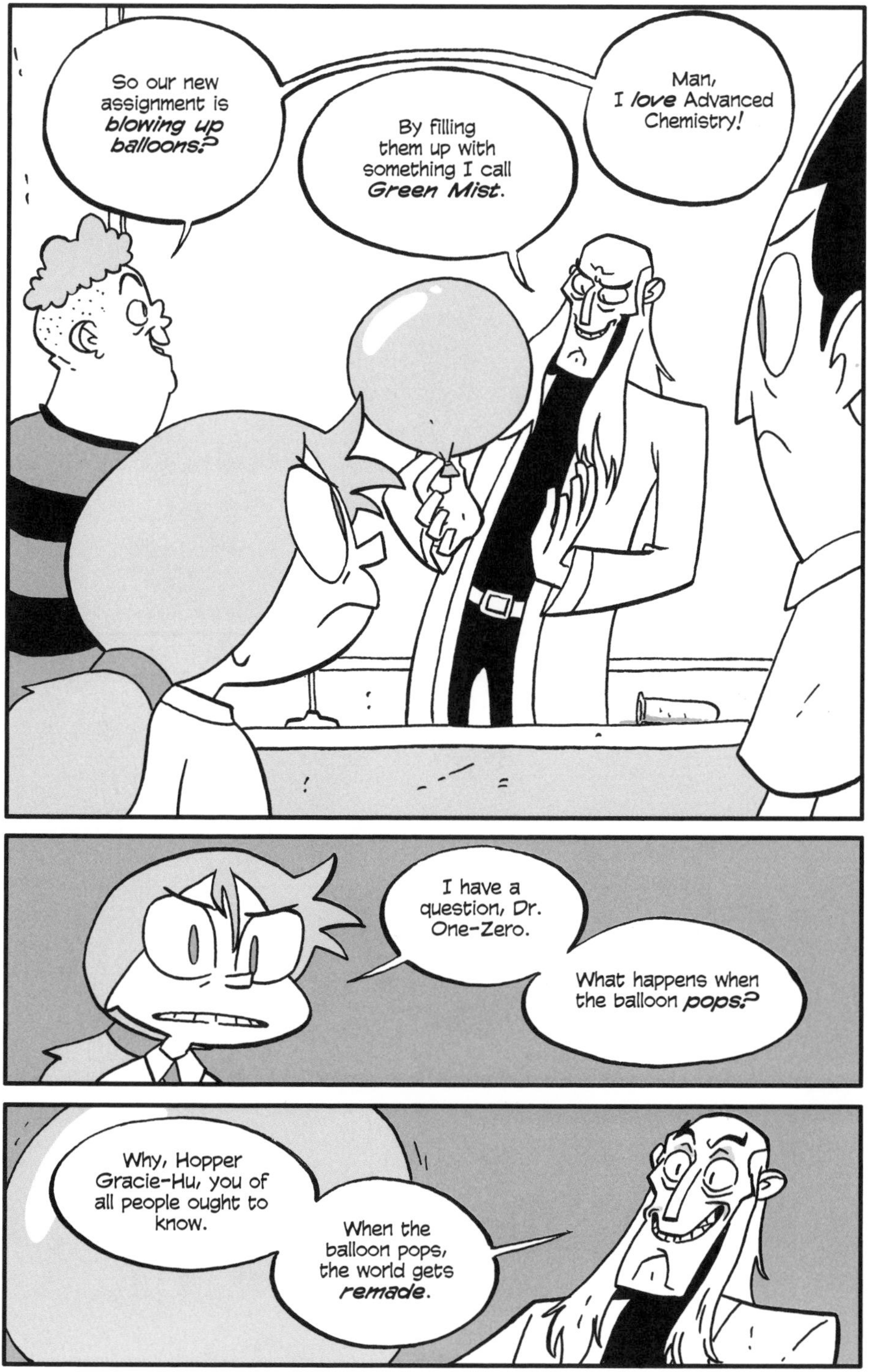
So our new assignment is *blowing up balloons?*
By filling them up with something I call *Green Mist*.
Man, I *love* Advanced Chemistry!
I have a question, Dr. One-Zero.
What happens when the balloon *pops?*
Why, Hopper Gracie-Hu, you of all people ought to know.
When the balloon pops, the world gets *remade*.

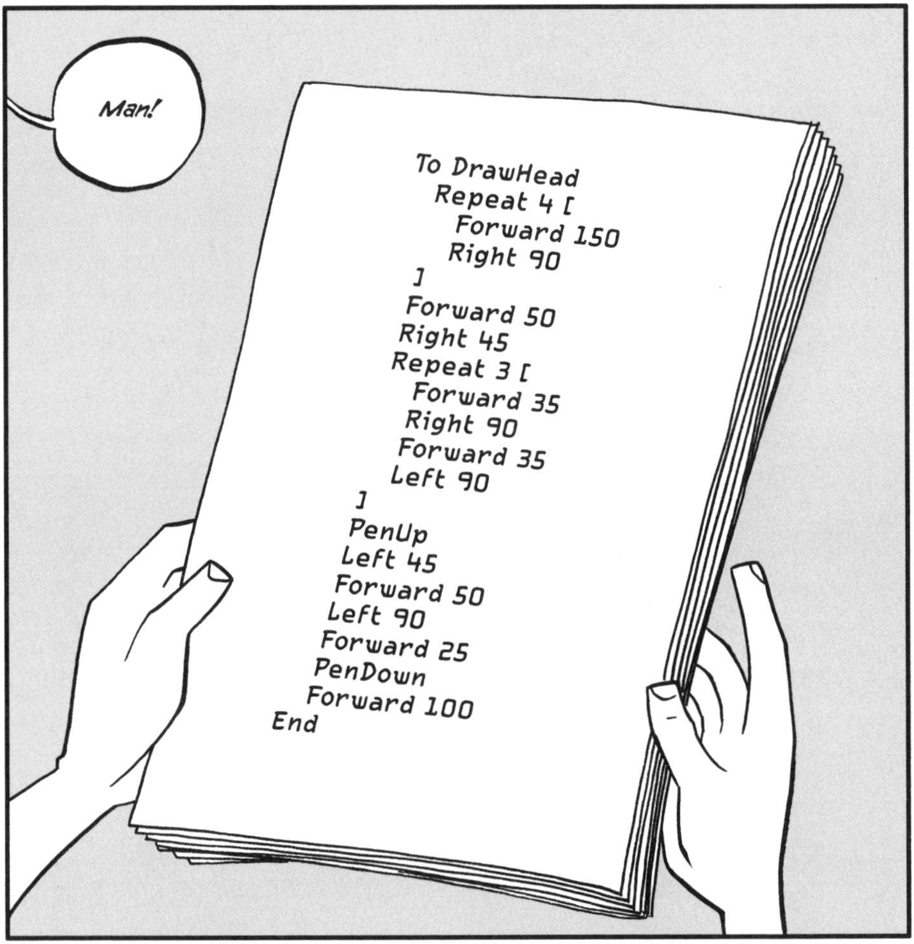
Man!
To DrawHead
Repeat 4 [
Forward 150
Right 90
]
Forward 50
Right 45
Repeat 3 [
Forward 35
Right 90
Forward 35
Left 90
]
PenUp
Left 45
Forward 50
Left 90
Forward 25
PenDown
Forward 100
End

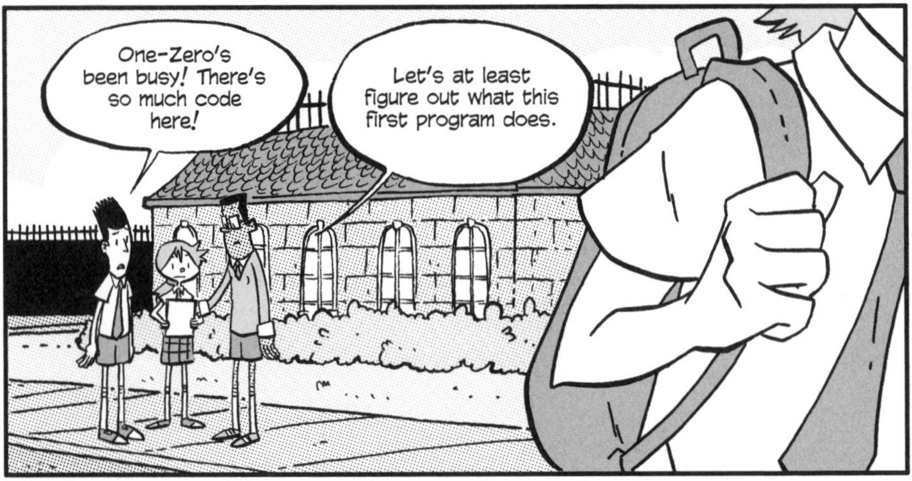
One-Zero's been busy! There's so much code here!
Let's at least figure out what this first program does.

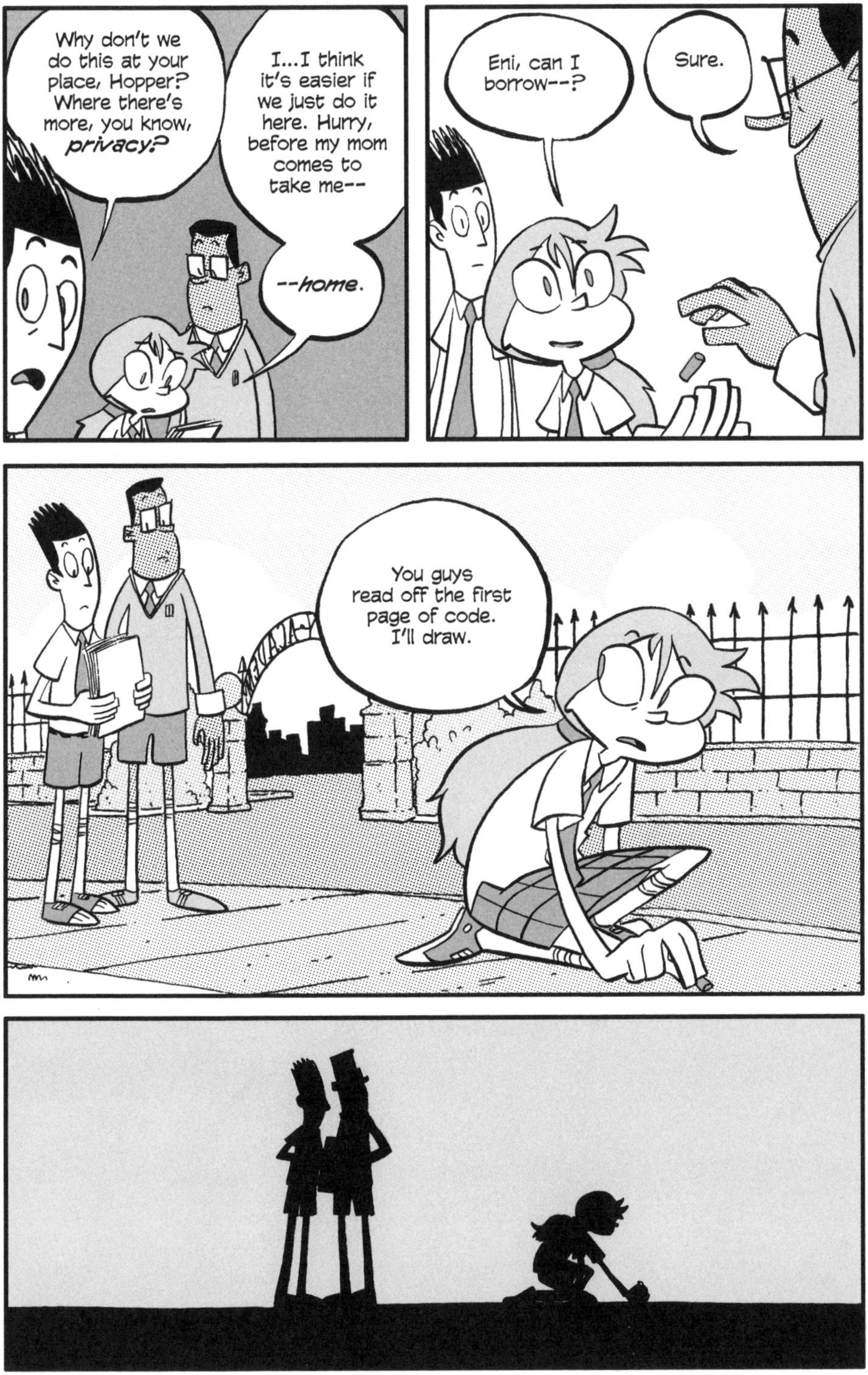
Why don't we do this at your place, Hopper? Where there's more, you know, *privacy?*
I...I think it's easier if we just do it here. Hurry, before my mom comes to take me--
--*home*.
Eni, can I borrow--?
Sure.
You guys read off the first page of code. I'll draw.

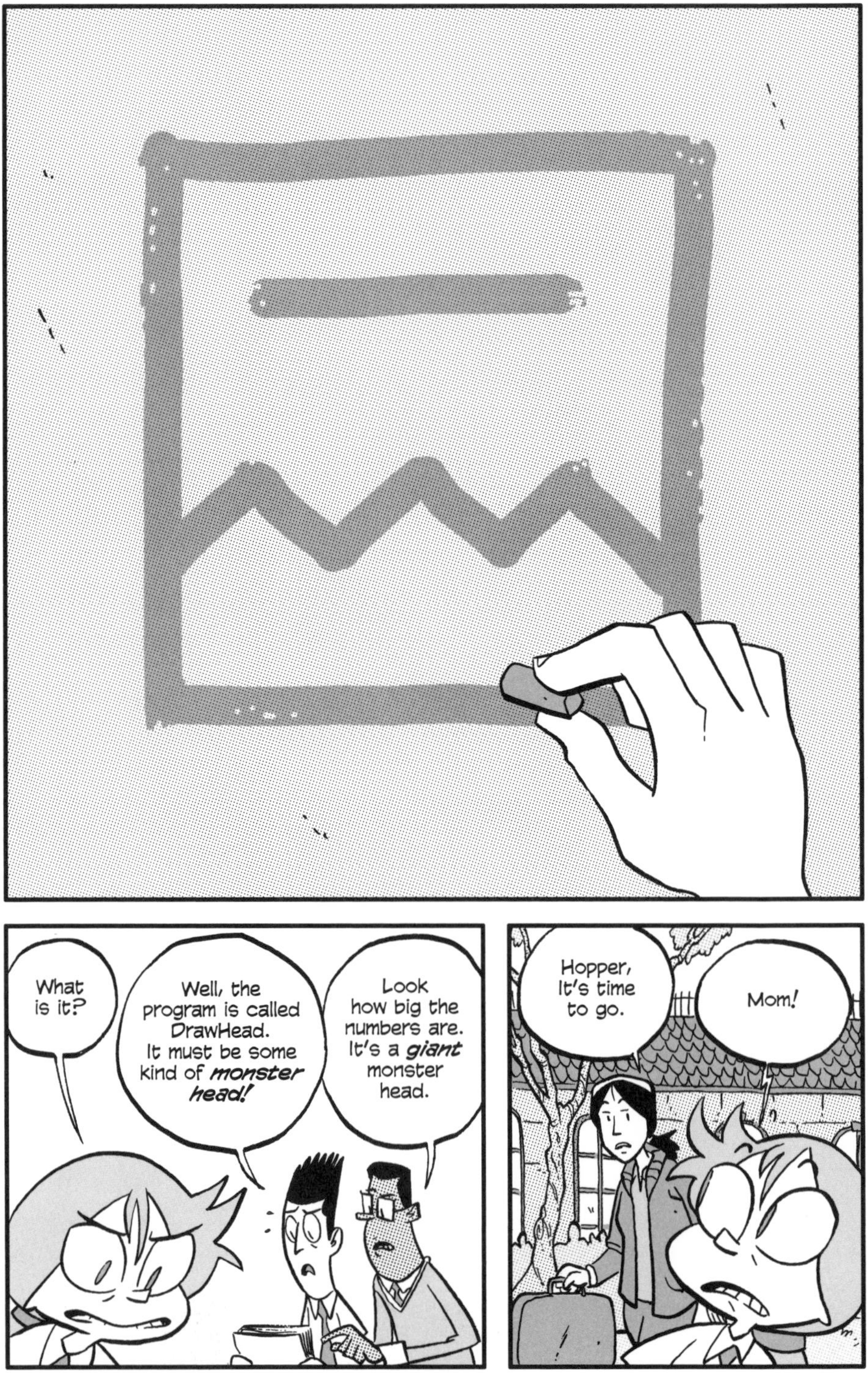
What is it?
Well, the program is called DrawHead. It must be some kind of *monster head!*
Look how big the numbers are. It's a *giant* monster head.
Hopper, It's time to go.
Mom!

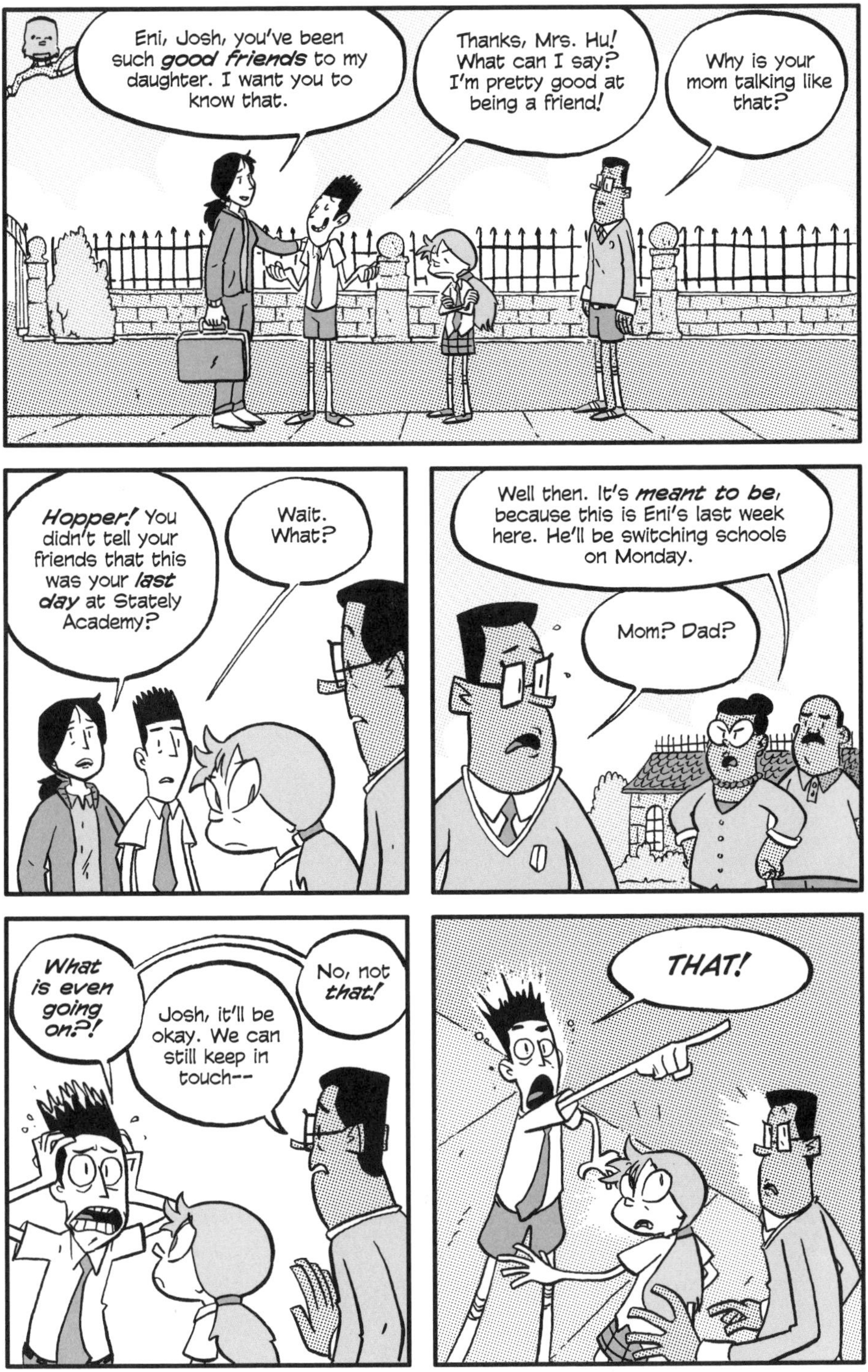
Eni, Josh, you've been such **good friends** to my daughter. I want you to know that.
Thanks, Mrs. Hu! What can I say? I'm pretty good at being a friend!
Why is your mom talking like that?
Hopper! You didn't tell your friends that this was your **last day** at Stately Academy?
Wait. What?
Well then. It's **meant to be**, because this is Eni's last week here. He'll be switching schools on Monday.
Mom? Dad?
What is even going on?!
Josh, it'll be okay. We can still keep in touch--
No, not **that!**
THAT!

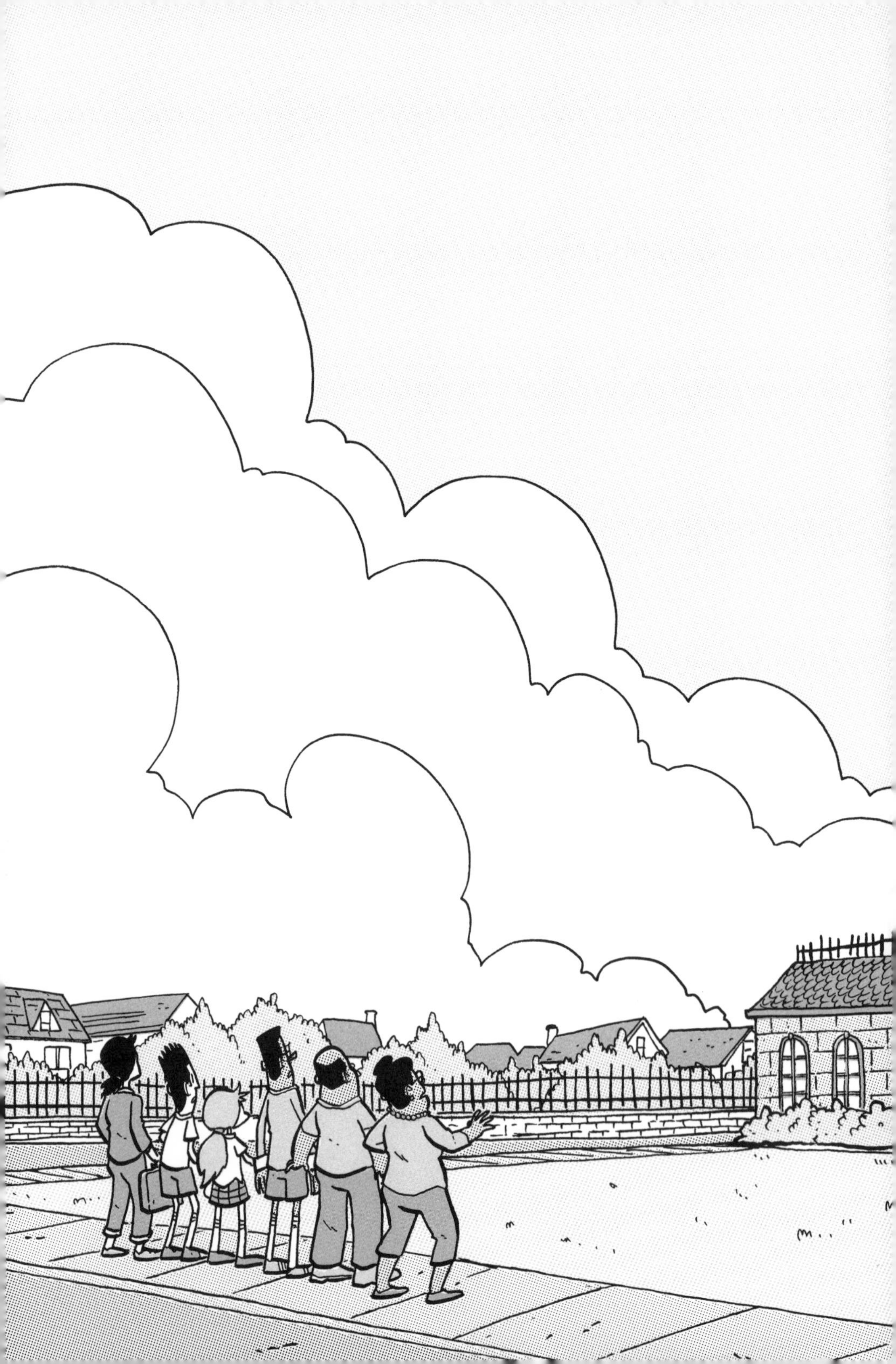

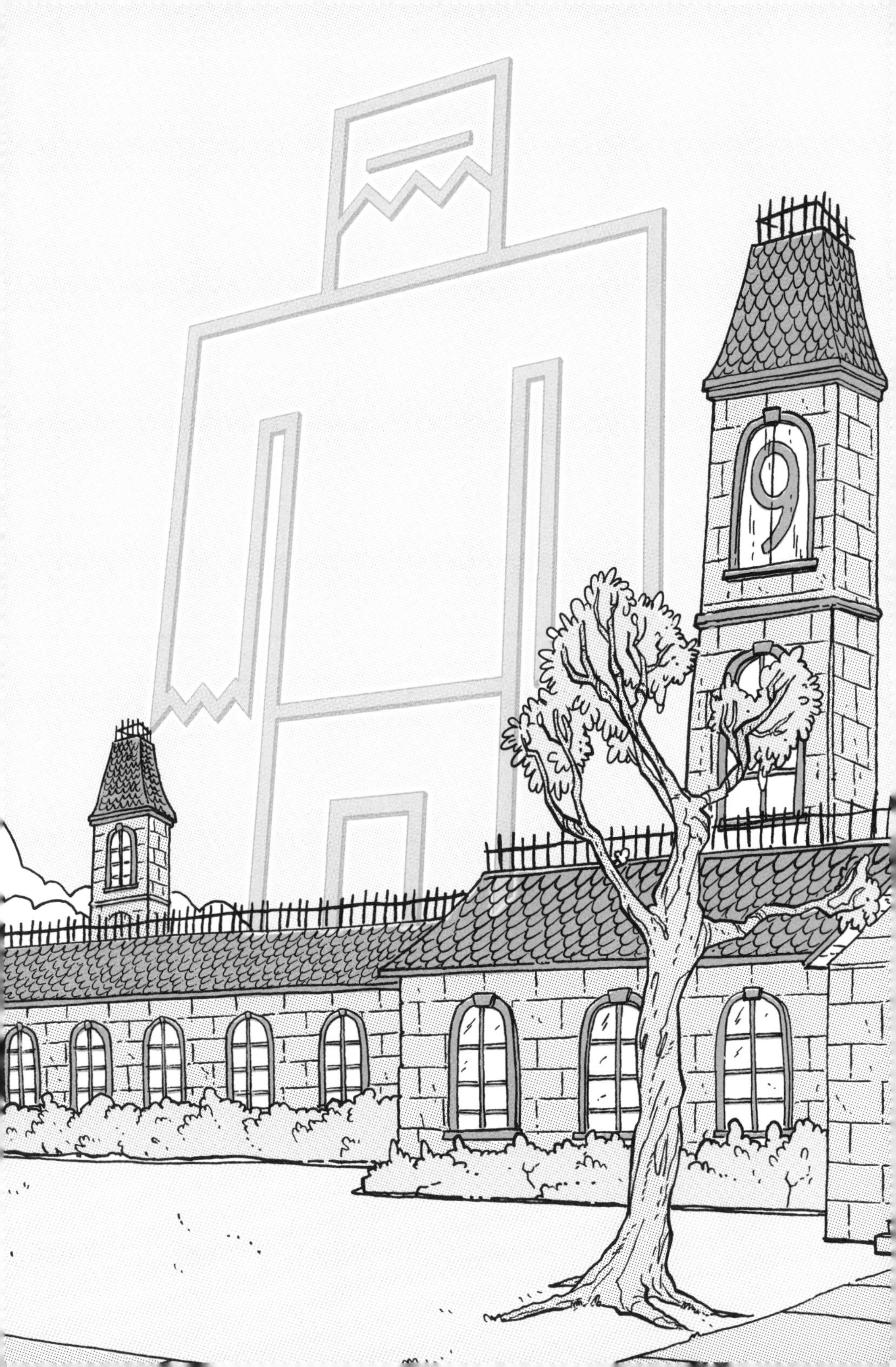
9

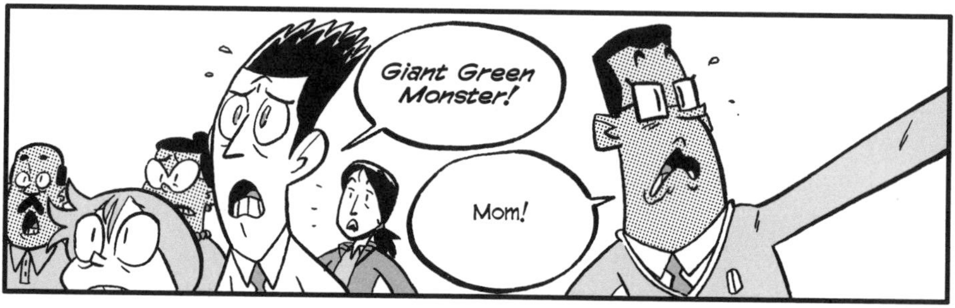
Giant Green Monster!
Mom!

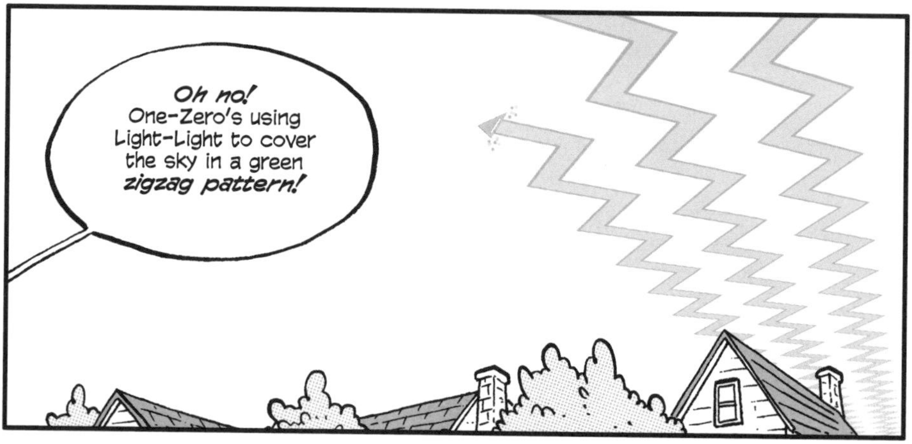
Oh no! One-Zero's using Light-Light to cover the sky in a green zigzag pattern!

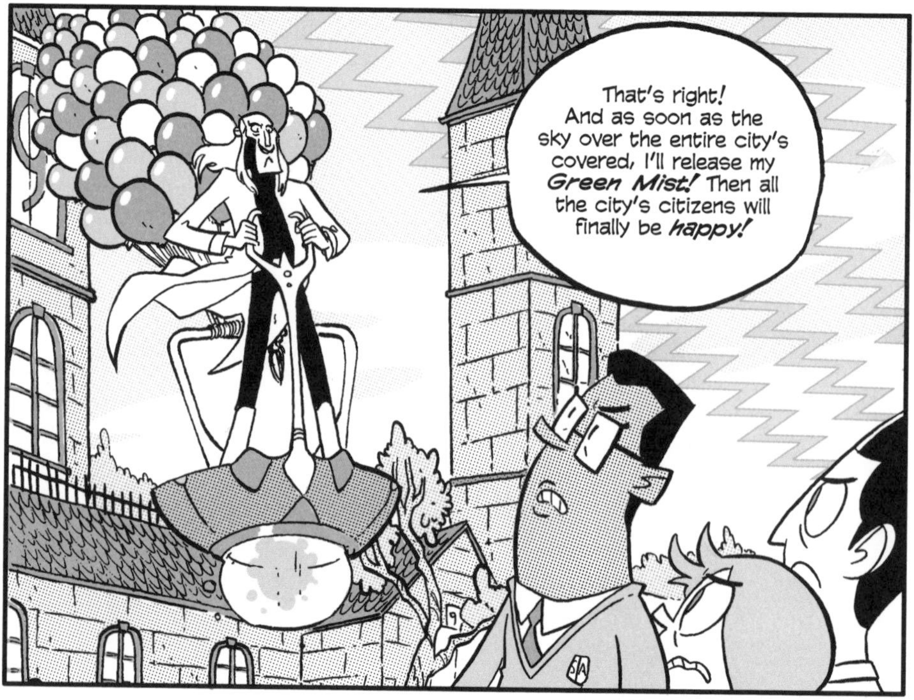
That's right! And as soon as the sky over the entire city's covered, I'll release my Green Mist! Then all the city's citizens will finally be happy!

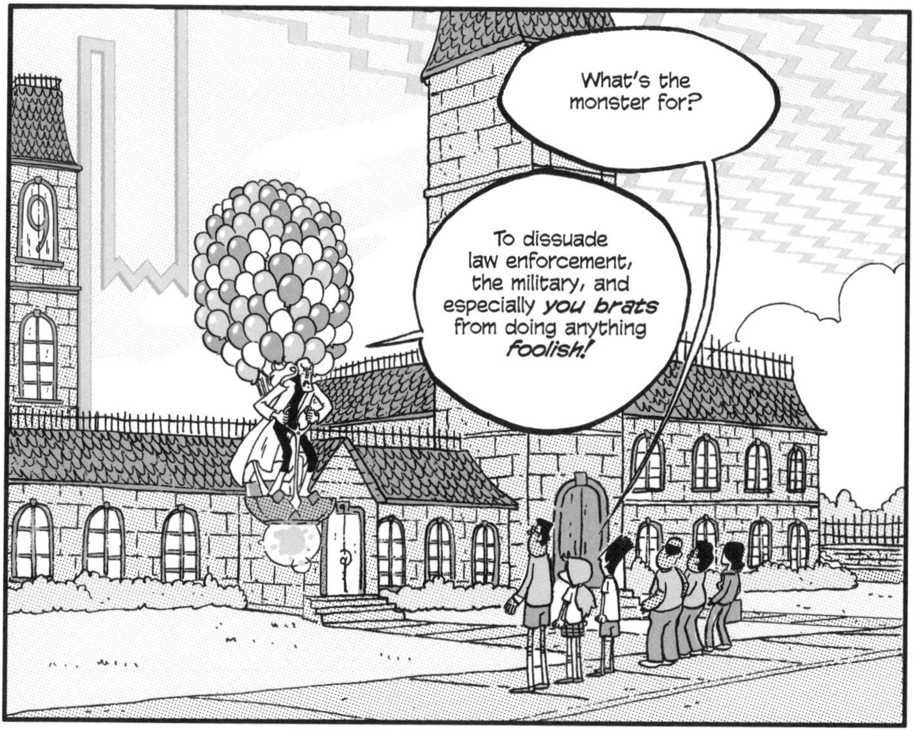
What's the monster for?
To dissuade law enforcement, the military, and especially *you brats* from doing anything *foolish!*

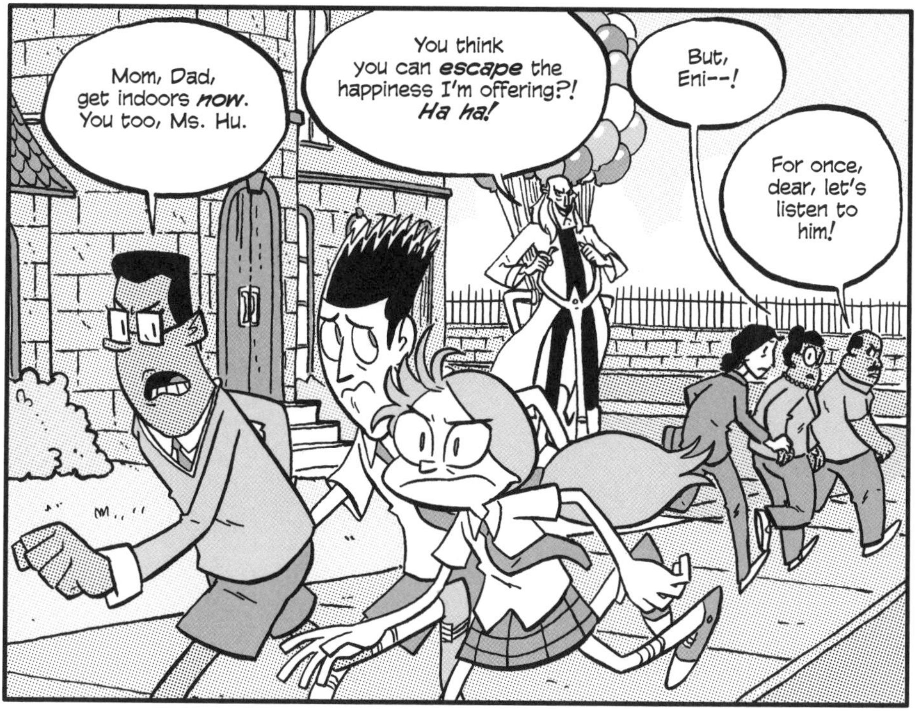
Mom, Dad, get indoors *now*. You too, Ms. Hu.
You think you can *escape* the happiness I'm offering?! *Ha ha!*
But, Eni--!
For once, dear, let's listen to him!

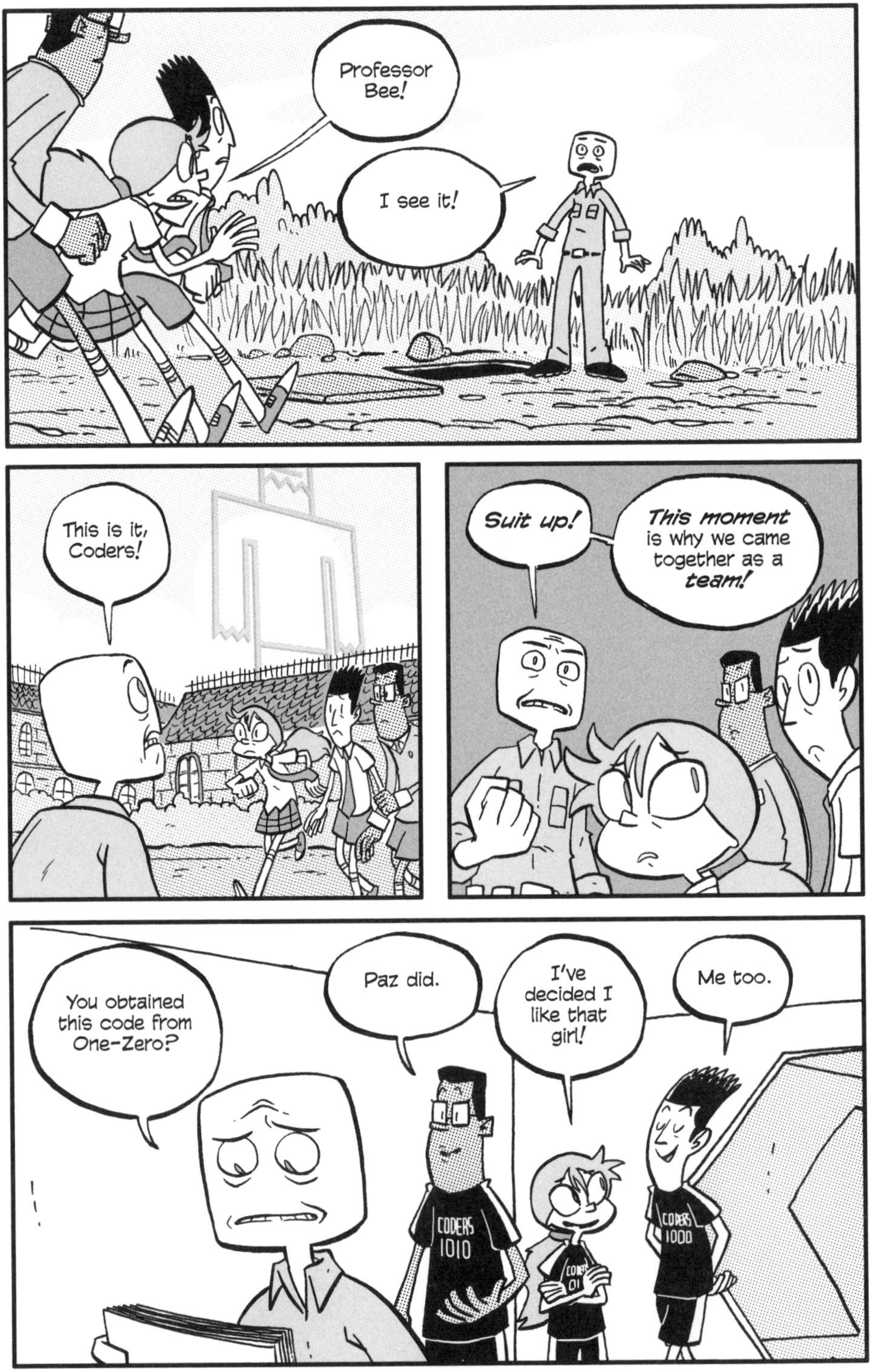
Professor Bee!
I see it!
This is it, Coders!
Suit up!
This moment is why we came together as a team!
You obtained this code from One-Zero?
Paz did.
I've decided I like that girl!
Me too.
CODERS 1010
CODERS 1000

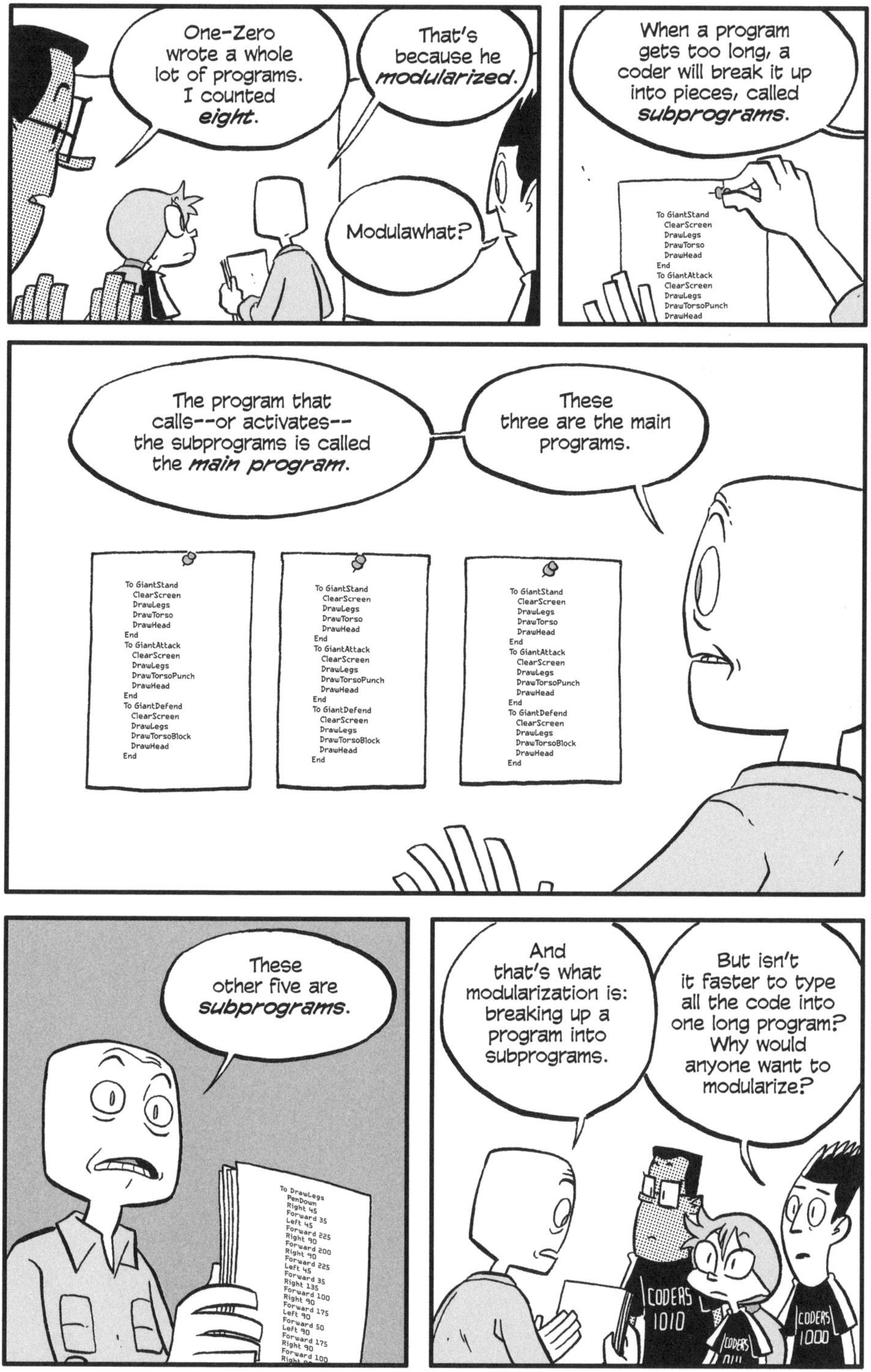
One-Zero wrote a whole lot of programs. I counted *eight*.
That's because he *modularized*.
Modulawhat?
When a program gets too long, a coder will break it up into pieces, called *subprograms*.
To GiantStand
ClearScreen
DrawLegs
DrawTorso
DrawHead
End
To GiantAttack
ClearScreen
DrawLegs
DrawTorsoPunch
DrawHead
The program that calls--or activates--the subprograms is called the *main program*.
These three are the main programs.
To GiantStand
ClearScreen
DrawLegs
DrawTorso
DrawHead
End
To GiantAttack
ClearScreen
DrawLegs
DrawTorsoPunch
DrawHead
End
To GiantDefend
ClearScreen
DrawLegs
DrawTorsoBlock
DrawHead
End
These other five are *subprograms*.
And that's what modularization is: breaking up a program into subprograms.
But isn't it faster to type all the code into one long program? Why would anyone want to modularize?
CODERS 1010
CODERS 1000

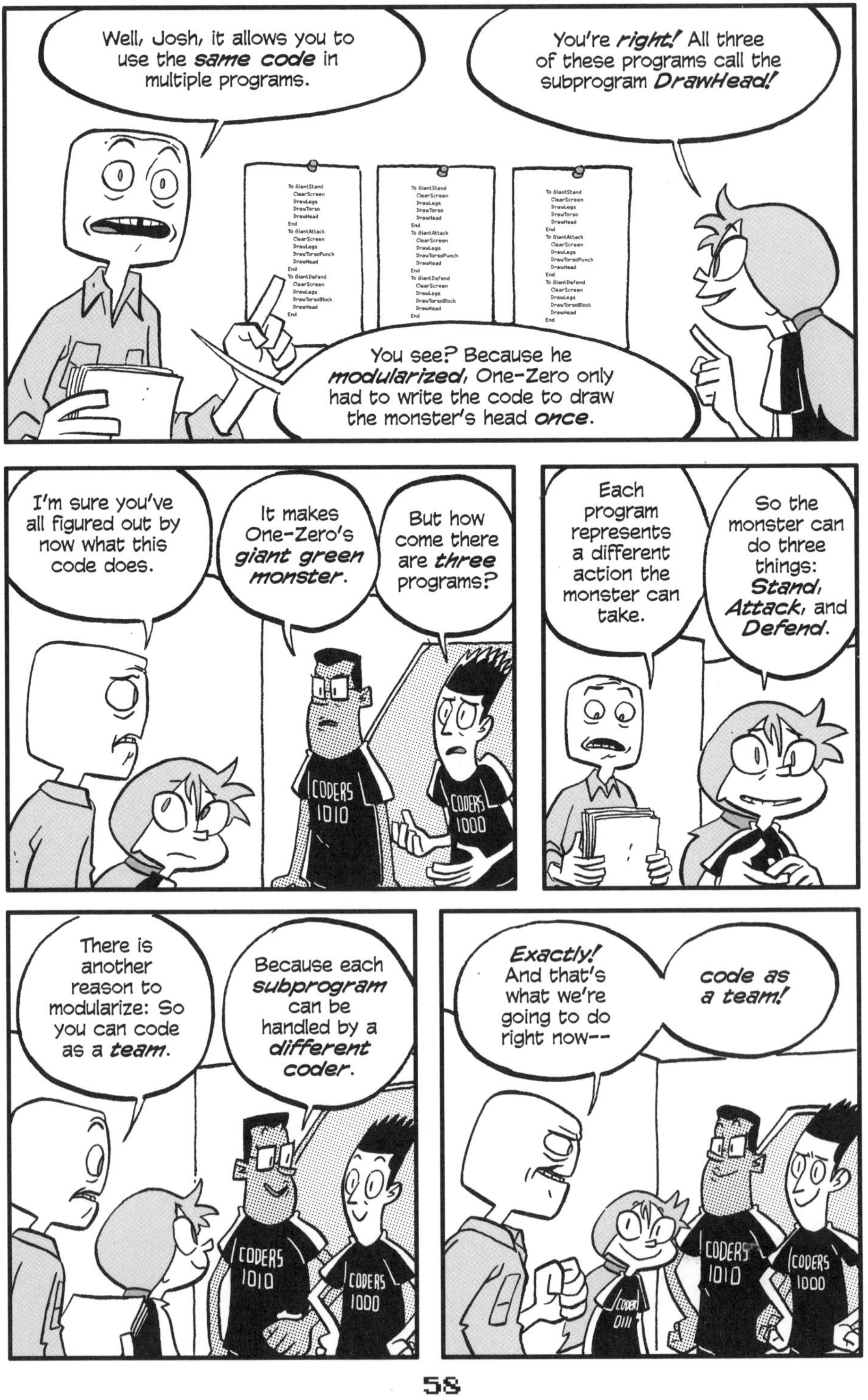
Well, Josh, it allows you to use the *same code* in multiple programs.
You're *right!* All three of these programs call the subprogram *DrawHead!*
To GiantStand
ClearScreen
DrawLegs
DrawTorso
DrawHead
End
To GiantAttack
ClearScreen
DrawLegs
DrawTorsoPunch
DrawHead
End
To GiantDefend
ClearScreen
DrawLegs
DrawTorsoBlock
DrawHead
End
To GiantStand
ClearScreen
DrawLegs
DrawTorso
DrawHead
End
To GiantAttack
ClearScreen
DrawLegs
DrawTorsoPunch
DrawHead
End
To GiantDefend
ClearScreen
DrawLegs
DrawTorsoBlock
DrawHead
End
To GiantStand
ClearScreen
DrawLegs
DrawTorso
DrawHead
End
To GiantAttack
ClearScreen
DrawLegs
DrawTorsoPunch
DrawHead
End
To GiantDefend
ClearScreen
DrawLegs
DrawTorsoBlock
DrawHead
End
You see? Because he *modularized*, One-Zero only had to write the code to draw the monster's head *once*.
I'm sure you've all figured out by now what this code does.
It makes One-Zero's *giant green monster*.
But how come there are *three* programs?
CODERS 1010
CODERS 1000
Each program represents a different action the monster can take.
So the monster can do three things: *Stand*, *Attack*, and *Defend*.
There is another reason to modularize: So you can code as a *team*.
Because each *subprogram* can be handled by a *different coder*.
CODERS 1010
CODERS 1000
Exactly! And that's what we're going to do right now--
code as a team!
CODERS 1010
CODERS 1000

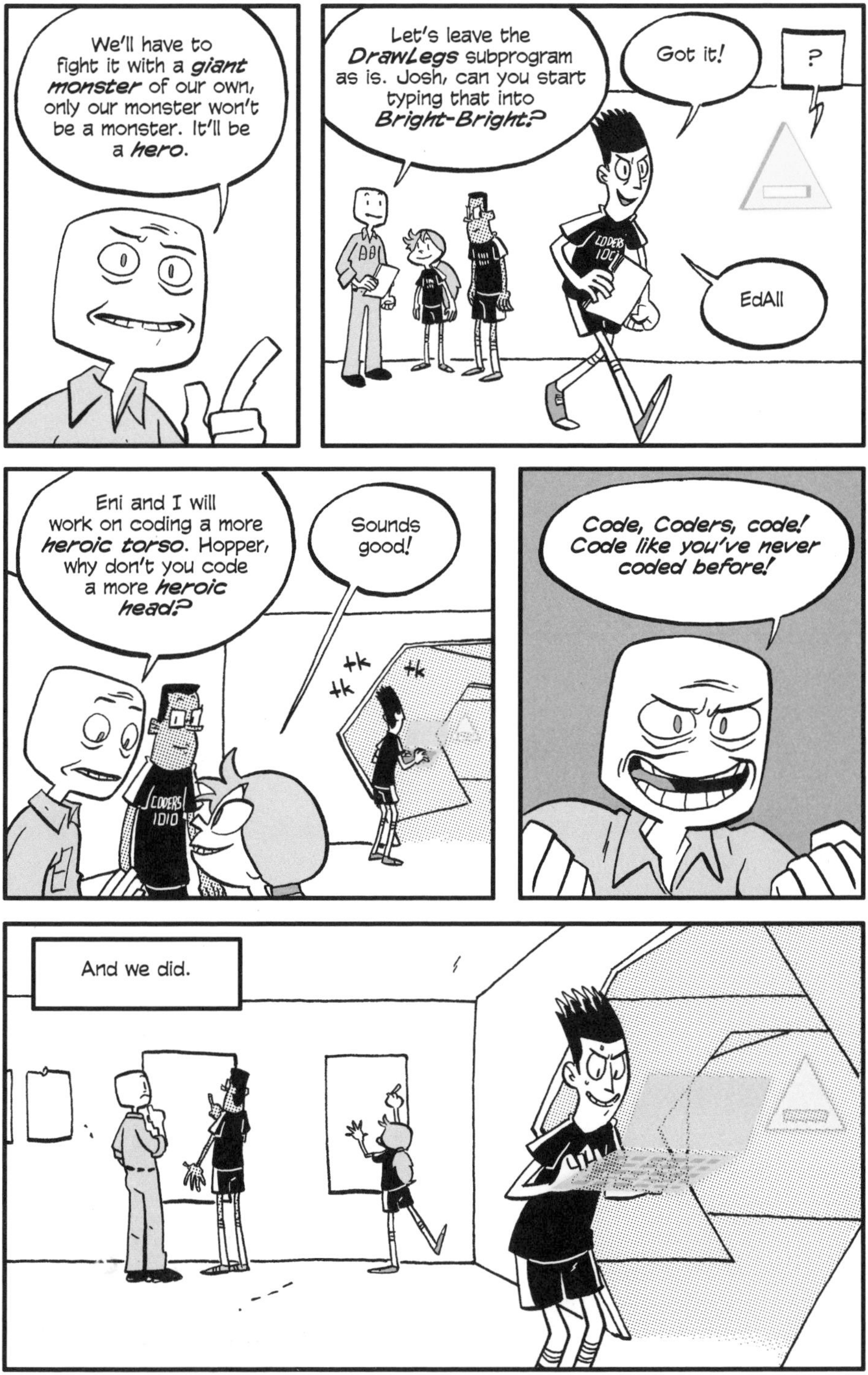

We'll have to fight it with a giant monster of our own, only our monster won't be a monster. It'll be a hero.
Let's leave the DrawLegs subprogram as is. Josh, can you start typing that into Bright-Bright?
Got it!
?
CODERS 101
EdAll
Eni and I will work on coding a more heroic torso. Hopper, why don't you code a more heroic head?
Sounds good!
tk
tk
tk
CODERS 101
Code, Coders, code! Code like you've never coded before!
And we did.

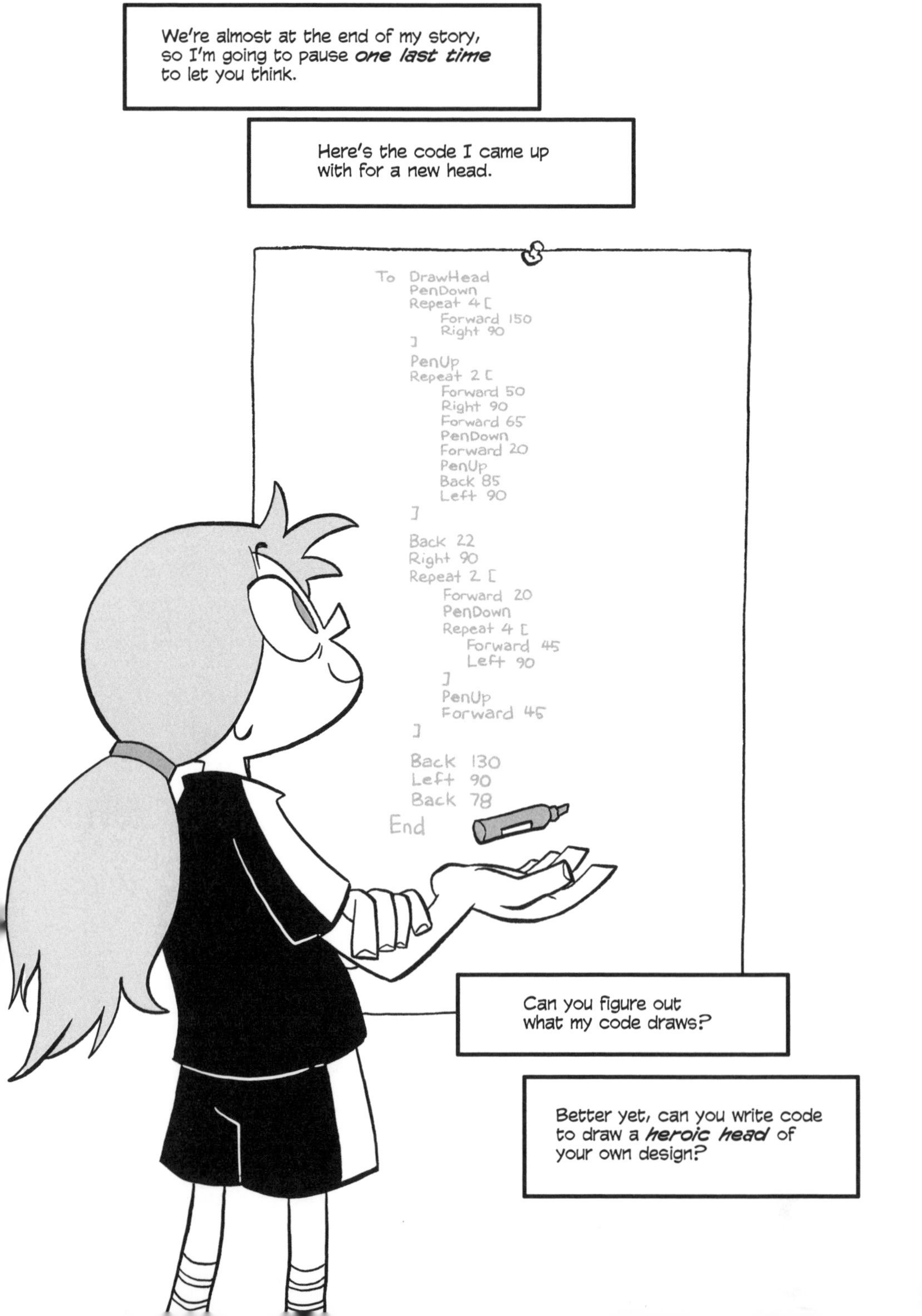
We're almost at the end of my story, so I'm going to pause *one last time* to let you think.
Here's the code I came up with for a new head.
To DrawHead
PenDown
Repeat 4 [
Forward 150
Right 90
]
PenUp
Repeat 2 [
Forward 50
Right 90
Forward 65
PenDown
Forward 20
PenUp
Back 85
Left 90
]
Back 22
Right 90
Repeat 2 [
Forward 20
PenDown
Repeat 4 [
Forward 45
Left 90
]
PenUp
Forward 45
]
Back 130
Left 90
Back 78
End
Can you figure out what my code draws?
Better yet, can you write code to draw a *heroic head* of your own design?

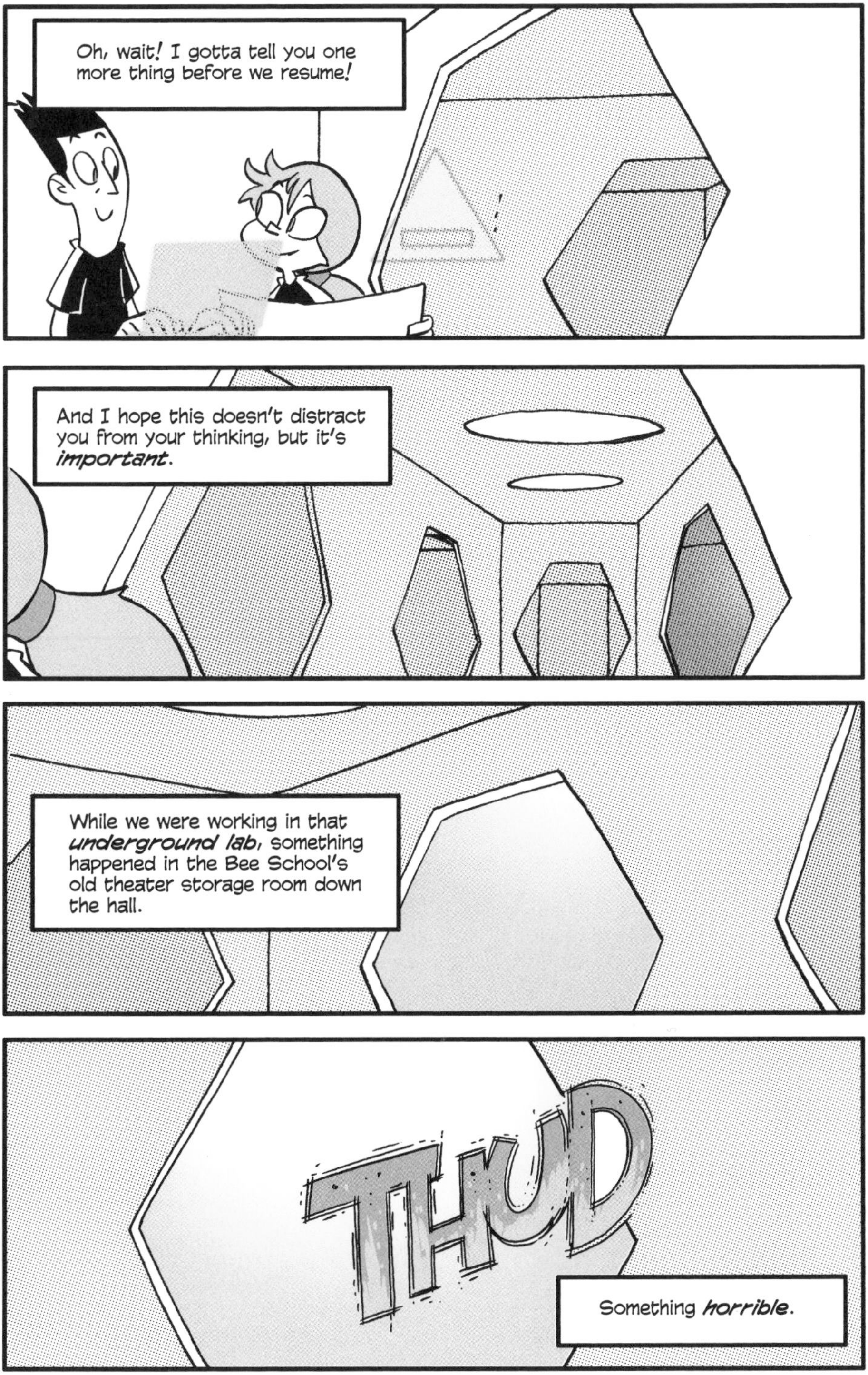
Oh, wait! I gotta tell you one more thing before we resume!
And I hope this doesn't distract you from your thinking, but it's *important*.
While we were working in that *underground lab*, something happened in the Bee School's old theater storage room down the hall.
THUD
Something *horrible*.

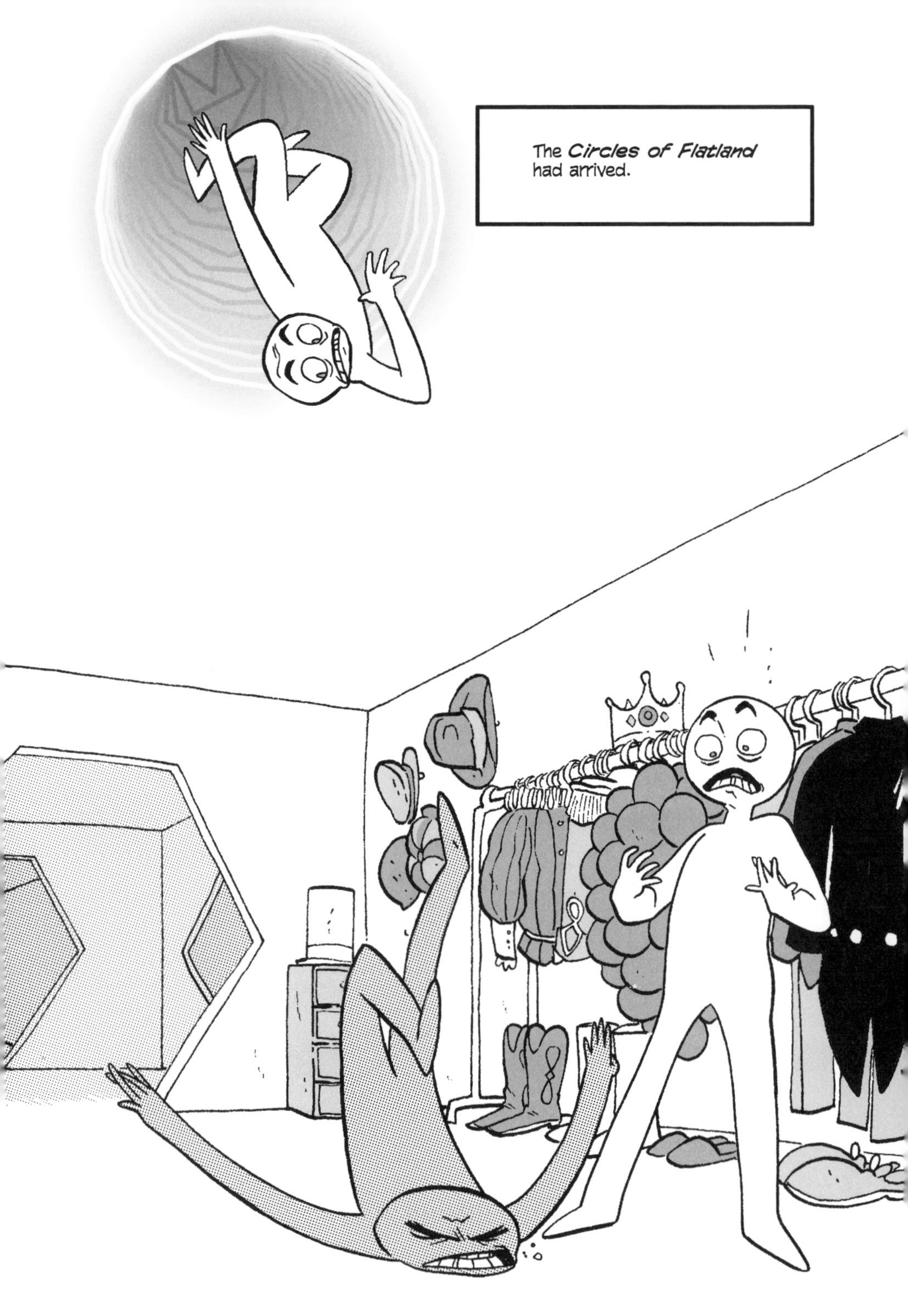
The *Circles of Flatland* had arrived.

Chapter

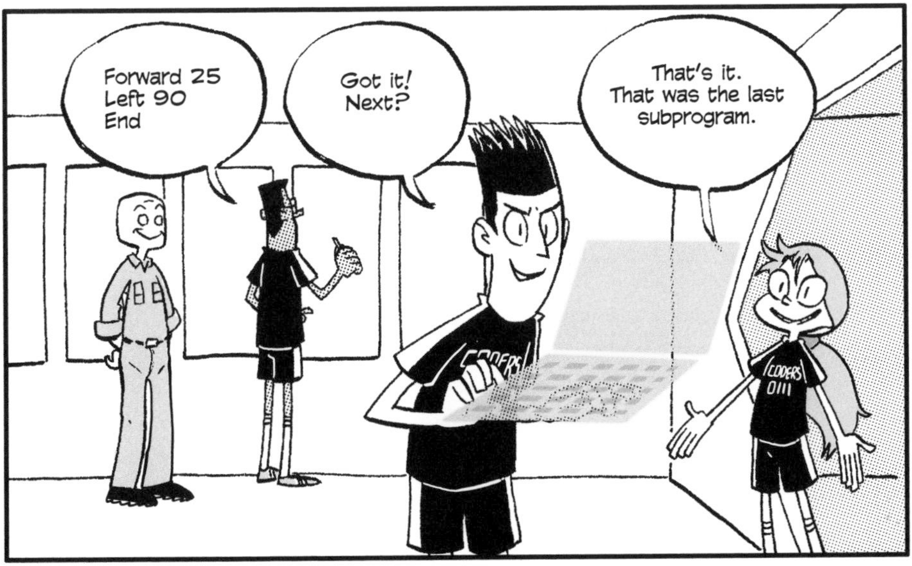
Forward 25
Left 90
End
Got it! Next?
That's it. That was the last subprogram.
CODERS
CODERS 0111

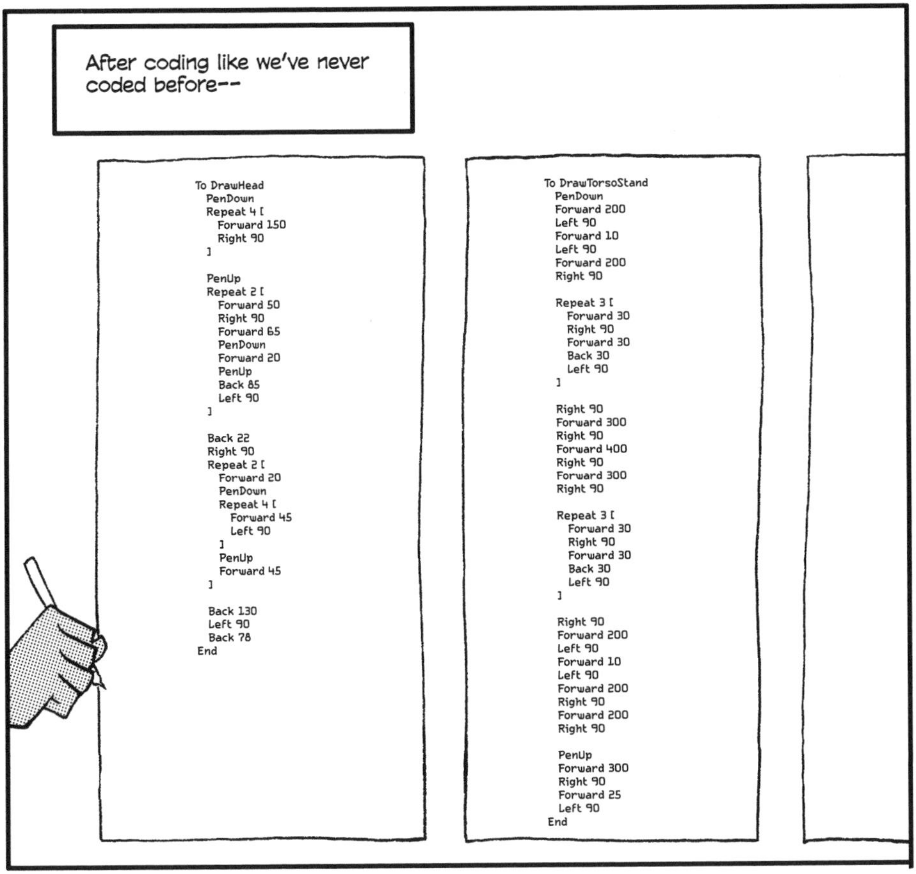
After coding like we've never coded before--
To DrawHead
PenDown
Repeat 4 [
Forward 150
Right 90
]
PenUp
Repeat 2 [
Forward 50
Right 90
Forward 65
PenDown
Forward 20
PenUp
Back 85
Left 90
]
Back 22
Right 90
Repeat 2 [
Forward 20
PenDown
Repeat 4 [
Forward 45
Left 90
]
PenUp
Forward 45
]
Back 130
Left 90
Back 78
End
To DrawTorsoStand
PenDown
Forward 200
Left 90
Forward 10
Left 90
Forward 200
Right 90
Repeat 3 [
Forward 30
Right 90
Forward 30
Back 30
Left 90
]
Right 90
Forward 300
Right 90
Forward 400
Right 90
Forward 300
Right 90
Repeat 3 [
Forward 30
Right 90
Forward 30
Back 30
Left 90
]
Right 90
Forward 200
Left 90
Forward 10
Left 90
Forward 200
Right 90
Forward 200
Right 90
PenUp
Forward 300
Right 90
Forward 25
Left 90
End

--we created six subprograms.

That's one more than One-Zero had because Josh added one called *DrawCrouchingLegs*.

```
To DrawTorsoPunch
  PenDown
  Forward 200
  Left 90
  Forward 10
  Left 90
  Forward 200
  Right 90
  Repeat 3 [
    Forward 30
    Right 90
    Forward 30
    Back 30
    Left 90
  ]
  Right 90
  Forward 300
  Right 90
  Forward 525
  Right 90
  Repeat 3 [
    Forward 30
    Right 90
    Forward 30
    Back 30
    Left 90
  ]
  Right 90
  Forward 225
  Left 90
  Forward 210
  Right 90
  Forward 200
  Right 90
  PenUp
  Forward 300
  Right 90
  Forward 25
  Left 90
End
```

```
To DrawTorsoBlock
  PenDown
  Forward 200
  Left 90
  Forward 10
  Left 90
  Forward 200
  Right 90
  Repeat 3 [
    Forward 30
    Right 90
    Forward 30
    Back 30
    Left 90
  ]
  Right 90
  Forward 300
  Right 90
  Forward 350
  Left 90
  Forward 150
  Right 90
  Repeat 3 [
    Forward 30
    Right 90
    Forward 30
    Back 30
    Left 90
  ]
  Right 90
  Forward 240
  Right 90
  Forward 140
  Left 90
  Forward 210
  Right 90
  Forward 200
  Right 90
  PenUp
  Forward 300
  Right 90
  Forward 25
  Left 90
End
```

66

```
To DrawLegs
  PenDown
  Right 45
  Forward 35
  Left 45
  Forward 225
  Right 90
  Forward 200
  Right 90
  Forward 225
  Left 45
  Forward 35
  Right 135
  Forward 100
  Right 90
  Forward 175
  Left 90
  Forward 50
  Left 90
  Forward 175
  Right 90
  Forward 100
  Right 90
  PenUp
  Forward 250
  Right 90
  Forward 25
  Left 90
End
```

```
To DrawCrouchingLegs
  PenDown
  Right 45
  Forward 35
  Left 45
  Forward 150
  Right 90
  Forward 400
  Right 90
  Forward 150
  Left 45
  Forward 35
  Right 135
  Forward 100
  Right 90
  Forward 100
  Left 90
  Forward 250
  Left 90
  Forward 100
  Right 90
  Forward 100
  Right 90
  PenUp
  Forward 175
  Right 90
  Forward 125
  Left 90
End
```

What does *DrawCrouchingLegs* do?

It makes our hero *crouch down* so he can punch One-Zero's monster in the *gut! Ka-pow!*

Hey, that's not a bad idea, Josh! Then let's code one more main program: *HeroCrouchingAttack!*

67

We ended up with four **main programs** that called our six **subprograms**.

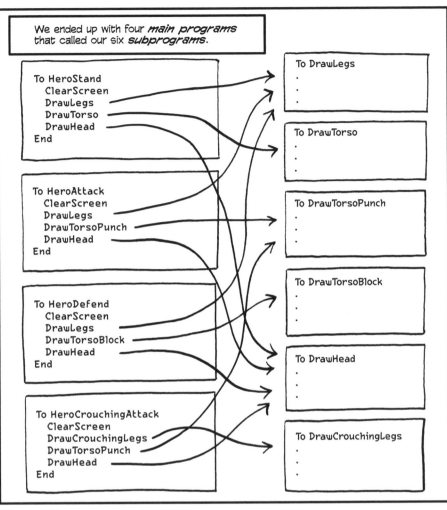

```
To HeroStand
  ClearScreen
  DrawLegs
  DrawTorso
  DrawHead
End

To HeroAttack
  ClearScreen
  DrawLegs
  DrawTorsoPunch
  DrawHead
End

To HeroDefend
  ClearScreen
  DrawLegs
  DrawTorsoBlock
  DrawHead
End

To HeroCrouchingAttack
  ClearScreen
  DrawCrouchingLegs
  DrawTorsoPunch
  DrawHead
End
```

```
To DrawLegs
  .
  .
  .

To DrawTorso
  .
  .
  .

To DrawTorsoPunch
  .
  .
  .

To DrawTorsoBlock
  .
  .
  .

To DrawHead
  .
  .
  .

To DrawCrouchingLegs
  .
  .
  .
```

Are we ready, Coders?

Ready as we'll ever be.

Ka-pow! Ka-pow!

Then it's time to save the city!

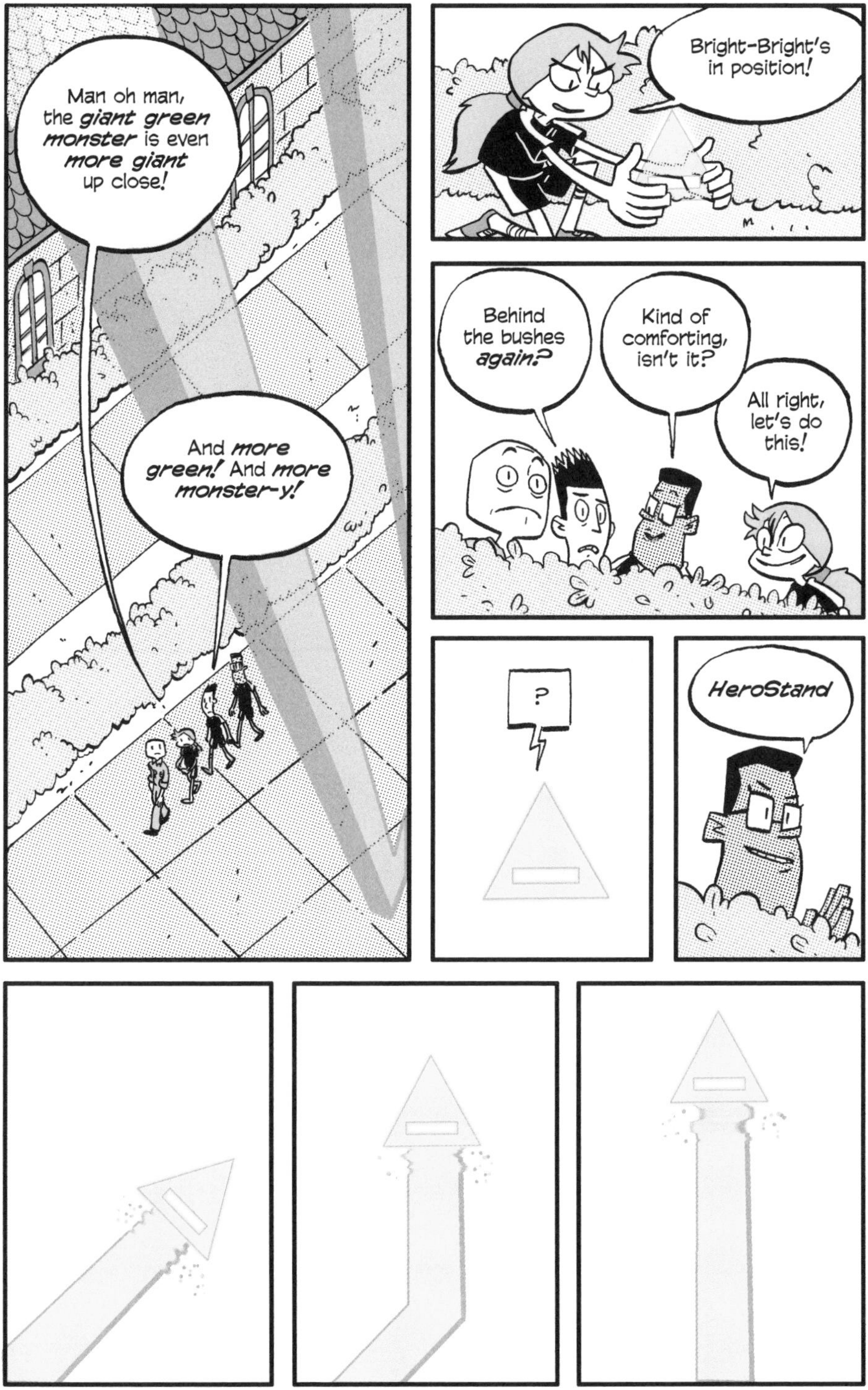
Man oh man, the giant green monster is even more giant up close!
And more green! And more monster-y!
Bright-Bright's in position!
Behind the bushes again?
Kind of comforting, isn't it?
All right, let's do this!
?
HeroStand

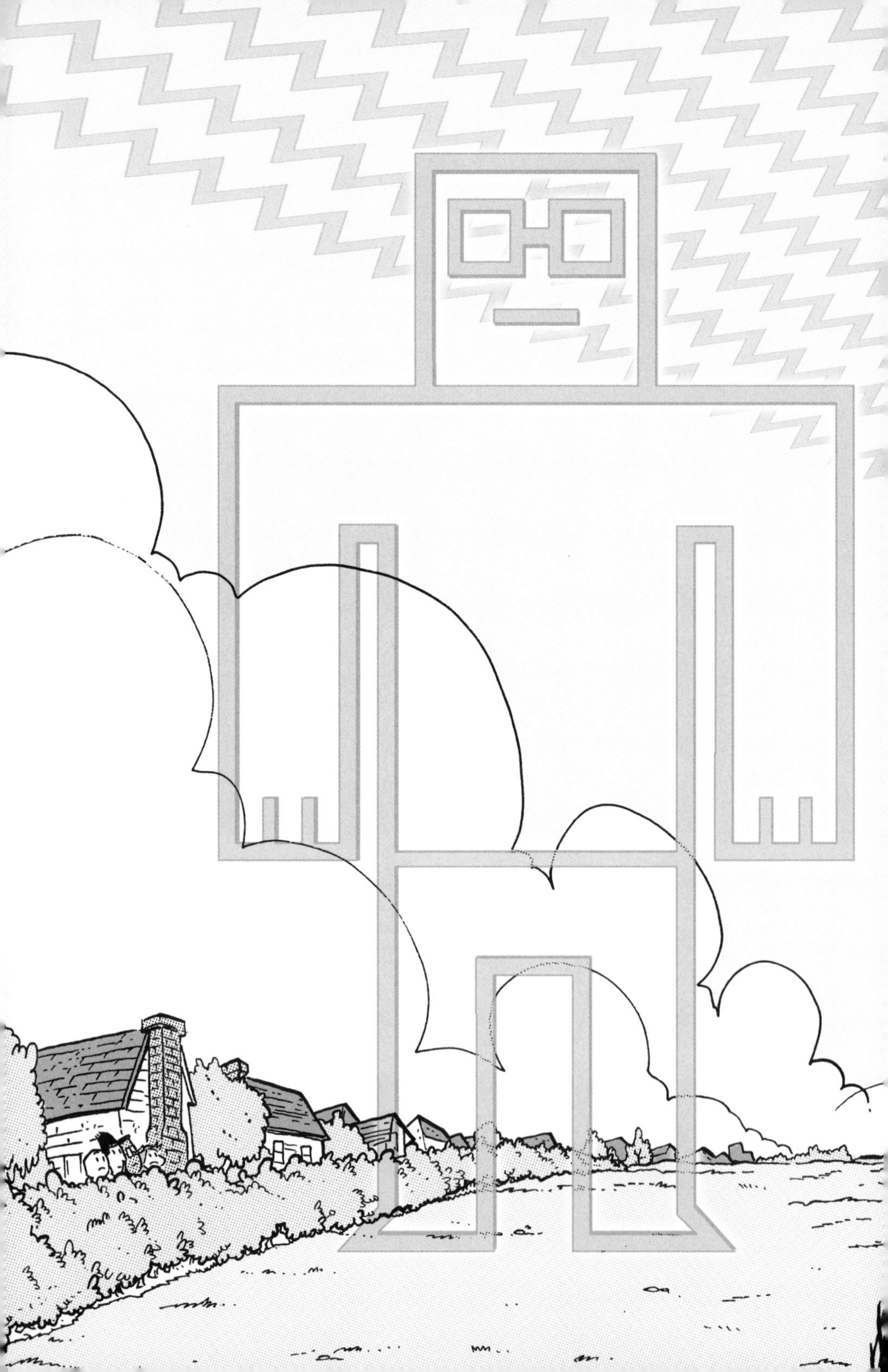

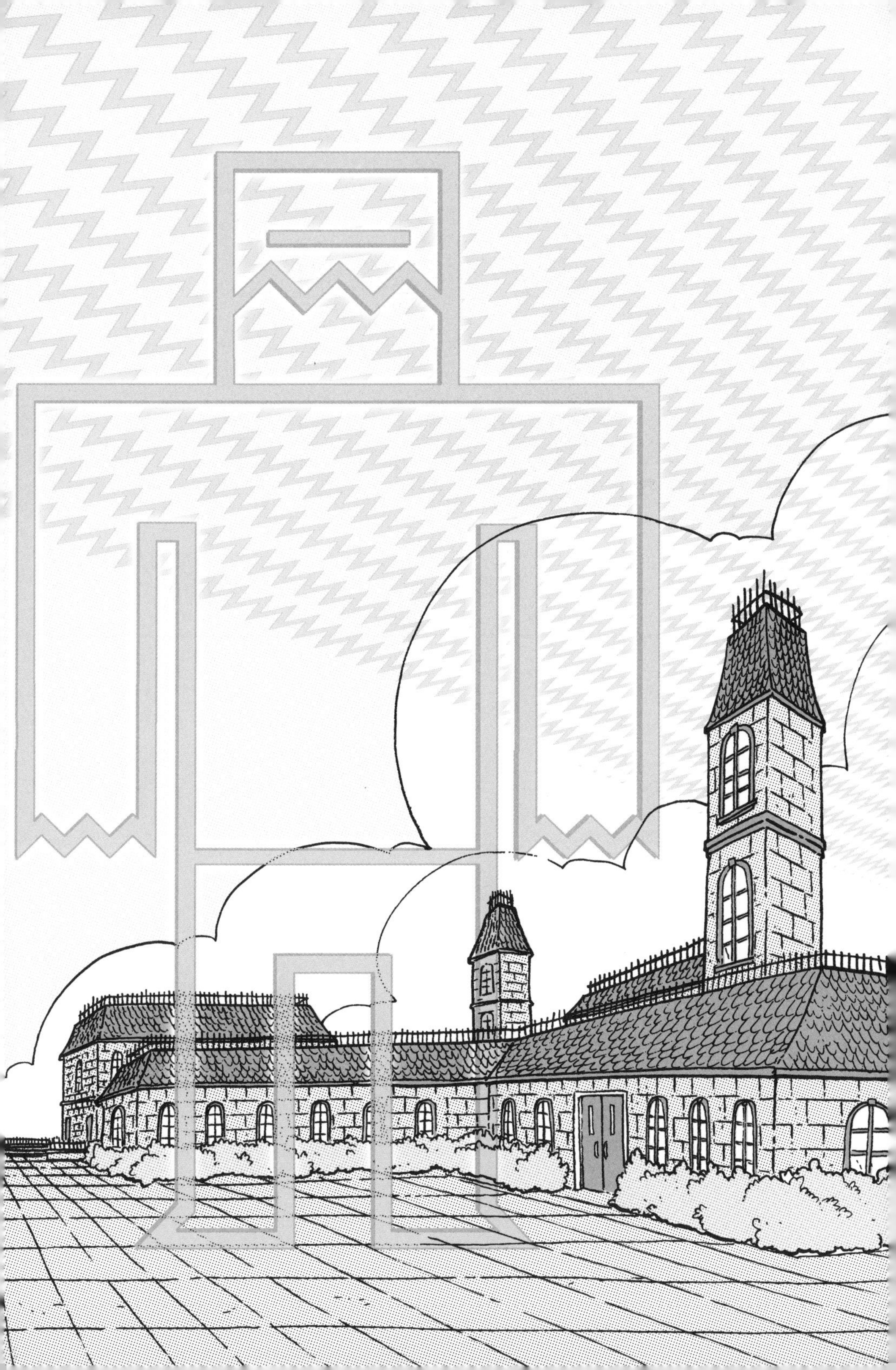

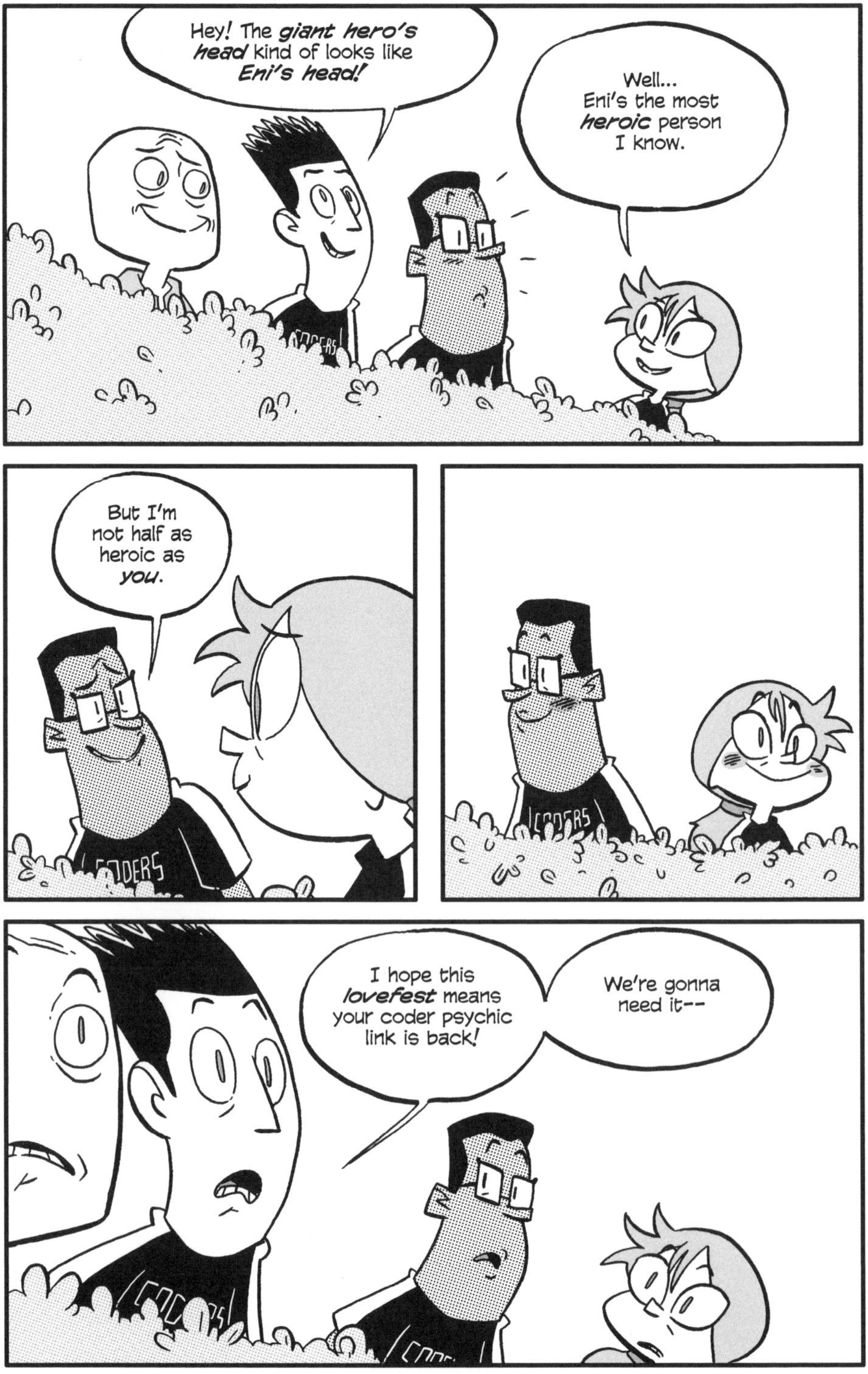
Hey! The giant hero's head kind of looks like Eni's head!
Well... Eni's the most heroic person I know.
But I'm not half as heroic as you.
I hope this lovefest means your coder psychic link is back!
We're gonna need it--

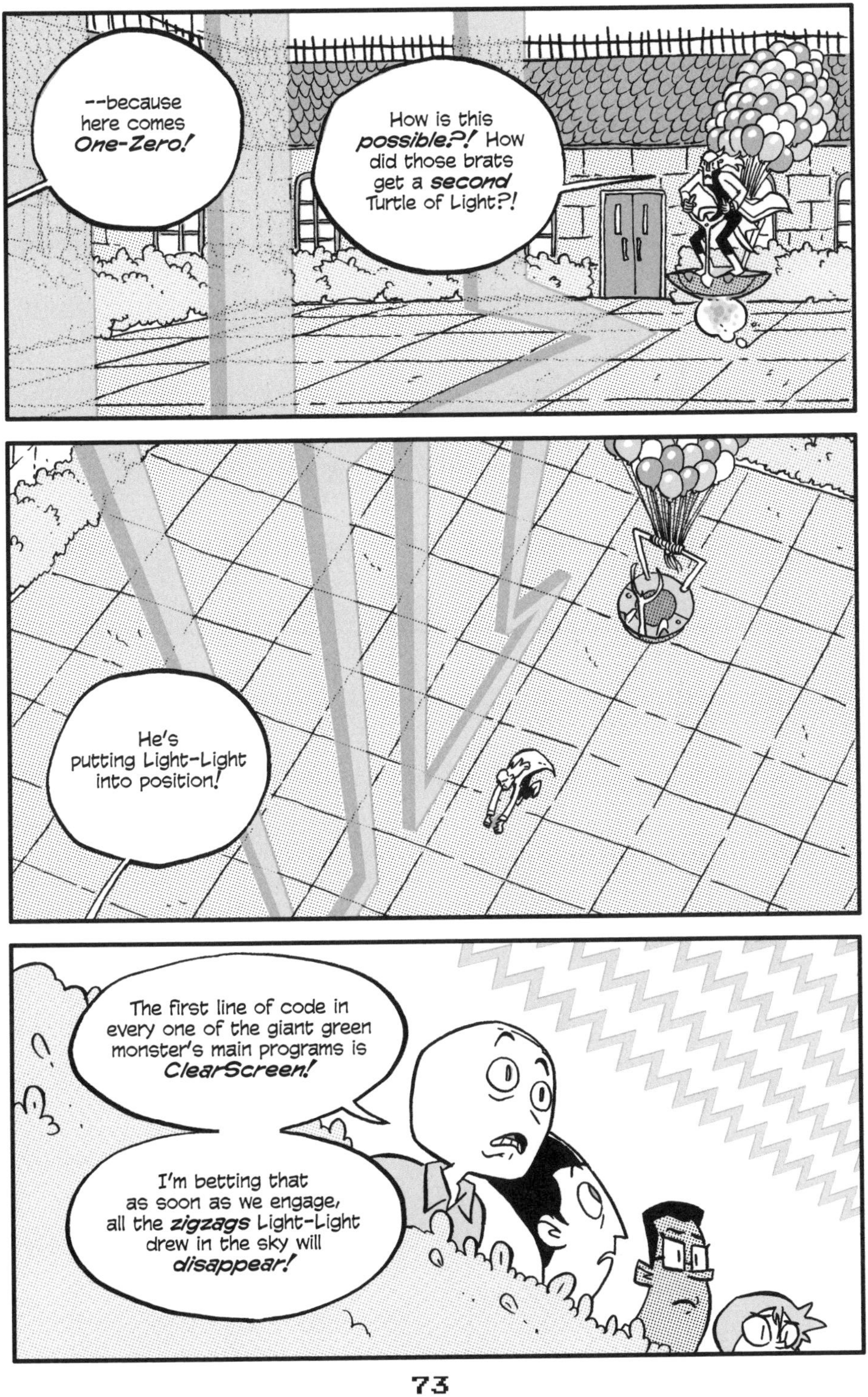

--because here comes One-Zero!
How is this possible?! How did those brats get a second Turtle of Light?!
He's putting Light-Light into position!
The first line of code in every one of the giant green monster's main programs is ClearScreen!
I'm betting that as soon as we engage, all the zigzags Light-Light drew in the sky will disappear!

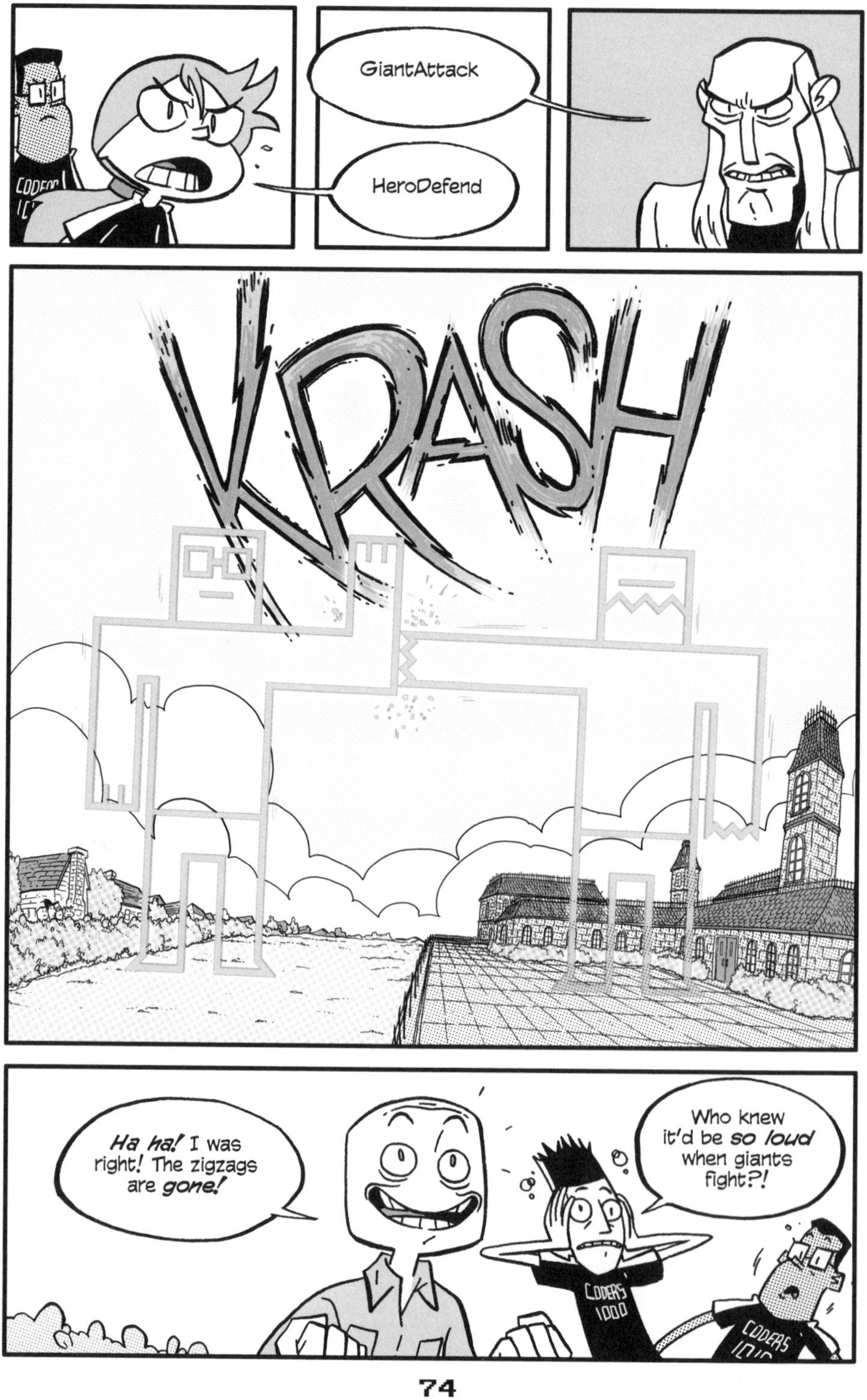
GiantAttack
HeroDefend
KRASH
Ha ha! I was right! The zigzags are gone!
Who knew it'd be so loud when giants fight?!

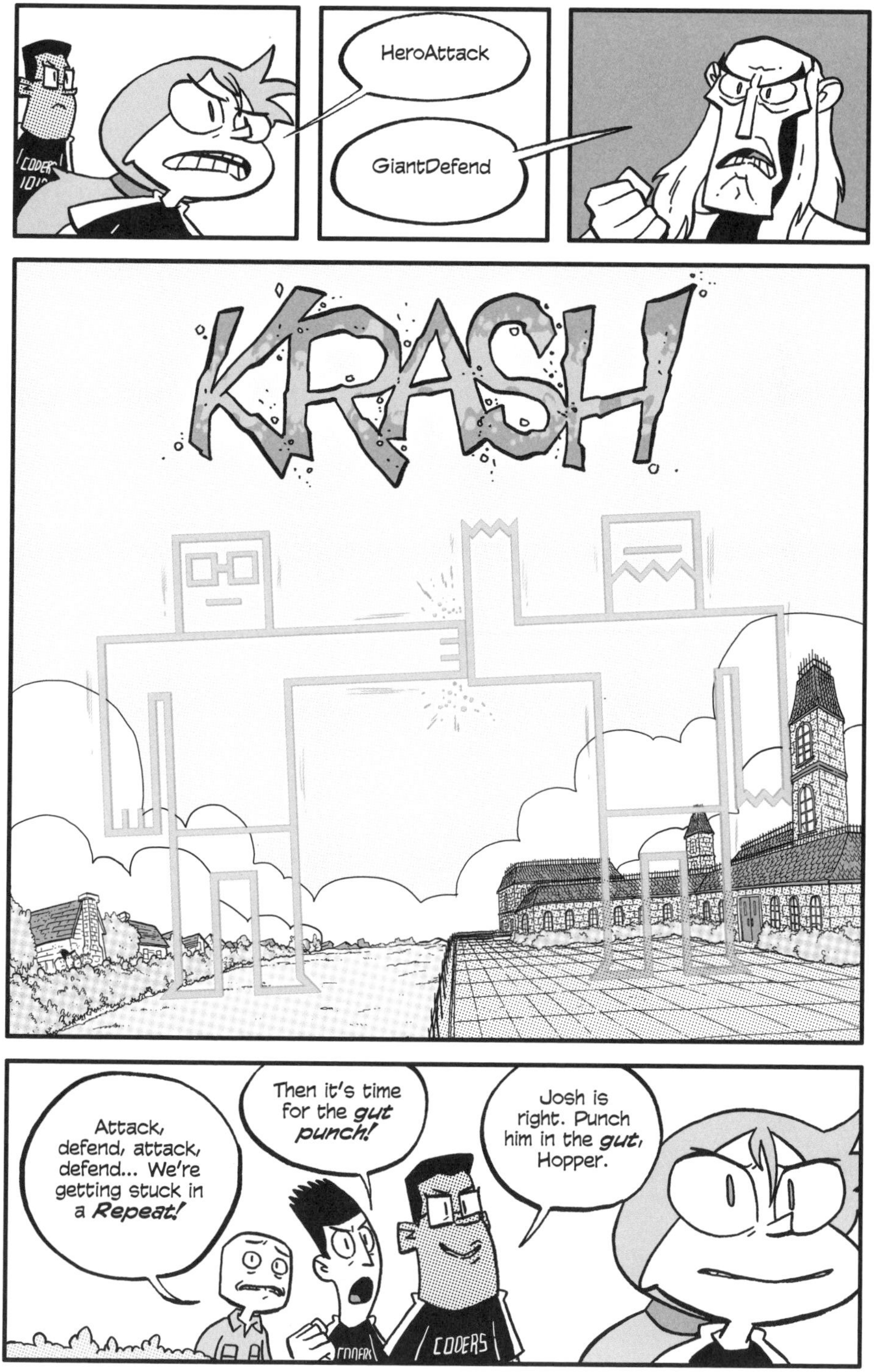

CODERS 101
HeroAttack
GiantDefend
KRASH
Attack, defend, attack, defend... We're getting stuck in a *Repeat!*
Then it's time for the *gut punch!*
Josh is right. Punch him in the *gut*, Hopper.
CODERS
CODERS

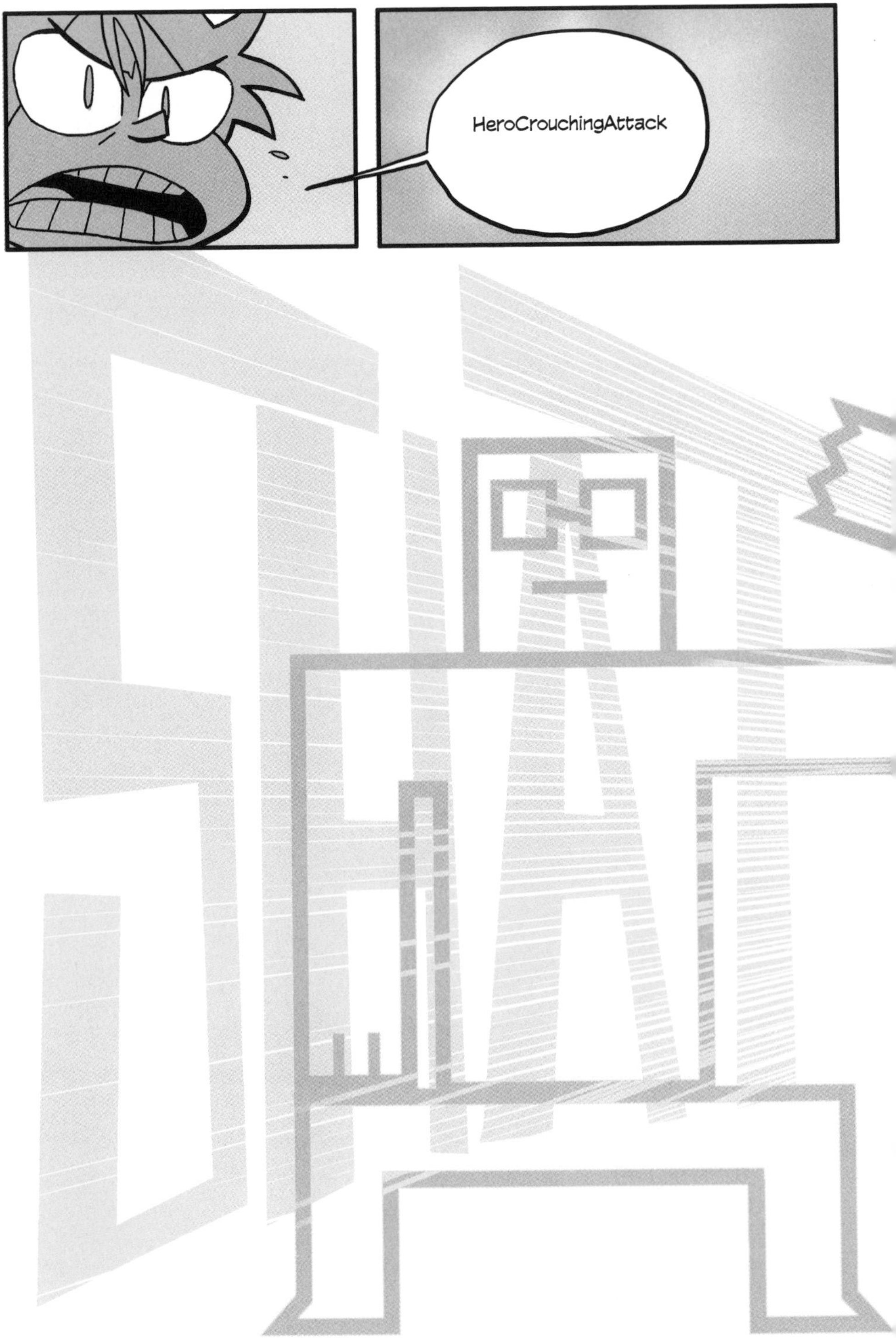
HeroCrouchingAttack

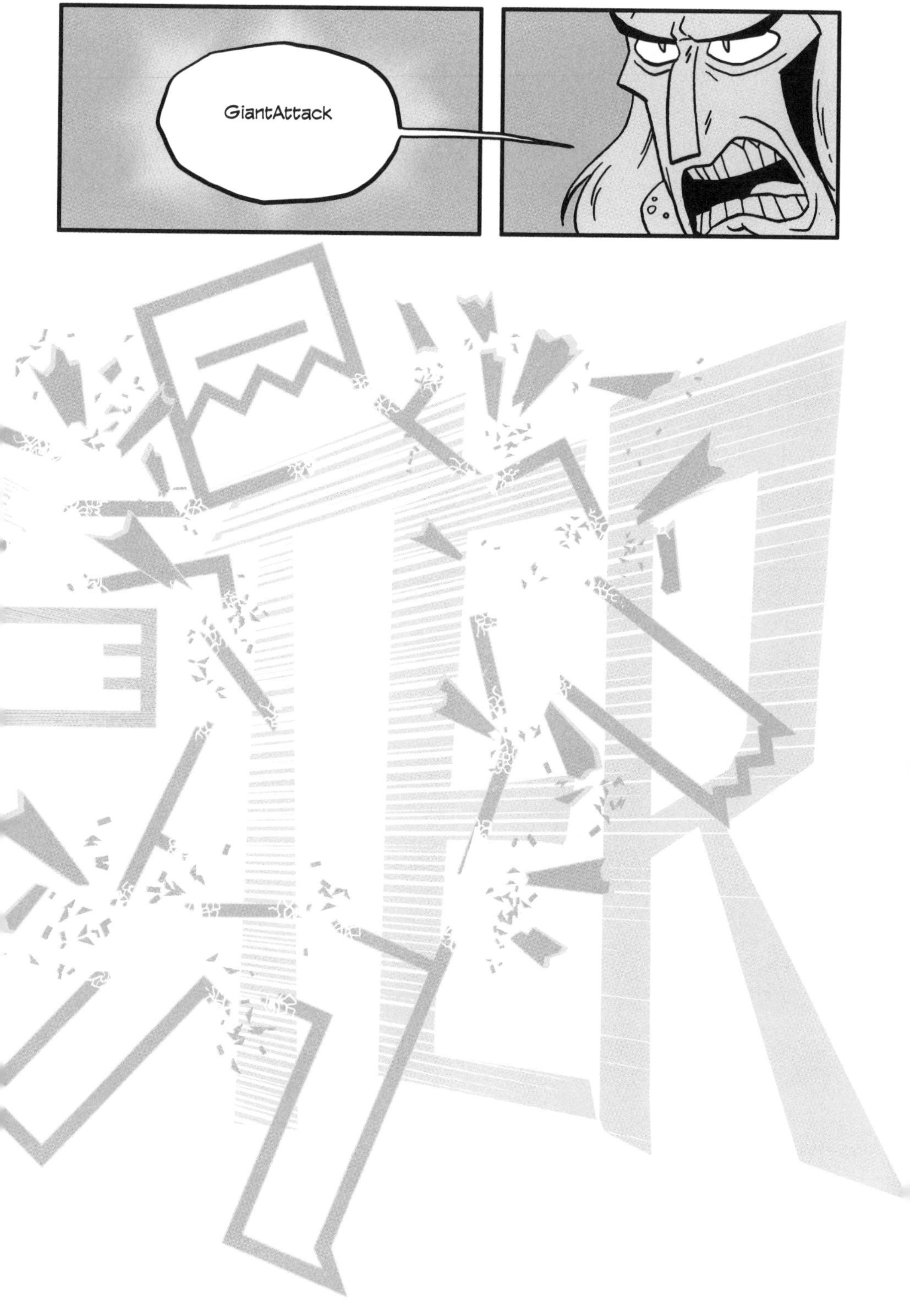
GiantAttack

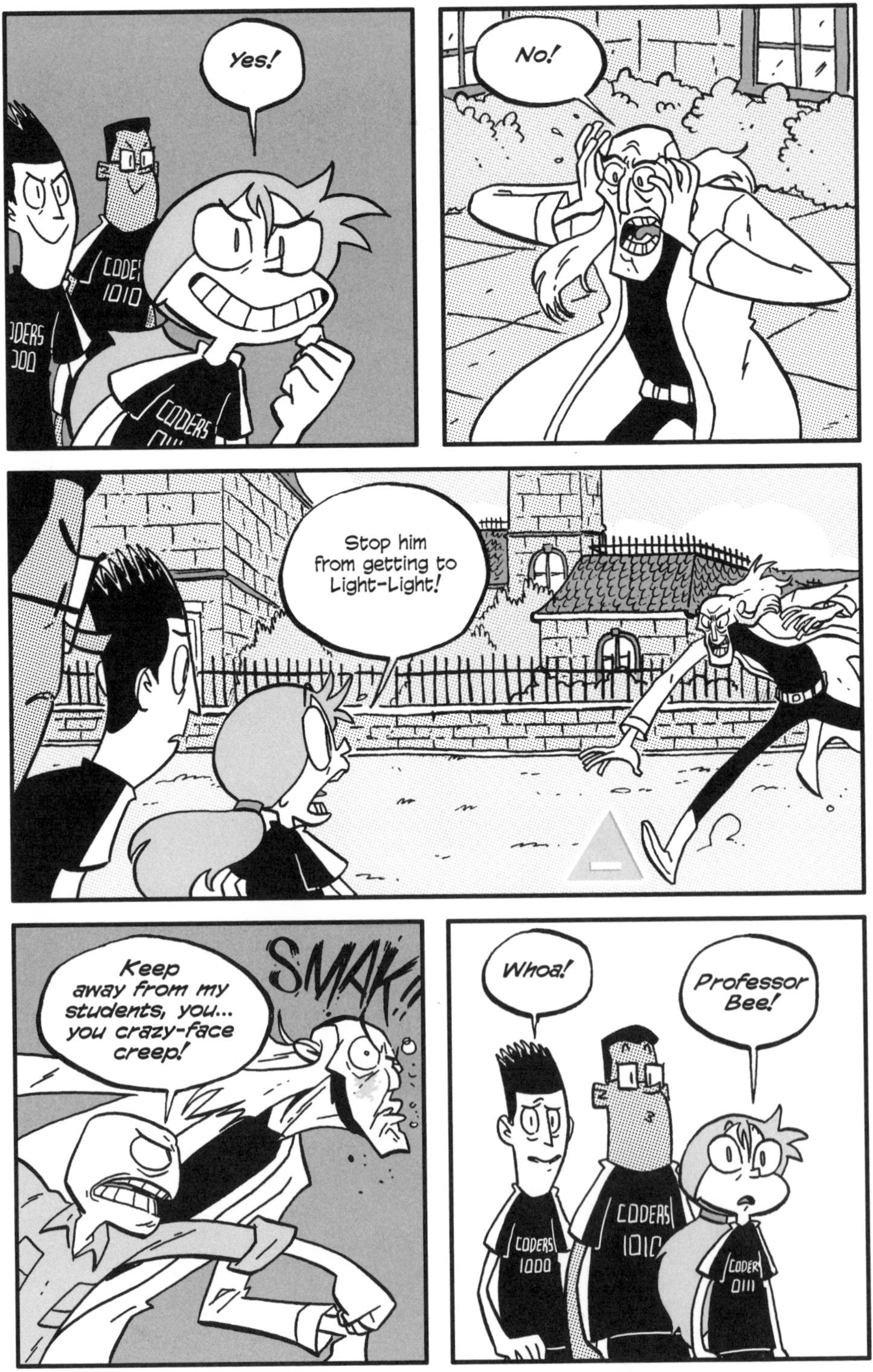
Yes!
No!
Stop him from getting to Light-Light!
Keep away from my students, you... you crazy-face creep!
SMAK!!
Whoa!
Professor Bee!
CODERS 1000
CODERS 1010

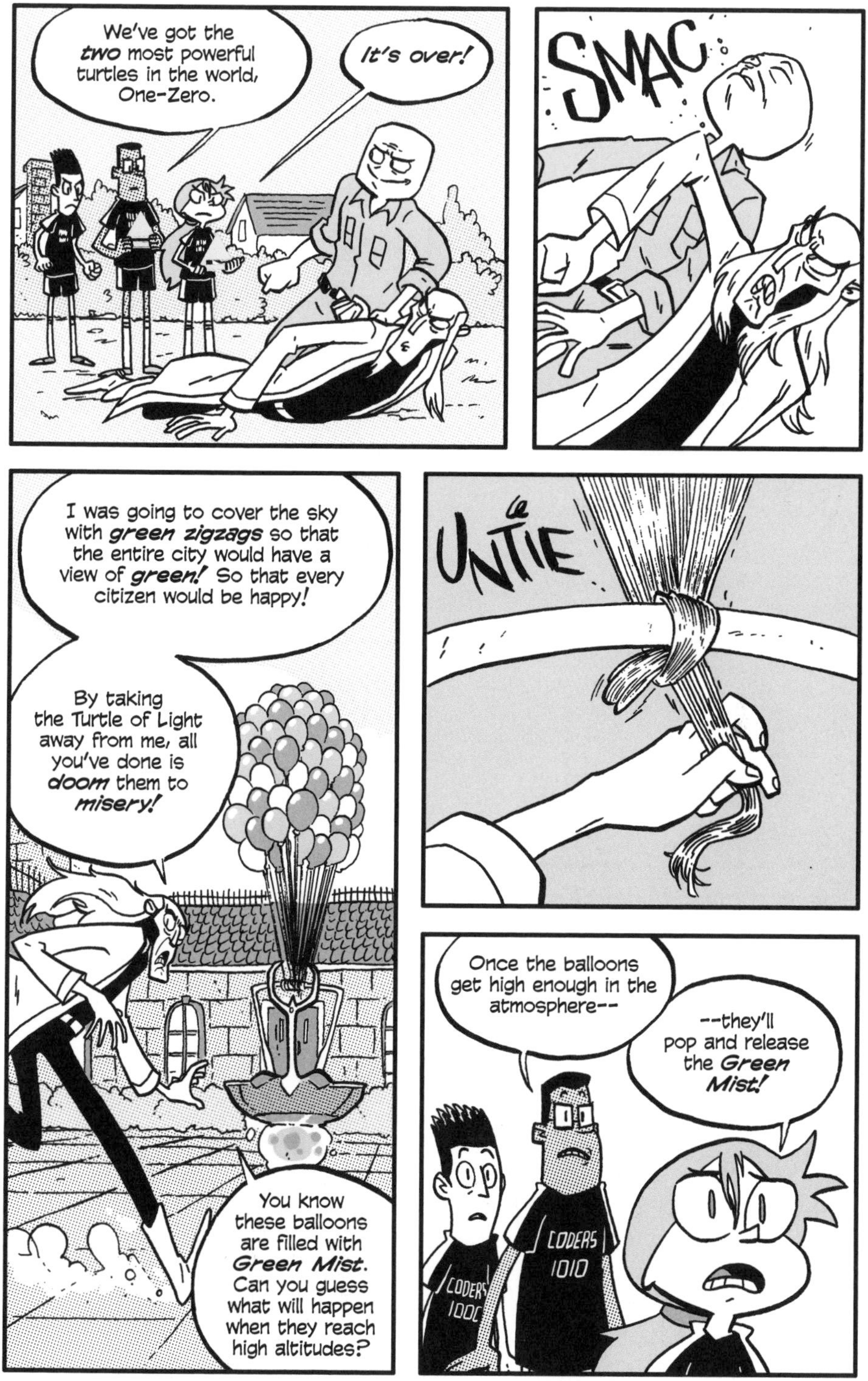

We've got the **two** most powerful turtles in the world, One-Zero.
It's over!
SMAC
I was going to cover the sky with ***green zigzags*** so that the entire city would have a view of ***green!*** So that every citizen would be happy!
By taking the Turtle of Light away from me, all you've done is ***doom*** them to ***misery!***
You know these balloons are filled with ***Green Mist***. Can you guess what will happen when they reach high altitudes?
UNTIE
Once the balloons get high enough in the atmosphere--
--they'll pop and release the ***Green Mist!***
CODERS 1010
CODERS 1010

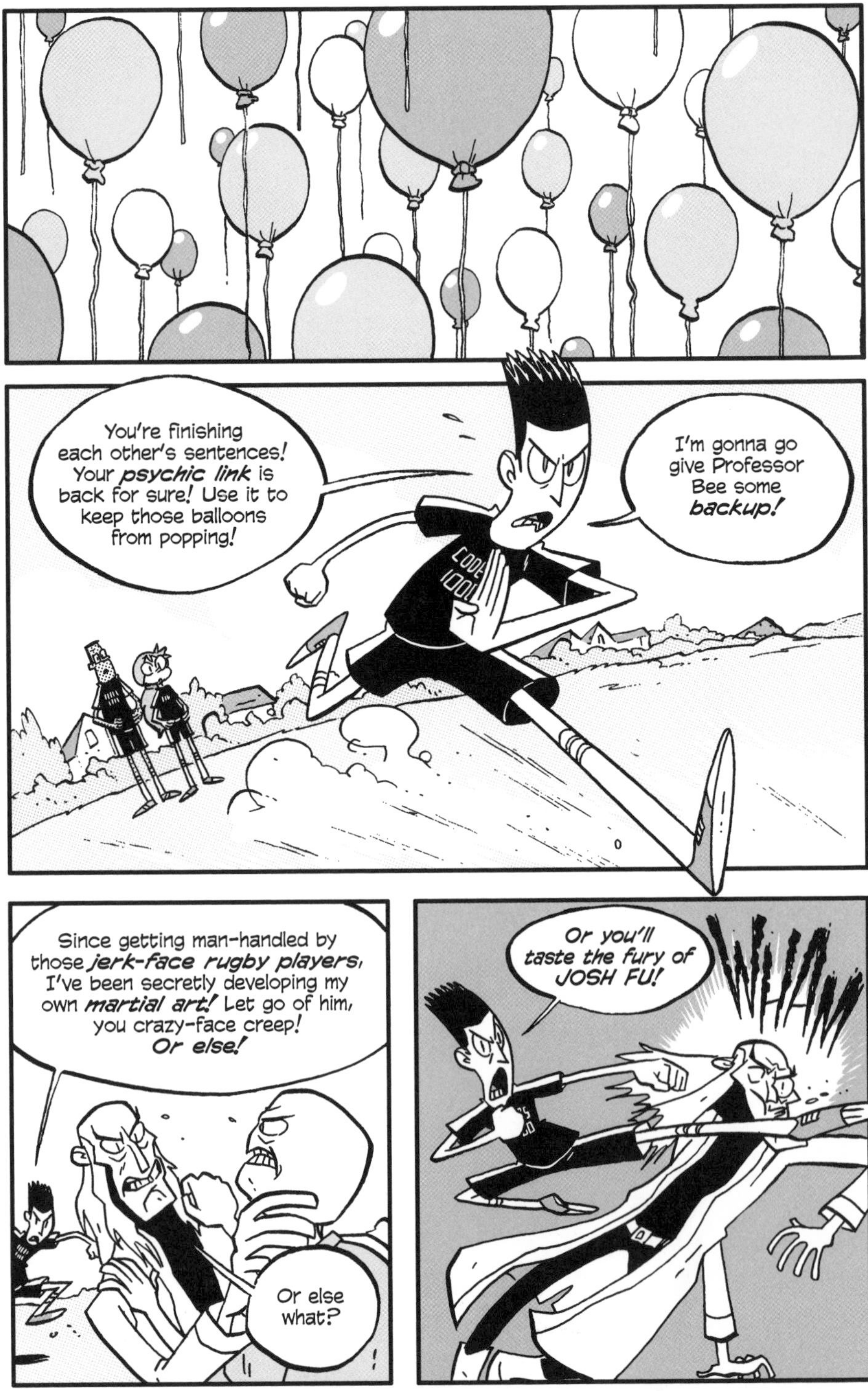
You're finishing each other's sentences! Your *psychic link* is back for sure! Use it to keep those balloons from popping!
I'm gonna go give Professor Bee some *backup!*
CODE 1001
Since getting man-handled by those *jerk-face rugby players*, I've been secretly developing my own *martial art!* Let go of him, you crazy-face creep! *Or else!*
Or else what?
Or you'll taste the fury of JOSH FU!
WHAM

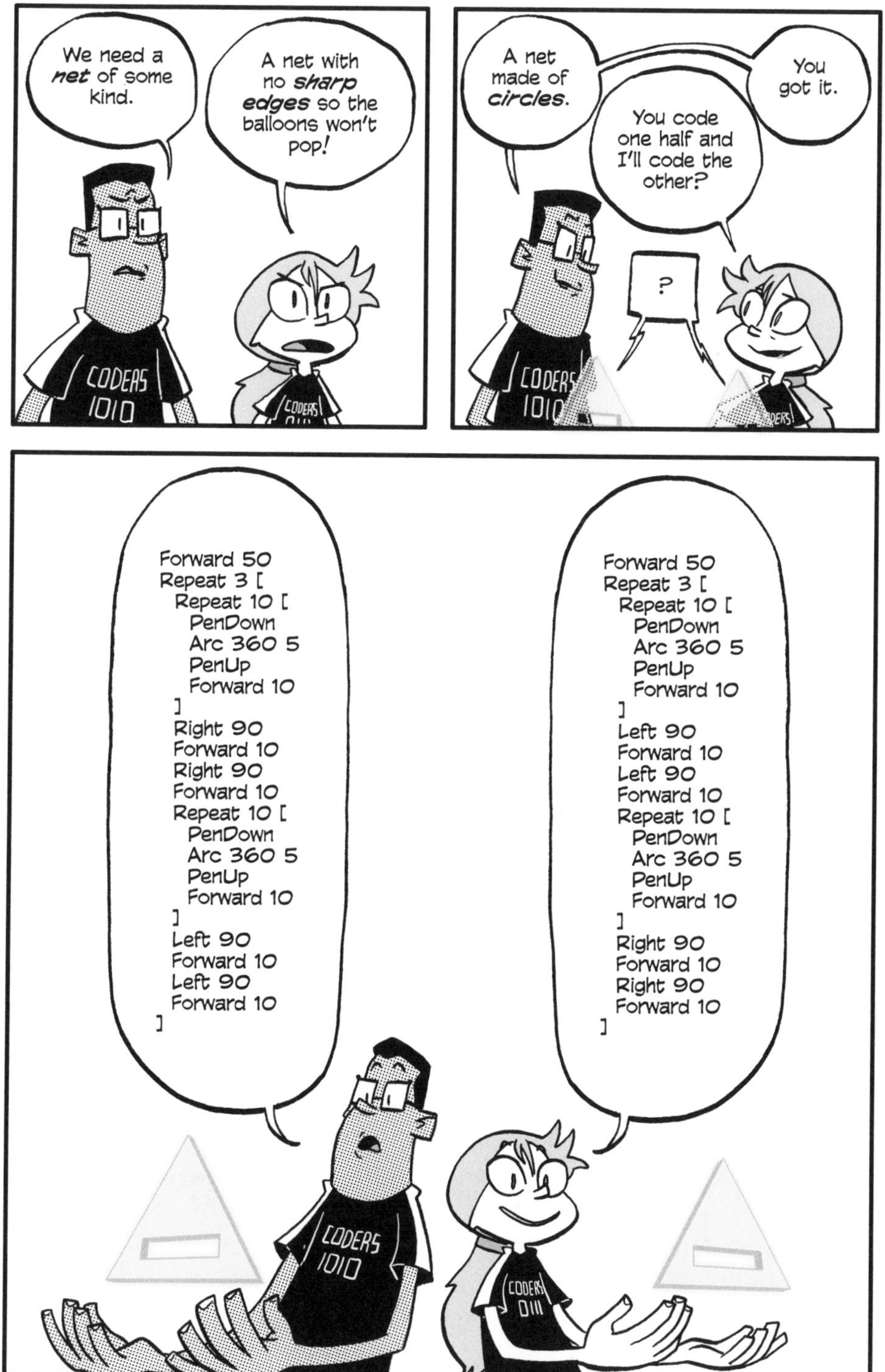
We need a *net* of some kind.
A net with no *sharp edges* so the balloons won't pop!
A net made of *circles*.
You code one half and I'll code the other?
You got it.
?
Forward 50
Repeat 3 [
Repeat 10 [
PenDown
Arc 360 5
PenUp
Forward 10
]
Right 90
Forward 10
Right 90
Forward 10
Repeat 10 [
PenDown
Arc 360 5
PenUp
Forward 10
]
Left 90
Forward 10
Left 90
Forward 10
]
Forward 50
Repeat 3 [
Repeat 10 [
PenDown
Arc 360 5
PenUp
Forward 10
]
Left 90
Forward 10
Left 90
Forward 10
Repeat 10 [
PenDown
Arc 360 5
PenUp
Forward 10
]
Right 90
Forward 10
Right 90
Forward 10
]

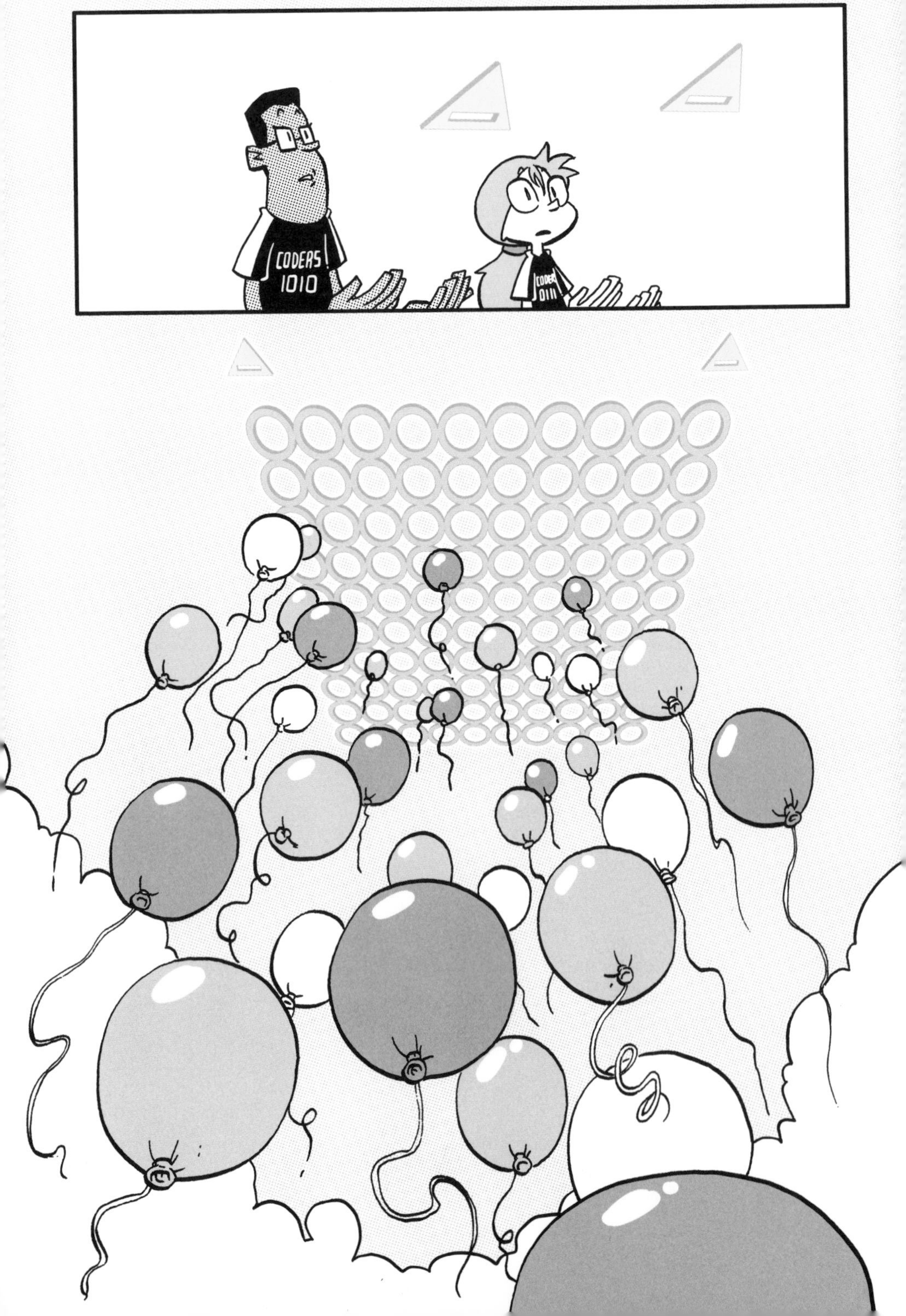
CODERS
1010

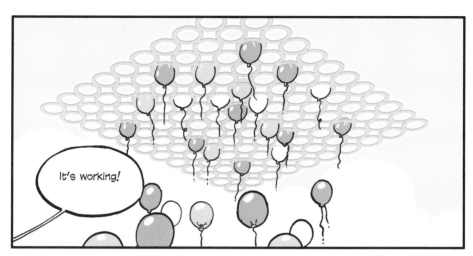

It's working!

HIGH-5!

Like eggs in an egg carton...

...only upside down!

CODERS

CODERS 0111

Blast it!

Josh Fu! Josh Fu! Josh Fu!

CODERS 1000

You kids think you're so clever, don't you?!

But are you clever enough to deal with ULTRAVIOLET MIST?!

Josh Fu...?

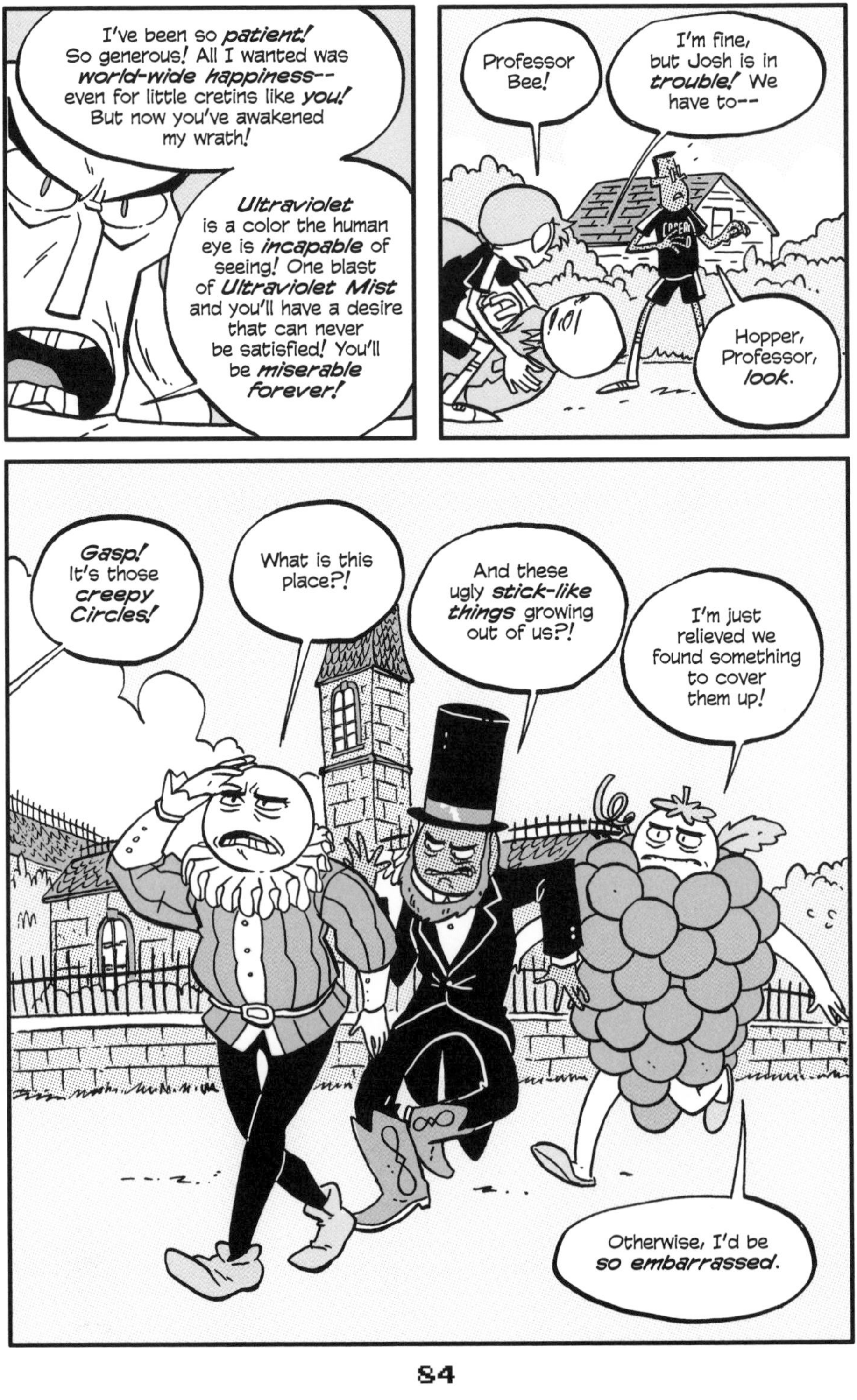
I've been so *patient!* So generous! All I wanted was *world-wide happiness*-- even for little cretins like *you!* But now you've awakened my wrath!
Ultraviolet is a color the human eye is *incapable* of seeing! One blast of *Ultraviolet Mist* and you'll have a desire that can never be satisfied! You'll be *miserable forever!*
Professor Bee!
I'm fine, but Josh is in *trouble!* We have to--
Hopper, Professor, *look*.
Gasp! It's those *creepy Circles!*
What is this place?!
And these ugly *stick-like things* growing out of us?!
I'm just relieved we found something to cover them up!
Otherwise, I'd be *so embarrassed*.

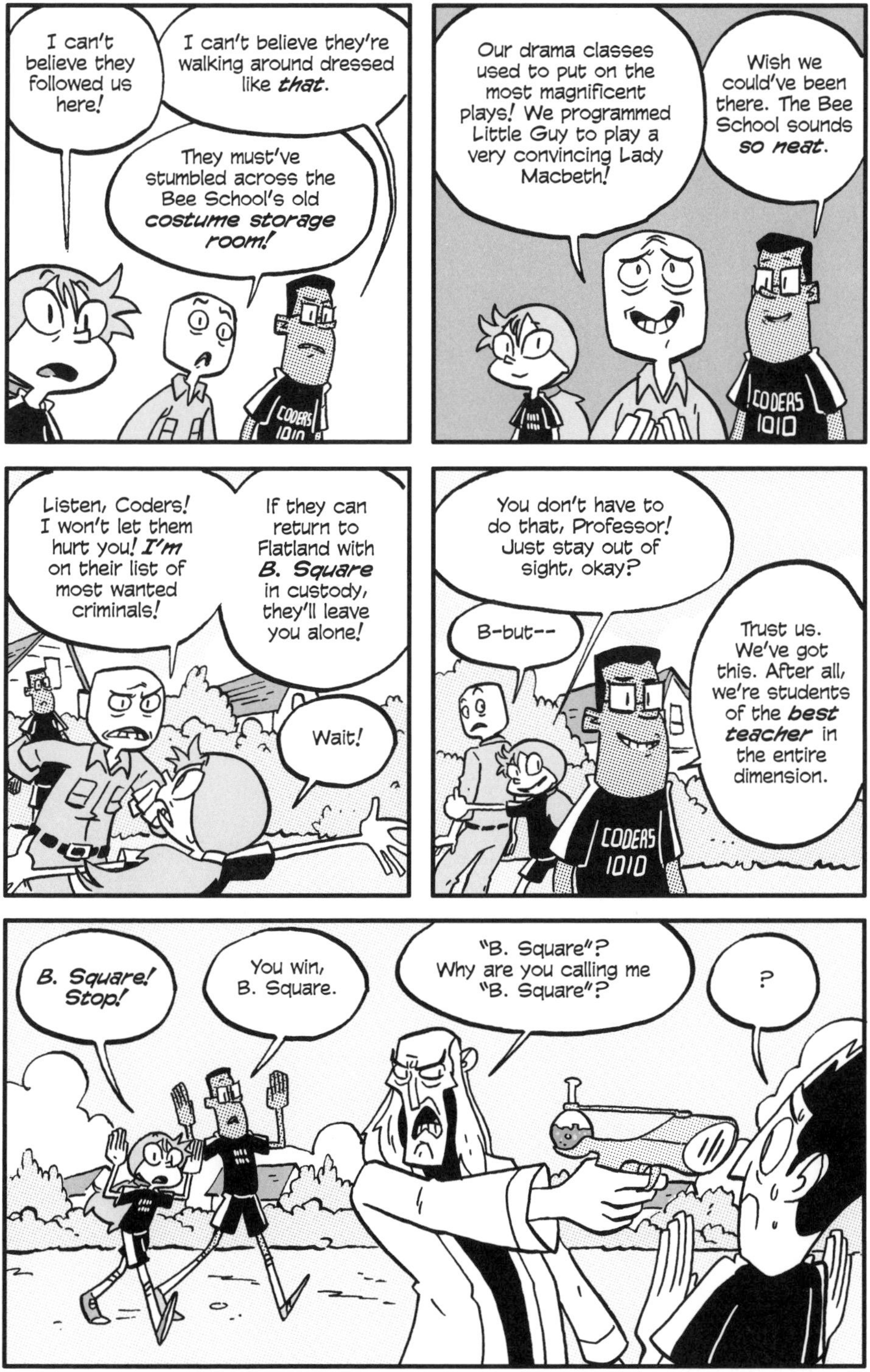
I can't believe they followed us here!
I can't believe they're walking around dressed like *that*.
They must've stumbled across the Bee School's old *costume storage room!*
CODERS 1010
Our drama classes used to put on the most magnificent plays! We programmed Little Guy to play a very convincing Lady Macbeth!
Wish we could've been there. The Bee School sounds *so neat*.
CODERS 1010
Listen, Coders! I won't let them hurt you! *I'm* on their list of most wanted criminals!
If they can return to Flatland with *B. Square* in custody, they'll leave you alone!
Wait!
You don't have to do that, Professor! Just stay out of sight, okay?
B-but--
Trust us. We've got this. After all, we're students of the *best teacher* in the entire dimension.
CODERS 1010
B. Square! Stop!
You win, B. Square.
"B. Square"? Why are you calling me "B. Square"?
?

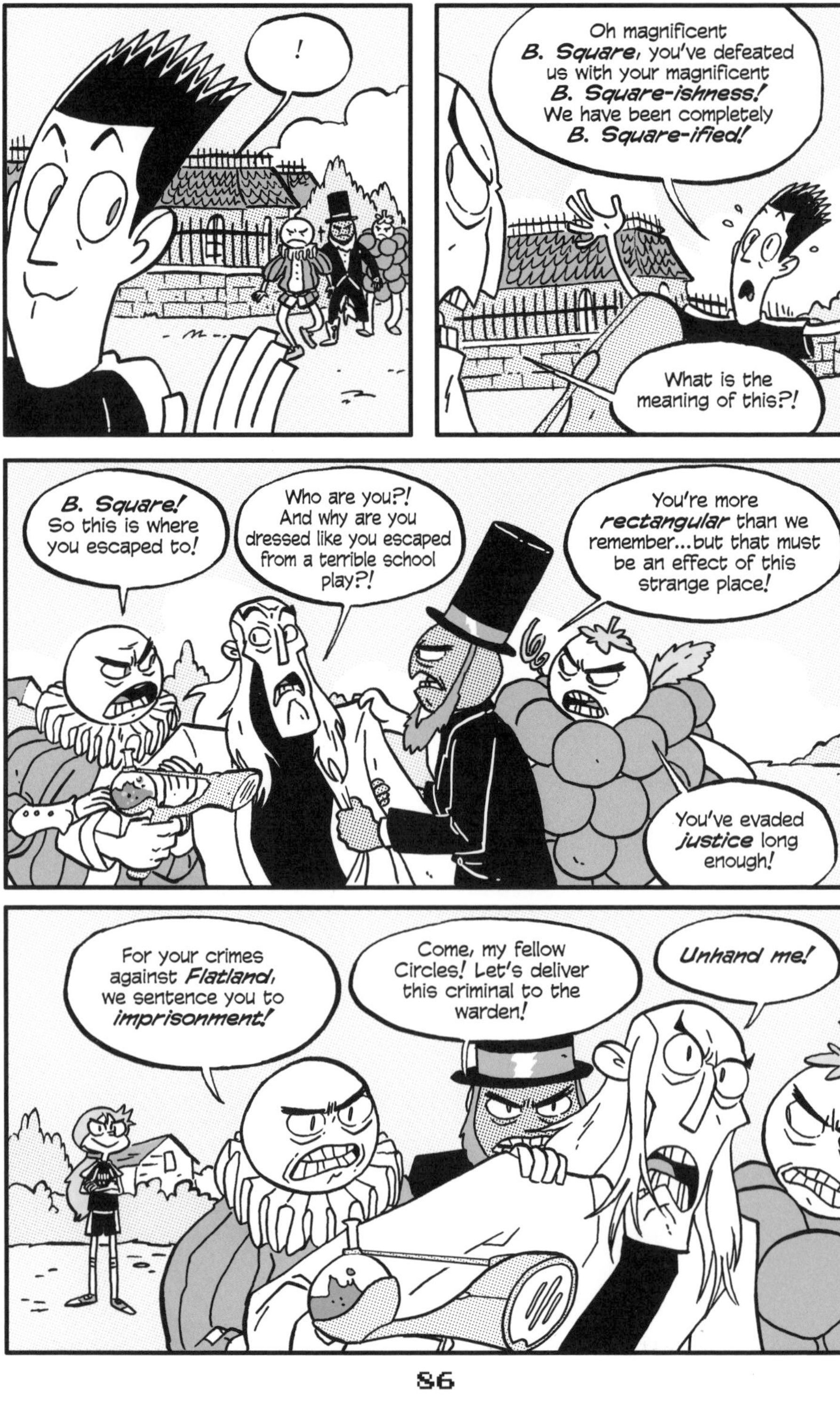
!
Oh magnificent **B. Square**, you've defeated us with your magnificent **B. Square-ishness!** We have been completely **B. Square-ified!**
What is the meaning of this?!
B. Square! So this is where you escaped to!
Who are you?! And why are you dressed like you escaped from a terrible school play?!
You're more **rectangular** than we remember...but that must be an effect of this strange place!
You've evaded **justice** long enough!
For your crimes against **Flatland**, we sentence you to **imprisonment!**
Come, my fellow Circles! Let's deliver this criminal to the warden!
Unhand me!

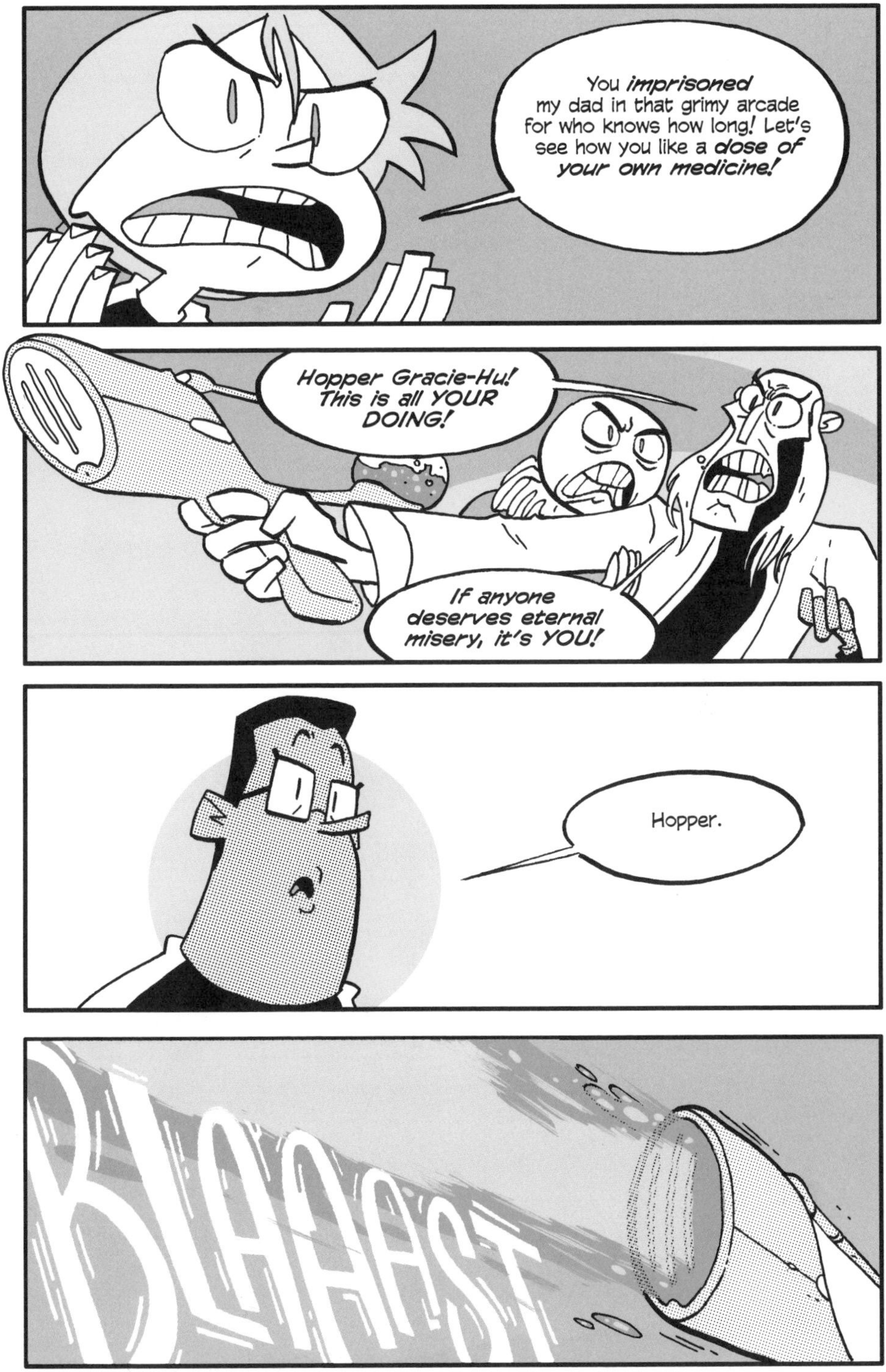
You *imprisoned* my dad in that grimy arcade for who knows how long! Let's see how you like a ***dose of your own medicine!***
Hopper Gracie-Hu! This is all YOUR DOING!
If anyone deserves eternal misery, it's YOU!
Hopper.
BLAAAST

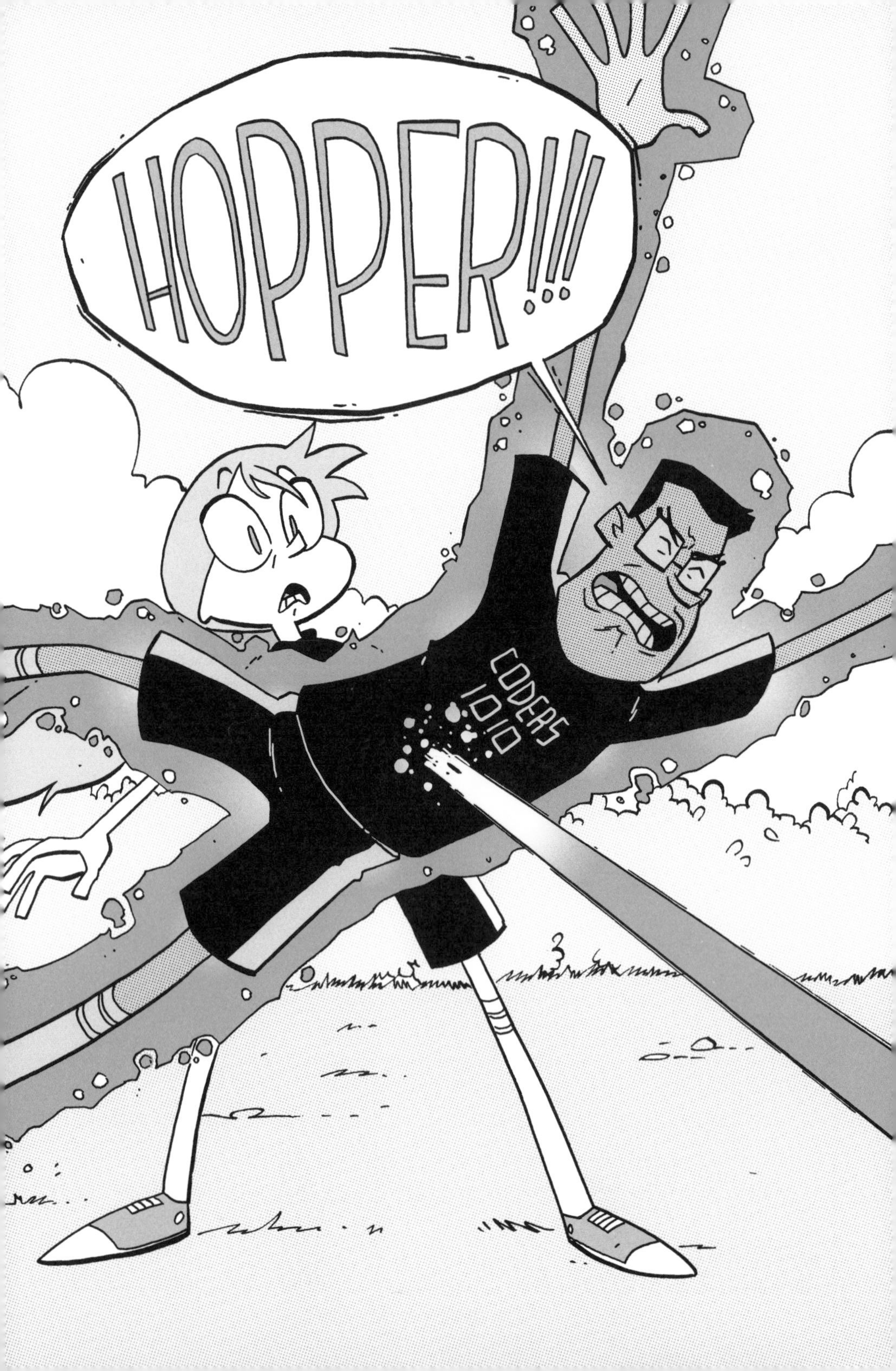
HOPPER!!!
CODERS
1010

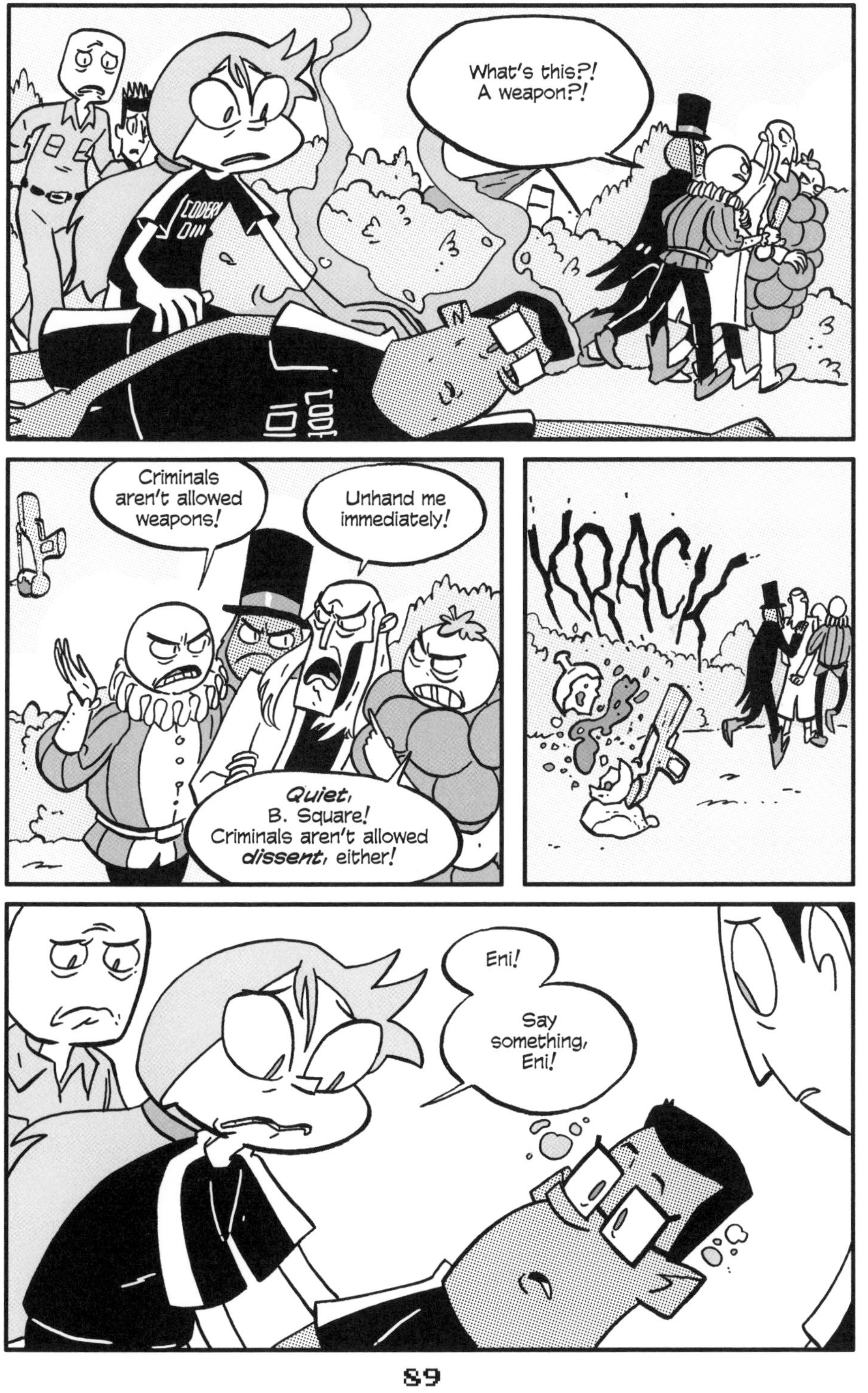
What's this?! A weapon?!
Criminals aren't allowed weapons!
Unhand me immediately!
Quiet, B. Square! Criminals aren't allowed dissent, either!
KRACK
Eni!
Say something, Eni!

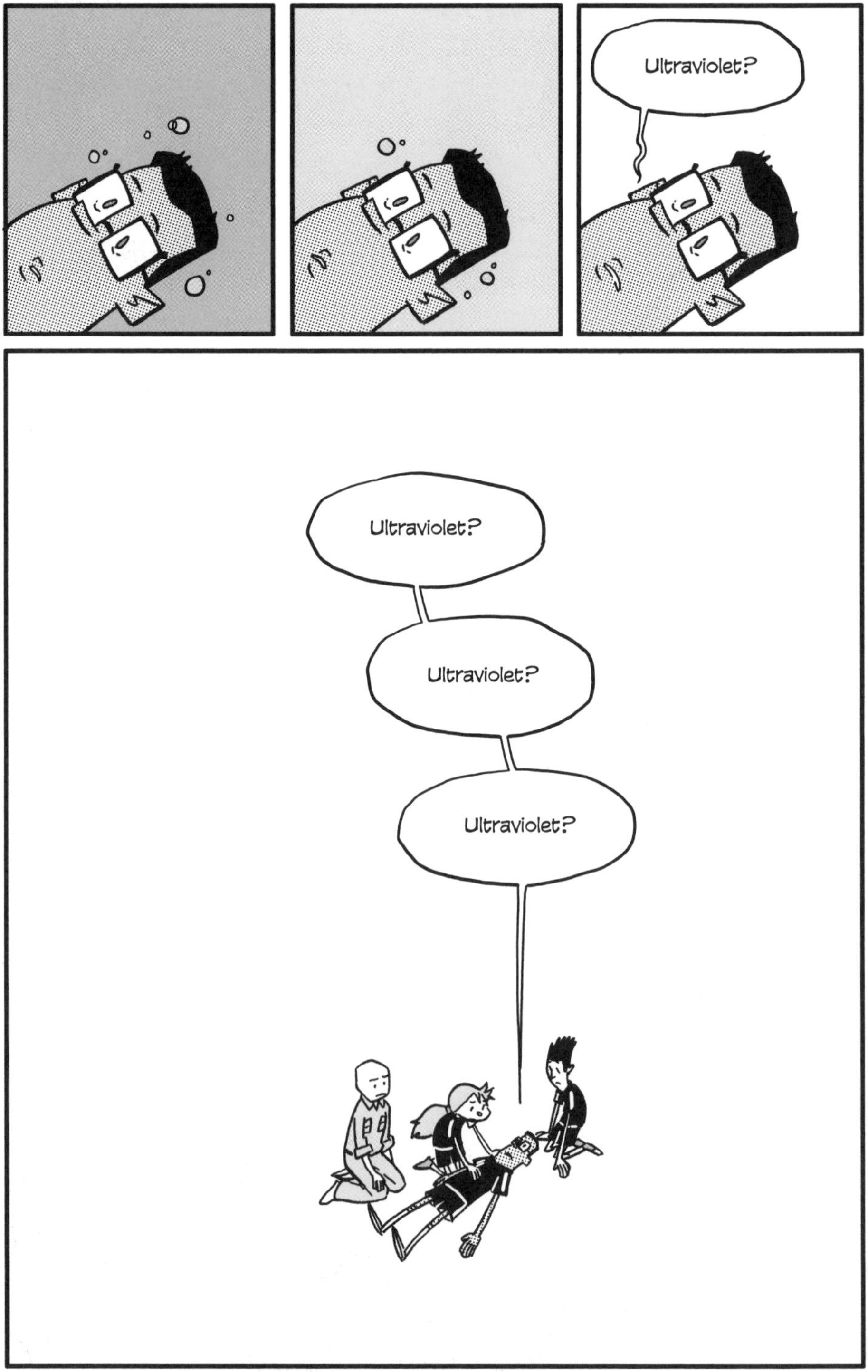
Ultraviolet?
Ultraviolet?
Ultraviolet?
Ultraviolet?

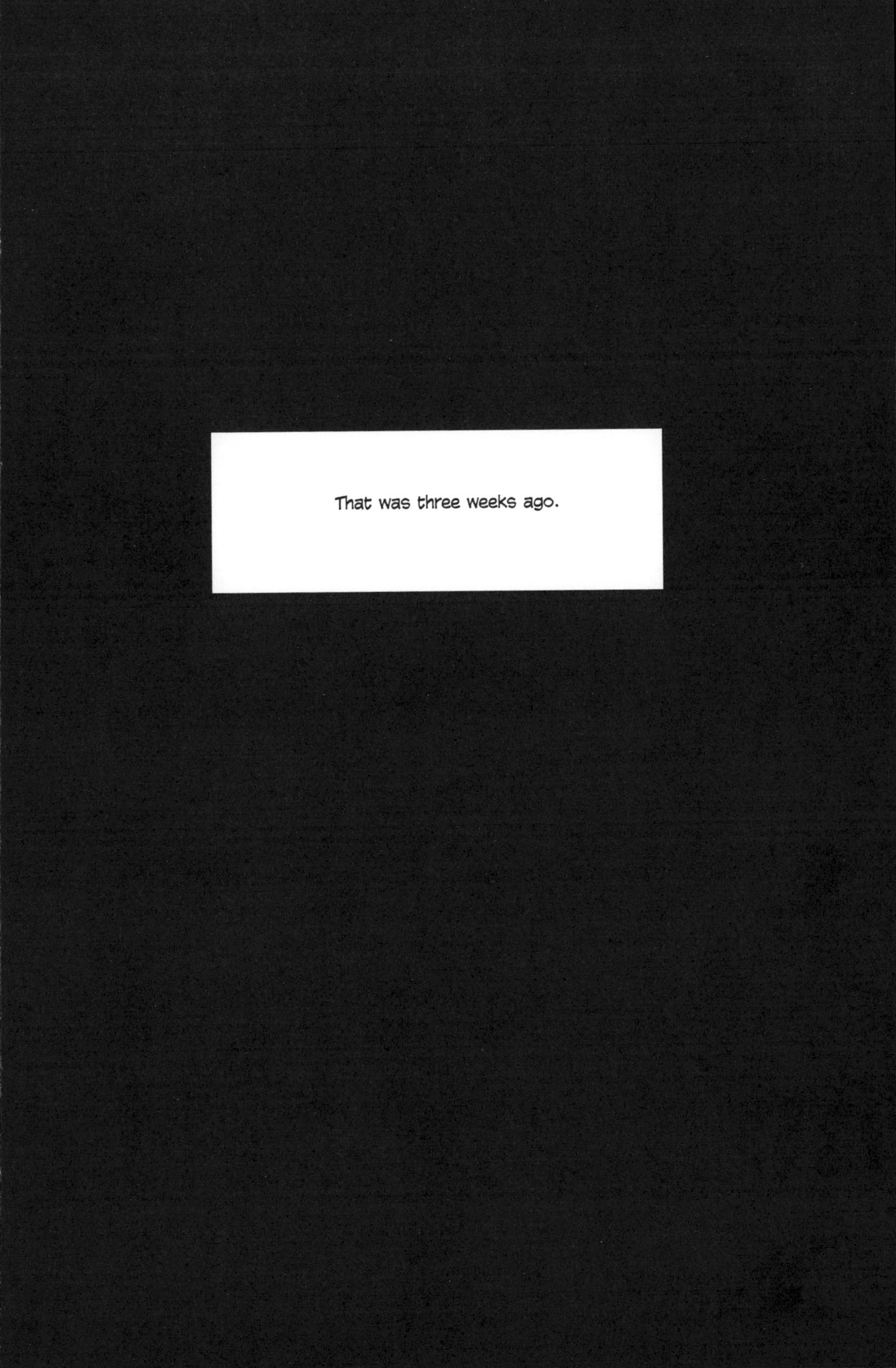
That was three weeks ago.

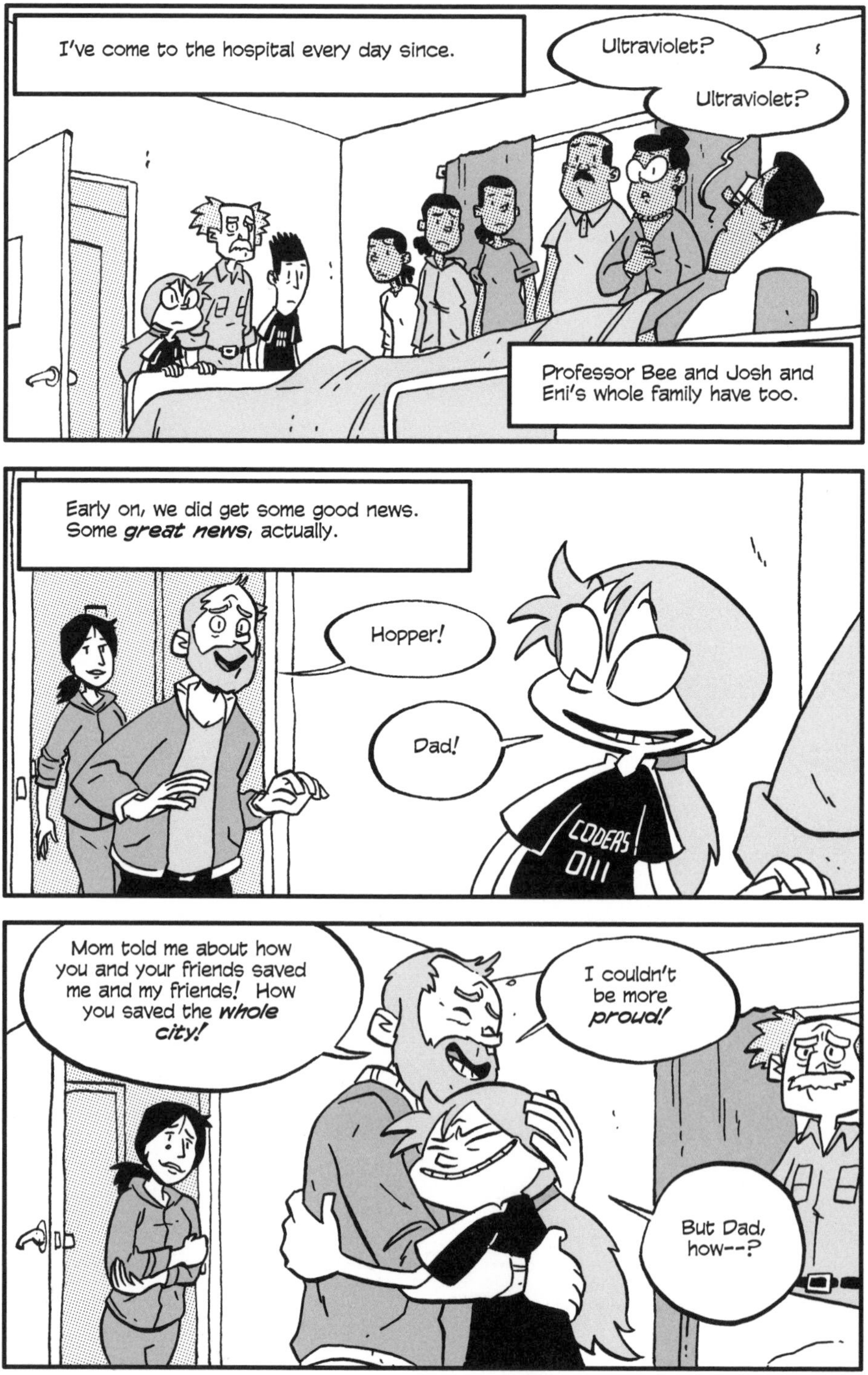
I've come to the hospital every day since.
Ultraviolet?
Ultraviolet?
Professor Bee and Josh and Eni's whole family have too.
Early on, we did get some good news. Some *great news*, actually.
Hopper!
Dad!
CODERS 0111
Mom told me about how you and your friends saved me and my friends! How you saved the *whole city!*
I couldn't be more *proud!*
But Dad, how--?

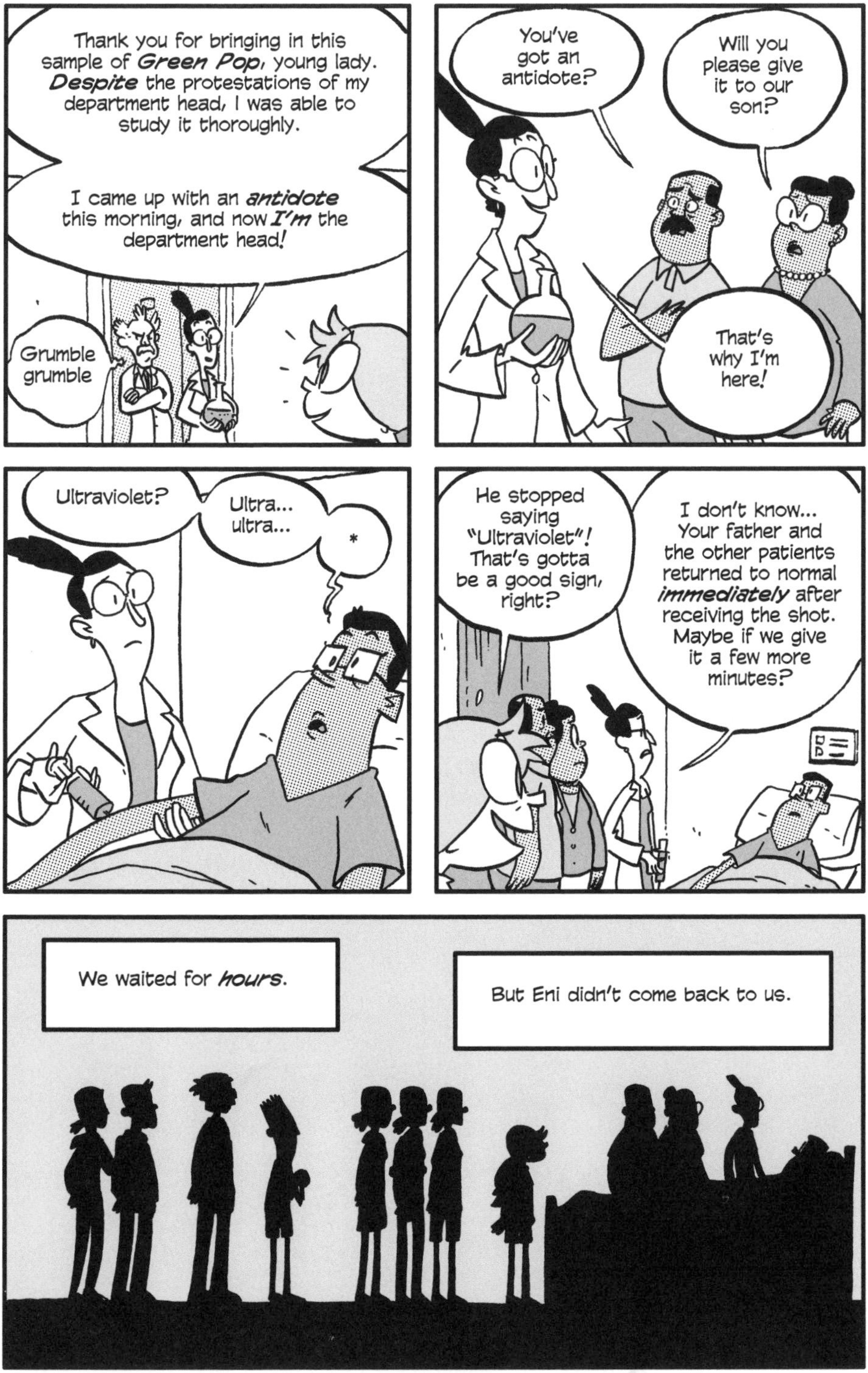
Thank you for bringing in this sample of Green Pop, young lady. Despite the protestations of my department head, I was able to study it thoroughly.
I came up with an antidote this morning, and now I'm the department head!
Grumble grumble
You've got an antidote?
Will you please give it to our son?
That's why I'm here!
Ultraviolet?
Ultra... ultra...
*
He stopped saying "Ultraviolet"! That's gotta be a good sign, right?
I don't know... Your father and the other patients returned to normal immediately after receiving the shot. Maybe if we give it a few more minutes?
We waited for hours.
But Eni didn't come back to us.

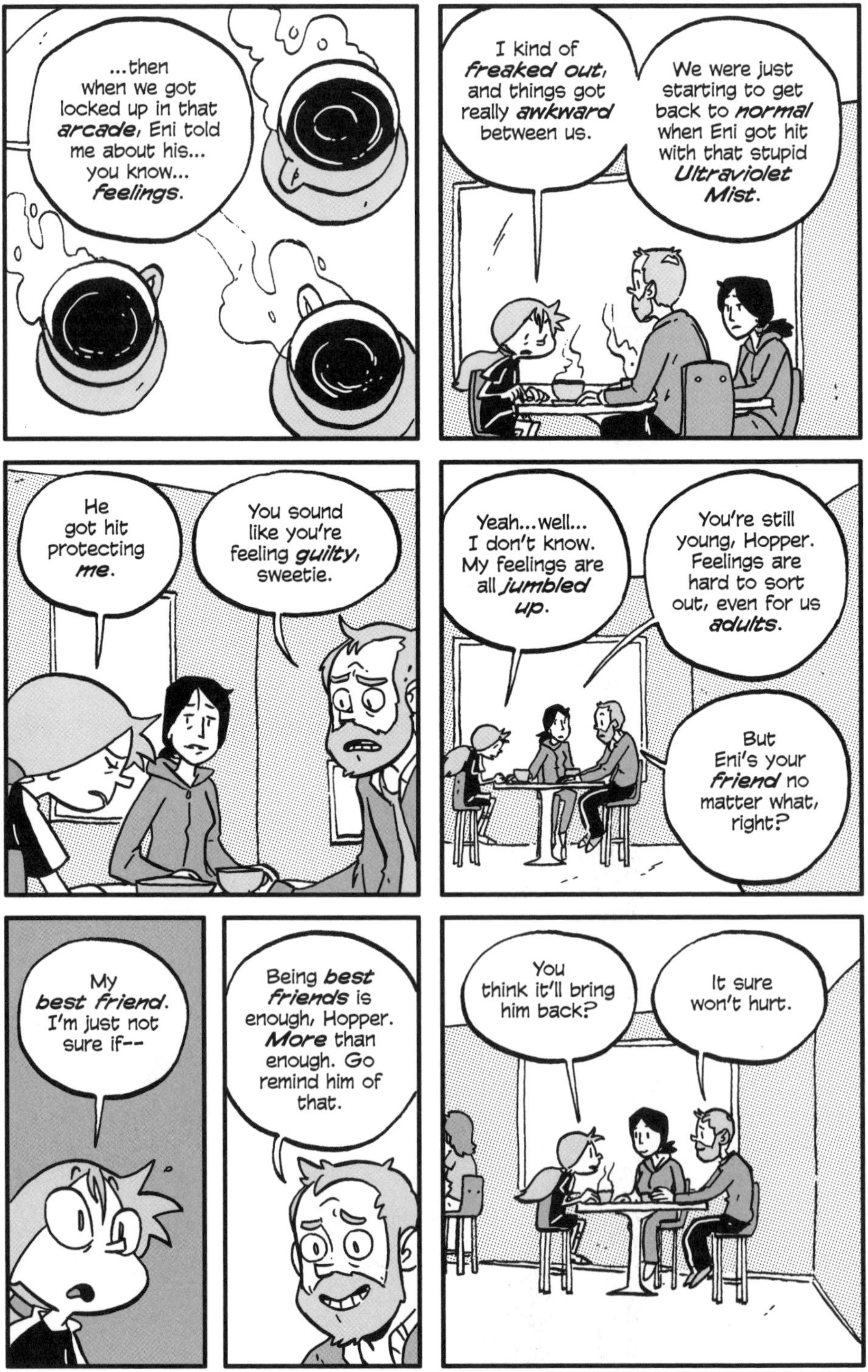
...then when we got locked up in that *arcade*, Eni told me about his... you know... *feelings*.
I kind of *freaked out*, and things got really *awkward* between us.
We were just starting to get back to *normal* when Eni got hit with that stupid *Ultraviolet Mist*.
He got hit protecting *me*.
You sound like you're feeling *guilty*, sweetie.
Yeah...well... I don't know. My feelings are all *jumbled up*.
You're still young, Hopper. Feelings are hard to sort out, even for us *adults*.
But Eni's your *friend* no matter what, right?
My *best friend*. I'm just not sure if--
Being *best friends* is enough, Hopper. *More* than enough. Go remind him of that.
You think it'll bring him back?
It sure won't hurt.

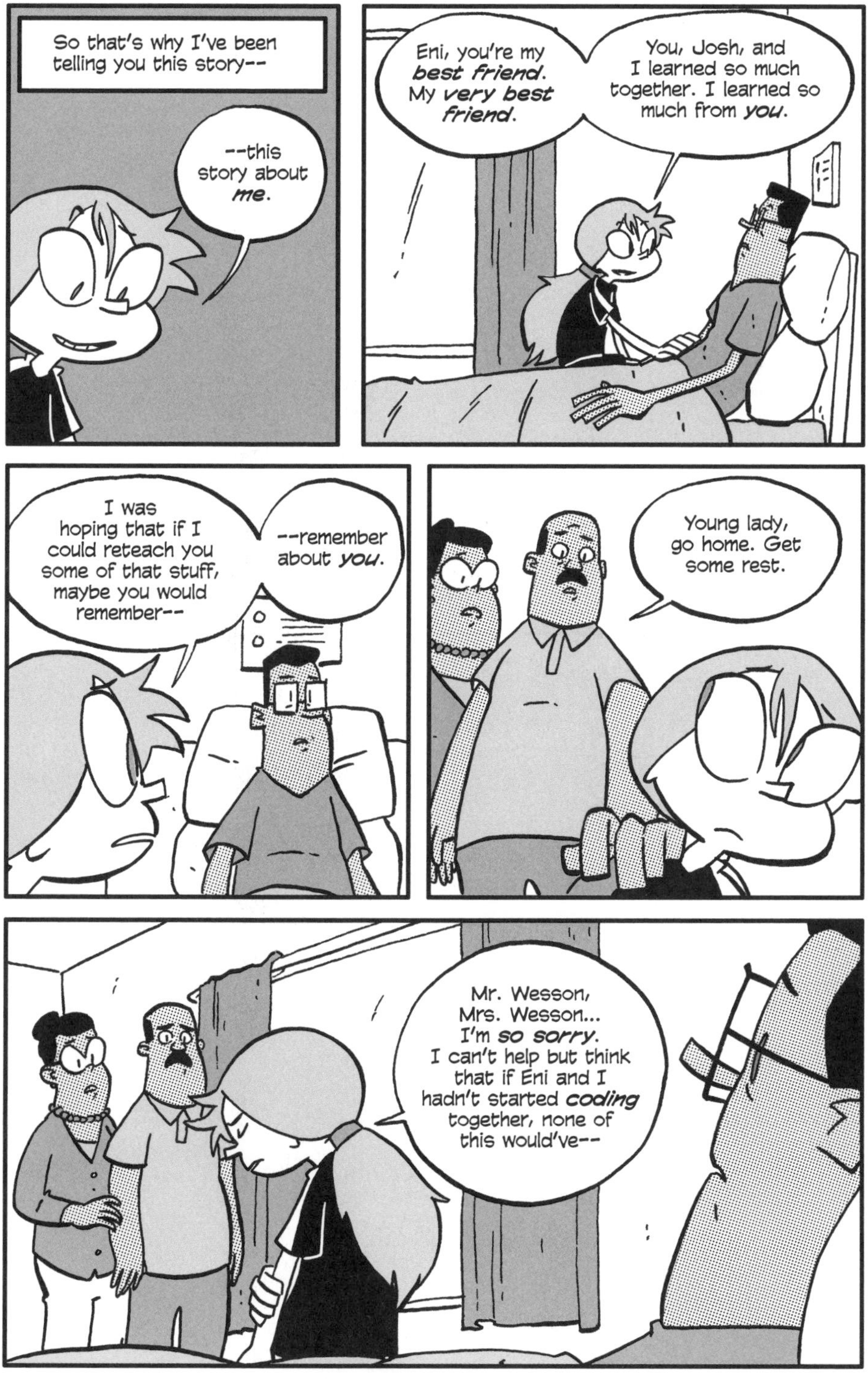
So that's why I've been telling you this story--
--this story about *me*.
Eni, you're my *best friend*. My *very best friend*.
You, Josh, and I learned so much together. I learned so much from *you*.
I was hoping that if I could reteach you some of that stuff, maybe you would remember--
--remember about *you*.
Young lady, go home. Get some rest.
Mr. Wesson, Mrs. Wesson... I'm *so sorry*. I can't help but think that if Eni and I hadn't started *coding* together, none of this would've--

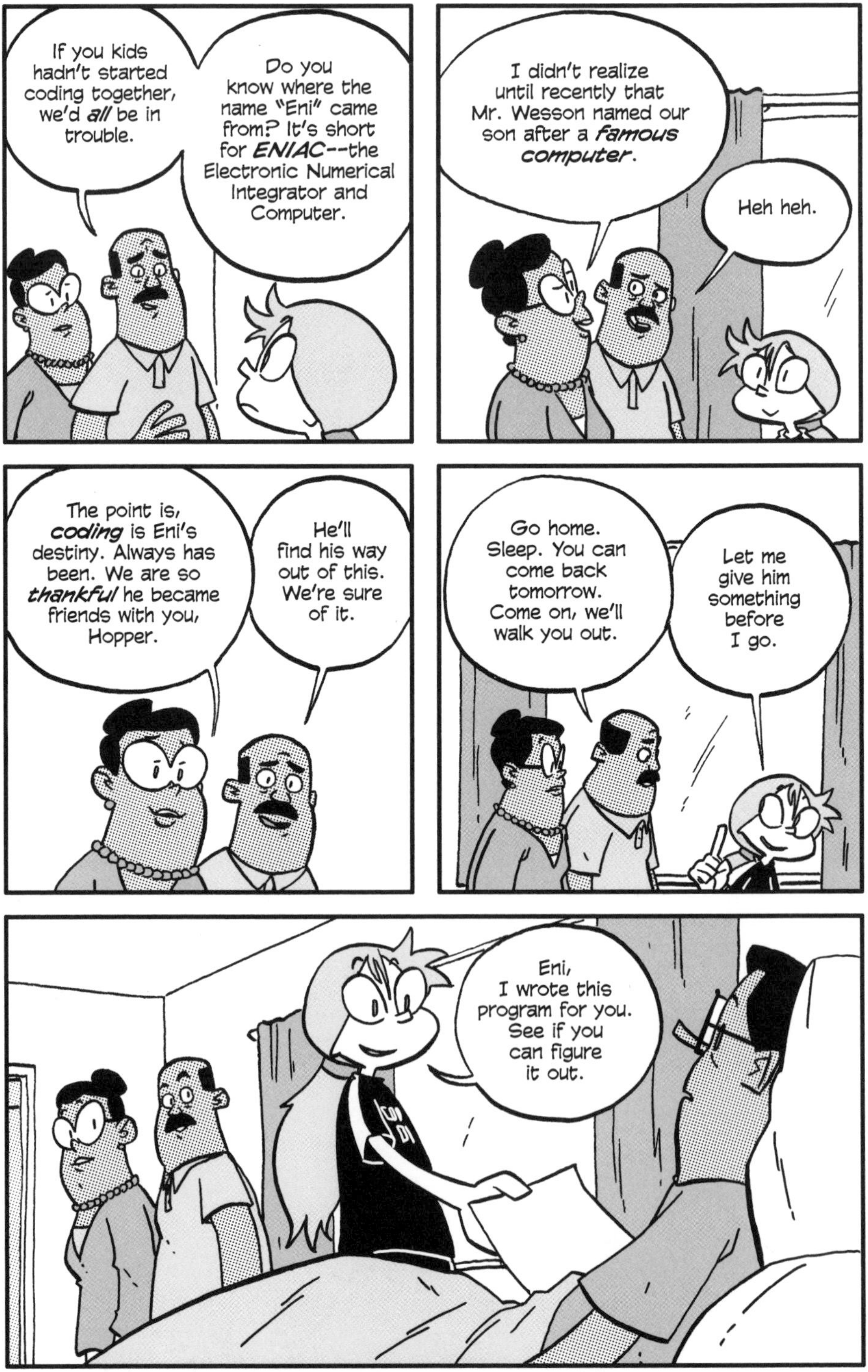

If you kids hadn't started coding together, we'd *all* be in trouble.
Do you know where the name "Eni" came from? It's short for *ENIAC*--the Electronic Numerical Integrator and Computer.
I didn't realize until recently that Mr. Wesson named our son after a *famous computer*.
Heh heh.
The point is, *coding* is Eni's destiny. Always has been. We are so *thankful* he became friends with you, Hopper.
He'll find his way out of this. We're sure of it.
Go home. Sleep. You can come back tomorrow. Come on, we'll walk you out.
Let me give him something before I go.
Eni, I wrote this program for you. See if you can figure it out.

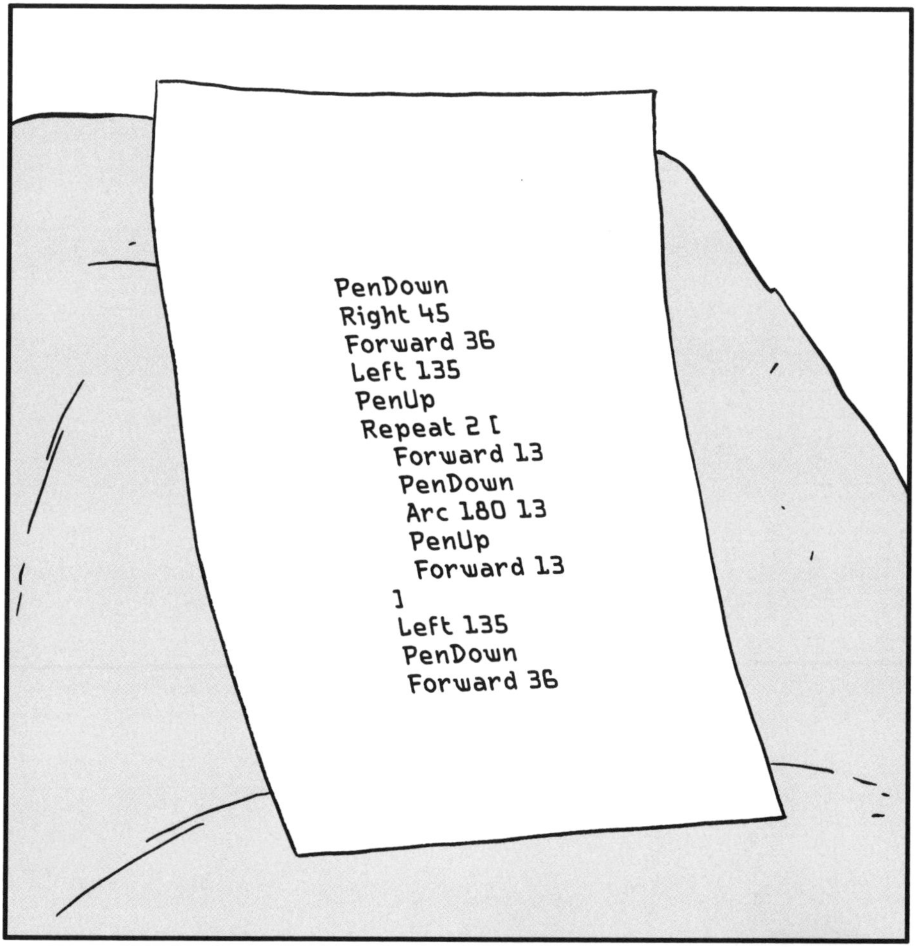
PenDown
Right 45
Forward 36
Left 135
PenUp
Repeat 2 [
Forward 13
PenDown
Arc 180 13
PenUp
Forward 13
]
Left 135
PenDown
Forward 36

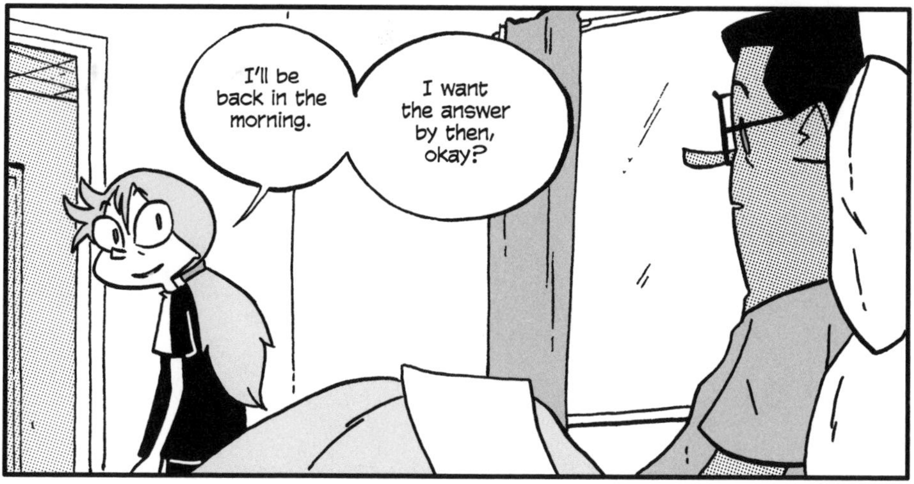
I'll be back in the morning.
I want the answer by then, okay?

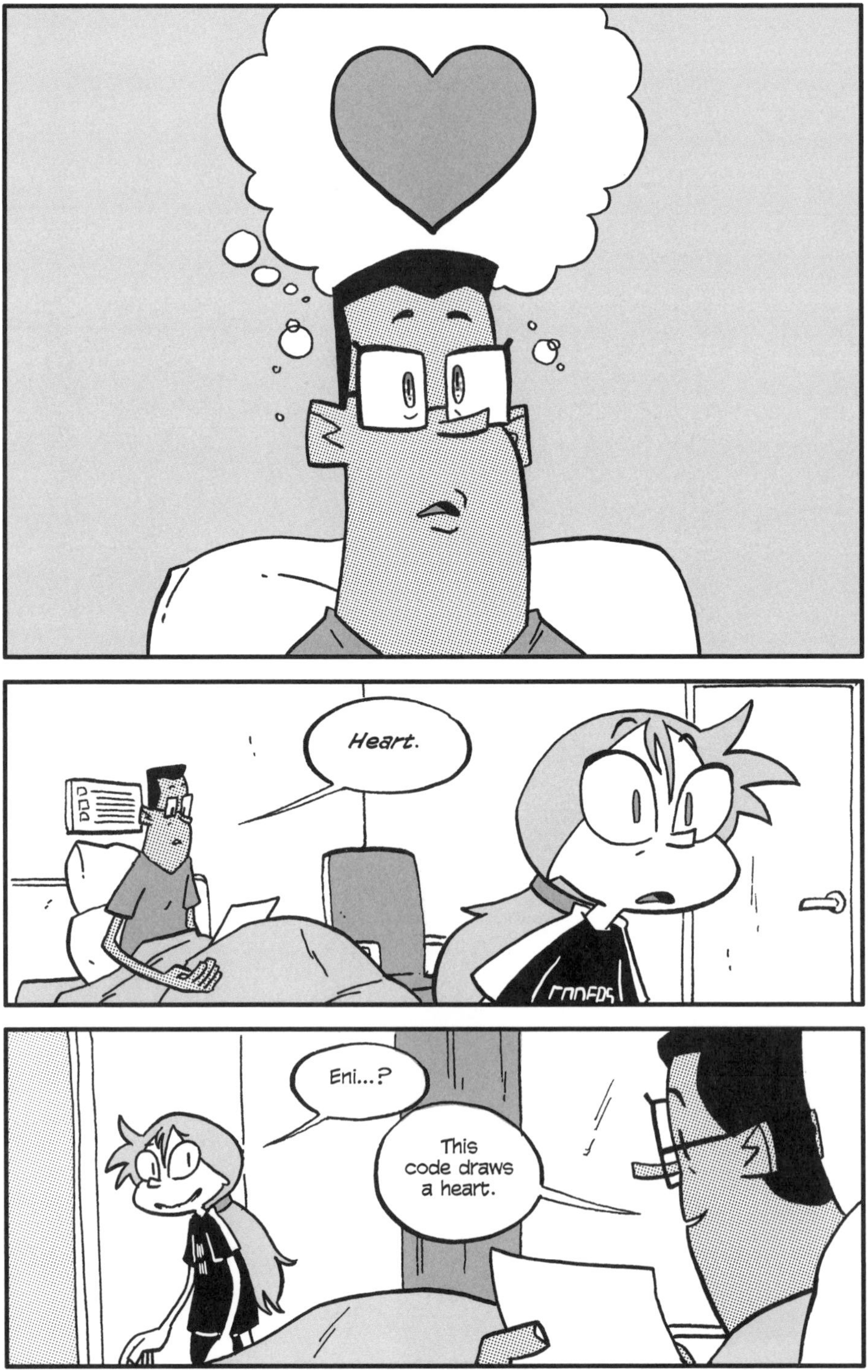
Heart.
Eni...?
This code draws a heart.

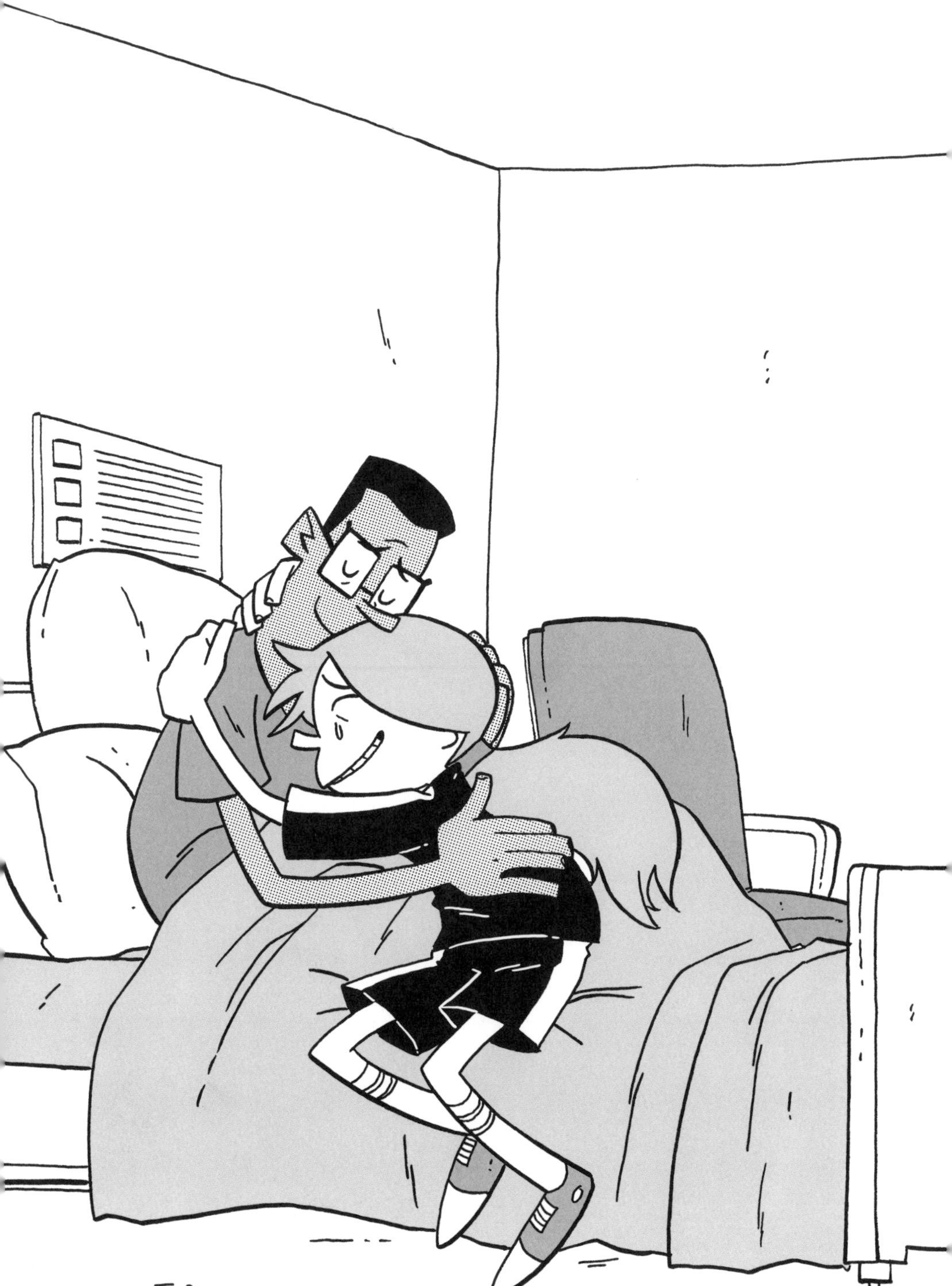

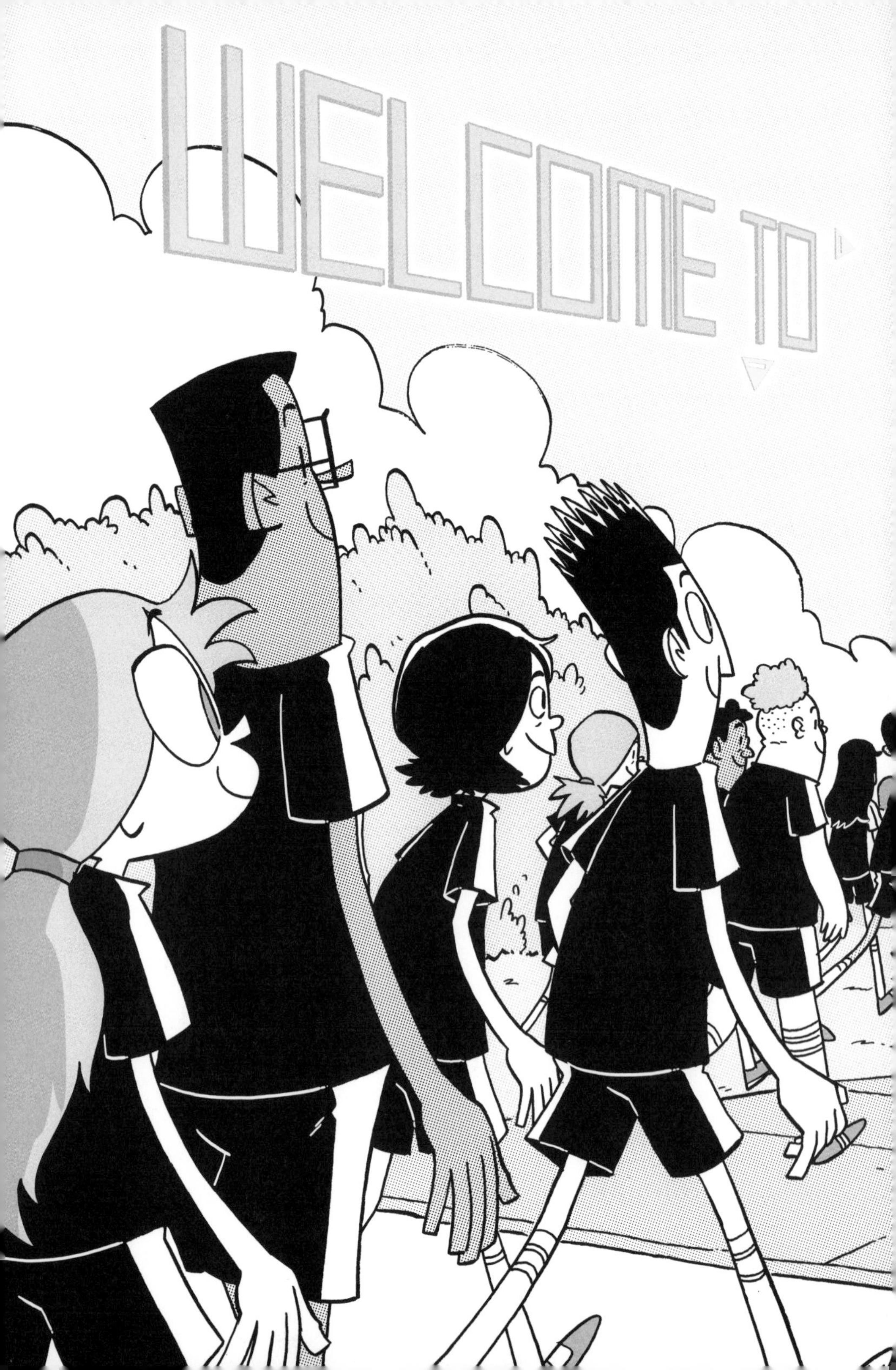
WELCOME TO

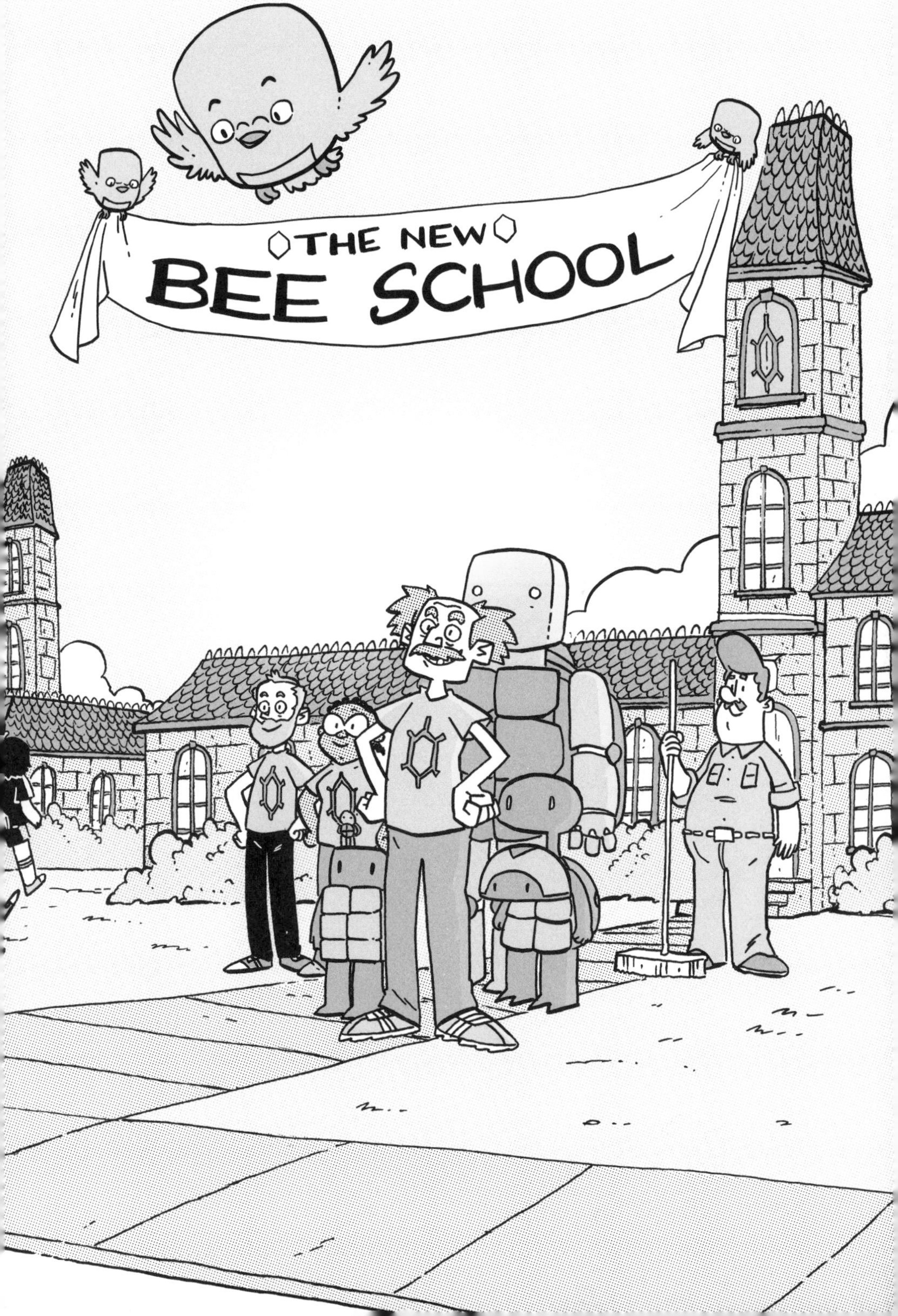
THE NEW
BEE SCHOOL

01010100
01001000
01000101
01000101
01001110
01000100

Ready to start coding?

Visit www.secret-coders.com

Check out these other books
in the Secret Coders series!

Secret Coders
Paths & Portals
Secrets & Sequences
Robots & Repeats
Potions & Parameters

The Making of Secret Coders

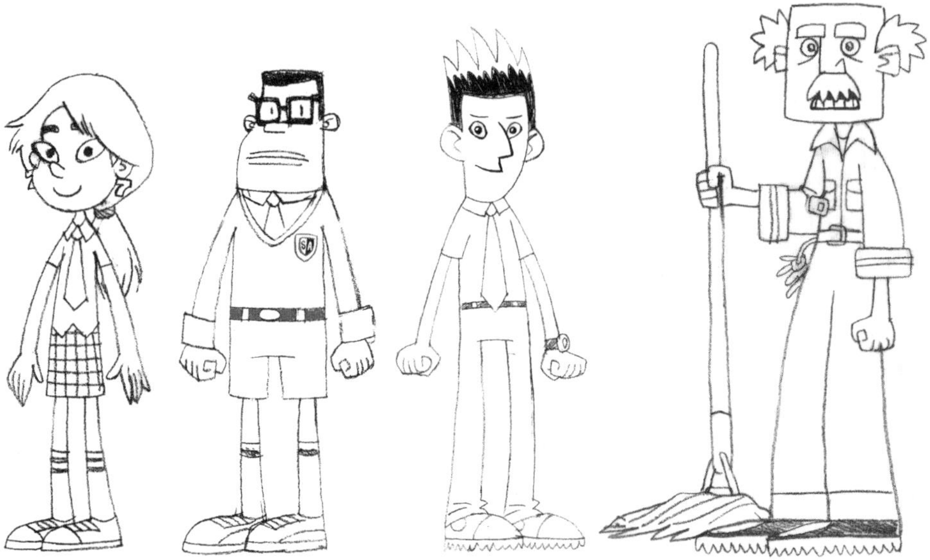

From the beginning, I knew Professor Bee would be a square. I don't mean somebody who's boring, I mean a shape with four equal, straight sides and four right angles. This character was inspired by *Flatland*, a science fiction classic first published in 1884. In that book, author Edwin Abbott firmly establishes his square-ness.

I decided to base the rest of my character designs on shapes too. It's hard to tell now, but Hopper's design started with circles. Eni is made up of rectangles and Josh triangles.

I sent my initial drawings to Mike, who added his own flair, making the Coders look a thousand times better.

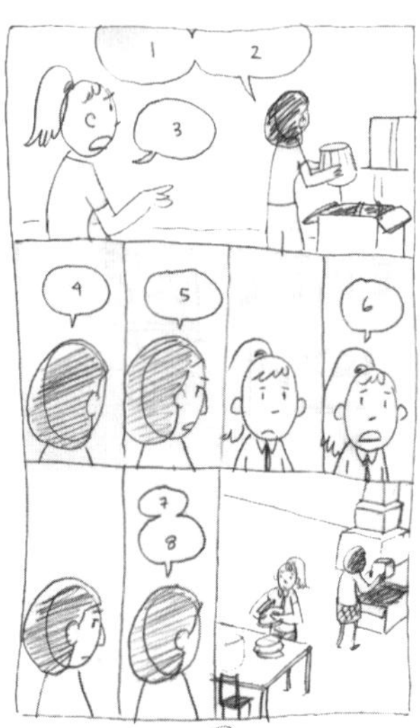
1
2
3
4
5
6
7
8
14

PAGE 16.

Panel 1.

MOM: [1]
I've already talked to your grandparents. We're going to live with them for a while.

[2]
We'll have your father transferred to a nearby hospital.

HOPPER: [3]
Mom, please--

Panel 2.

MOM: [4]
I need you to understand something, Hopper.

Panel 3.

MOM: [5]
These past few days… I've never lived in so much fear in all my life.

Panel 5.

HOPPER: [6]
Mom. Just one more day. Please.

Panel 7.

MOM: [7]
Fine.

MOM: [8]
One more day.

This is how I wrote Secret Coders. I did rough drawings (called thumbnails) of every page. Next I typed up the script. Then I scanned in the drawings and inserted them into my script. I found this to be an efficient way to get the story across to Mike.

—Gene

Most comic book writers only provide a script. I'm incredibly fortunate to have Gene as a creative partner on Secret Coders—Gene is a writer *and* an artist. Gene's thumbnails offered a basic blueprint of the comic page, and I built on that.

I penciled digitally on a twenty-two inch Cintiq tablet. I laid out the panels first, then dropped in the text (dialogue, narration, etc.) so that I could account for how much room was left for the art. The art and the words need the right balance of space. Once that was done, I sketched out word balloons and blocked out the backgrounds and characters. Then I did another layer of pencils with more emphasis on detail, facial expressions, and movement.

At that point I'm usually ready for inks, since I like my pencils loose—it gives a more spontaneous feel to the art. I'll print out the digital pencils on smooth two-ply Bristol paper. For the characters or anything organic I inked with a fine-tipped Zebra brush pen. For backgrounds or anything with straight lines I used .02 to .05 Micron felt-tipped pens. Then I scanned the page at a high resolution and cleaned up the artwork in Photoshop.

You may wonder why I don't ink digitally as well, and the truth is, I like inking by hand! It's almost relaxing—I can sit on the couch, put on a couple movies, and before you know it, my work is done for the day.

—Mike

Mike: You're shockingly talented. Working with you to bring Secret Coders to life has been an amazing experience. Thank you.

My wife and kids: Thank you for inspiring me every day with your love, care, and goofiness.

First Second Books: Thanks for taking a chance on such a nerdy project. A cartoonist could not ask for a better home.

My agent Judy Hansen: Thanks for all your help with the tiny print.

Every one of our readers: You are the best. THE BEST. You reading our story is a tremendous, tremendous honor. Keep reading and keep coding!

—Gene

To Gene Luen Yang: A thousand thanks for taking me on as a partner in this enterprise and teaching me about coding along the way—and for being a pretty awesome guy. Good luck, Gene—maybe one day you'll enjoy some success in comics.

—Mike

Secret Coders is dedicated to every student who has ever set foot in my computer lab at Bishop O'Dowd High School.

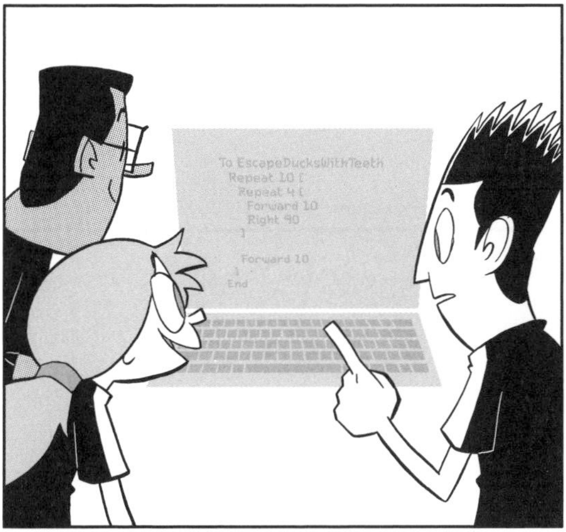
To EscapeDucksWithTeeth
Repeat 10 [
Repeat 4 [
Forward 10
Right 90
]
Forward 10
]
End

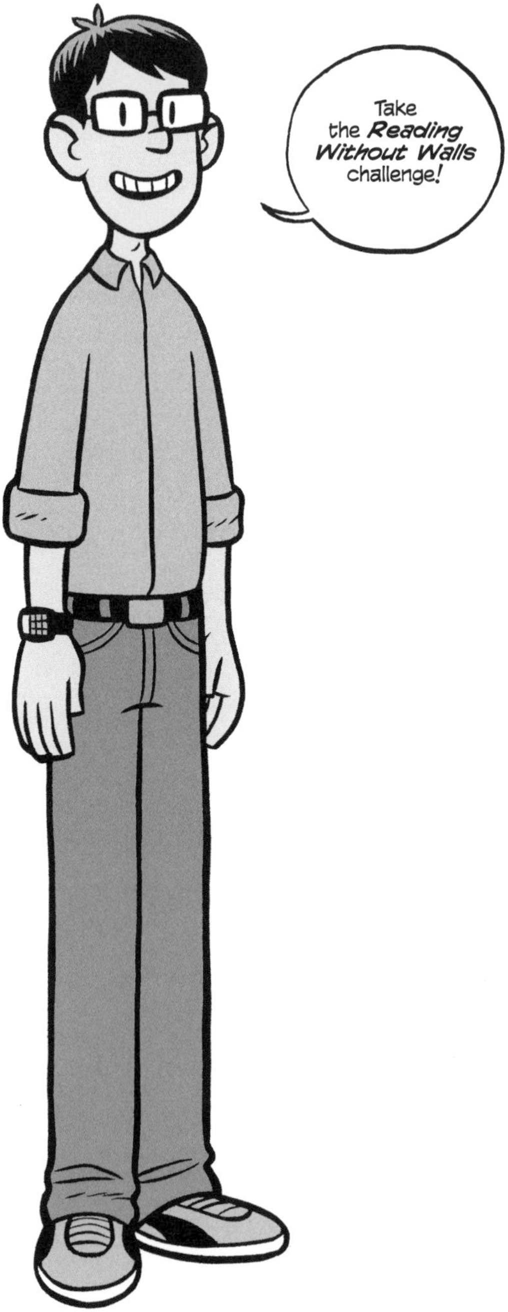
Take the *Reading Without Walls* challenge!

GENE LUEN YANG'S
READING WITHOUT WALLS
CHALLENGE

Read outside your comfort zone!

Read a book about a **character** who doesn't look or live like you.

Read a book about a **topic** you don't know much about.

Read a book in a **format** that you don't normally read for fun.

Learn more at **ReadingWithoutWalls.com**

GREAT GRAPHIC NOVELS

From the *New York Times*–Bestselling Author
Gene Luen Yang

978-1-59643-152-2

BOXERS

978-1-59643-359-5

SAINTS

978-1-59643-689-3

"Gene Luen Yang has created that rare article: a youthful tale with something new to say about American youth."
—*The New York Times*

"Read this, and come away shaking."
—Gary Schmidt, Newbery Honor–winning author

"A masterful work of historical fiction."
—Dave Eggers, author of
A Heartbreaking Work of Staggering Genius

THE EXCITING NEW SERIES

978-1-62672-075-6

"Brings computer coding to life."
—*Entertainment Weekly*

978-1-59643-697-8

★ **"A brilliant homage."**
—*BCCB*

978-1-59643-235-2

"Bravura storytelling."
—*Publishers Weekly*

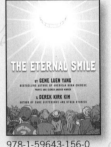

978-1-59643-156-0

★ **"Absolutely not to be missed."**
—*Booklist*

:01
First Second
NEW YORK